"A riveting, sensitive, and skillfully rendered story about the darker recesses of the human heart. Michael Sterba's expertise as a writer and his professional experiences working with troubled adolescents make him the perfect author for this mesmerizing tale."

Richard Dooling, National Book Award Finalist and Author of BRAIN STORM, WHITE MAN'S GRAVE, and CRITICAL CARE

"Abuse in our society is a reality and it is dealt with through the creative efforts addressed in **LITTLE VOICES***. As a parish priest, I found Michael Sterba's examples and experiences quite typical of the issues we priests deal with on a daily basis.* **LITTLE VOICES** *will prove to shed insight, understanding, and direction for those dealing with areas of abuse. Books like this one will have an impact on our society. Many will be inspired by this book. I couldn't put it down."*

Rev. Thomas M. Fangman, Pastor of Sacred Heart Church in Omaha, Nebraska.

*"***LITTLE VOICES** *is not only factually accurate in terms of the impact of abuse both early and later in life, but is an excellent and gripping story. Its protagonist provides a clear illustration of the importance of intervention, understanding, and forgiveness."*

Dr. Timothy Shaw, Licensed Clinical Psychologist (New Smyrna Beach, Florida) with 25 years of experience, much of which has focused on the treatment of adult survivors and child victims of physical and sexual abuse.

*"***LITTLE VOICES** *is, at its core, a book about the triumph of the spirit. Without resorting to sensationalism and gratuitousness, Michael Sterba captures the pain and impact of our society's most sickening depravity – the abuse of a child – and shows the reader that the broken among us can reclaim our eternal obligation to make the world a better place. And, he does this in a spellbinding pageturner that unmasks the guilty while keeping us guessing until the last page. Read this book if you want to be entertained on a topic of immense current interest!"*

Martin McCaslin, M.A., former Instructor of Composition and Rhetoric, Creighton University in Omaha, Nebraska.

Little Voices is a riveting story that is quite timely in its topic given recent widespread media coverage of the sexual abuse of children by trusted adults. Suspenseful from the first page to the last, it examines the betrayal of the sacred trust between helping professionals and innocent children. The story offers the reader easily accessible insight into therapeutic techniques to help troubled children and the profound impact that abuse can have throughout the victim's life.

Linda S. LaMarca, Ph.D.,Licensed Clinical Psychologist, NSB FL

Little Voices

By
Michael Sterba

Little Voices
ISBN 1-58853-055-8

Library of Congress Control Number: 2002106127

Author: **Michael Sterba**
Primary Editor: Martin McCaslin
Contributing Editors: Timothy Shaw, MD
                         Christy Bartholomew
Publisher: Richard Burgess

Cover Design: J. Spittler/Jamison Design, Nevada City, CA

Copyright © 2002 Michael Sterba
Copyright © 2002 Sensory Publishing, Inc.
And Michael Sterba
All rights reserved

Fictitious Persons
The characters and events in this book are fictitious and any resemblance to actual persons, living or dead, or events, past or present, is purely coincidental.

No part of this book may be reproduced or transmitted in any form or by any means, electronic or mechanical, including photocopying, recording, or by any information storage and retrieval system, without the written permission of Sensory Publishing, Inc., except where permitted by law.

Published by Sensory Publishing, Inc.
2000 Jefferson Davis Hwy, Ste. D, Alexandria, VA 22301

Acknowledgements

It takes more than just a writer to create a book, and my life has been blessed over the four years it took to write this novel with many people. To my wife, Fae: Your unwavering support and belief in me to achieve my dreams only reinforces why I love you. To my three kids who think that writing a book is a cool thing to do: You guys are what's cool. Thanks for showing me what's really important. To my parents, Ed and Norma, brothers, David and Pat, sisters, Jeannie and Jacki, father-in-law, Bob and mother-in-law, Connie, and to all my friends: Thank you for your enthusiasm and encouragement. You all helped me to come to know that writing is a noble, honorable, and worthy endeavor. To my writing therapists Marty McCaslin, Bob Huerter, Jami Spittler, and Connie Spittler: Your insights, patronage, and comradeship were, and will always remain, inspiring. To all my "readers" who took time to review the story at all stages: I thank you for having the same passion that I did to create the best story possible. To my publishers, Richard and Christy, at Sensory Publishing: Thanks for giving me the opportunity.

I would like to acknowledge the best priest there is, Father Tom Fangman. Tom, I am humbled by all that you have done for me and others and appreciate all that you continue to do. I admire your devotion and spirit. You are amazing.

A special tribute goes to my editor, Marty McCaslin. It's funny how people are brought into our lives at just the right moment. Marty, I will forever be indebted to you for your time and patience, knowledge and guidance, and belief in my story and me. I will always recall with fondness our work together in these pages and our many talks about writing and life. However, what I'm most appreciative of is that in this process I came to truly know you as a friend.

Without you, my dream would never have been fully realized. I am eternally grateful.

For Noah, Hannah, and Zoey – my little voices. May I always remember to listen.

For all the troubled little voices in the world who have no one: I pray that some caring souls enter your lives and heed your pleas, because many times that's all the little ones need.

CHAPTER 1

Bobby was late. He arrived out-of-breath and apologetic. David snapped at him for his shabby punctuality. It was just past dusk but there was enough light to see the black and blue swelling around Bobby's eye.

"What's up with the eye?" David said, snatching a beer from the twelve-pack Bobby had lugged to the playground.

"Umm..." Bobby straightened the glasses that sat crooked on his face. One earpiece was taped to the front of the frame. "Reggie Cempak."

David gulped down half of his first beer in one giant swallow, then looked at Bobby out of the corner of his eye. "Man, you gotta stay away from that dude. You're like target practice for him. What'd you do? Breathe wrong?"

"I didn't do nothin'." Bobby sat on the swing next to David and began swaying back and forth.

David chugged the rest of his beer, set the can on the ground and crushed it by stomping down hard. Then, he popped the tab on a fresh one and took a sip. "Come on, man. What happened?"

Bobby continued to swing. "Nothing. I...I was just walking home and Reggie started pushing me around."

"Did he punch you?"

"He...he pushed me...into a tree." Bobby started pumping harder, going higher and farther away from David.

David furrowed his brow and stopped in mid-sip. "He get you today?"

"Yep." Bobby was now flying through the air.

David rose from the swing seat he was sitting on and, as Bobby came rushing by, grabbed the chain.

"Hey!" Bobby said, after he came to a halt. "I almost fell off. What're you doing?"

David sat back down, took a swig and squinted sideways at Bobby. "I saw Reggie leaving town with his stepdad today."

Bobby's good eye grew wide; he took off his glasses and adjusted the broken earpiece. "Yeah, well, it happened this morning."

"When?"

Bobby looked away. "Why? What's it to you."

"Just looking out for you, buddy." David smirked, knowing he had Bobby trapped. "Come on, man, you can tell me. When did it happen?"

Bobby wrapped his arms tightly across his chest and began quickly rocking back and forth. Suddenly, he turned to David and said with an angry look, "Give me a beer."

David was shocked – and pleased – to see Bobby was finally boozing. But the small boy didn't know how to pace himself. David watched in amazement as Bobby guzzled down the entire beer as if it was ice-cold water on a hot day.

"Damn, you slammed that thing down like you knew what you were doing." David smiled and slapped Bobby on the back.

Bobby tossed the empty can aside and held out his hand. With no emotion, he said, "Another."

For the next hour and a half Bobby kept pounding; he guzzled eight beers to David's three. David continued to egg Bobby on with a mixture of phony approval and attention – that is, until David realized the booze was running out.

"Man, Bobby, slow down. You're drinking all the beer."

"Reggie...he didn't get me."

David reached into the sack for another beer; there was only one left. "Shit Bobby, they're all gone." David was pissed. He didn't even have a decent buzz going yet.

"It ain't Reggie – never was." Bobby went to take a drink from the open beer in his hand and managed to get some in his mouth. Most spilled down his chin and onto his clothes.

"What the hell you talking about?"

Bobby's head was drooping and swaying like a bobblehead doll. His glasses fell off. As he let go of one of the chains to try and catch his specs, he lost his balance and spilled out of the swing seat. He fell to the ground with a thud, landing on top of the glasses. Now both earpieces were snapped off. "Oh no!" he slurred. "He's gonna get me good now, David." Bobby started crying.

"Jeez, Bobby, chill out. Reggie's gone for a couple of days." David was already halfway through the last beer. "I heard he was going to Falls City to visit an uncle or something."

"Not him!"

"Man, you're all fucked up."

"He's gonna get me!" Bobby stood up, took one step and swayed, then fell down. "He's gonna hurt me…I don't want to hurt anymore. I just want him to stop. You gotta help me, David."

"What're you babbling about?'" Bobby was getting weird and David didn't like it. "I told you Reggie went—"

"Not him!" Bobby screamed. After a moment, he said softly, "My daddy…"

David got a pit in his stomach. He wanted to leave, but couldn't. After all, this was his alcohol pimp and he didn't want to blow a good thing.

"He hit you?" David really didn't want to know, and he didn't really care. Instead, he asked the question out of morbid curiosity.

Bobby started sobbing and curled up in a ball. "Make him stop," he moaned. "He drinks and beats me. Every night it's the same thing. David, you gotta help me. He says it's for my own good…it'll toughen me up. I'm not gonna be a star quarterback like he was. I don't wanna play football. I like reading...but he takes my books away. I gotta hide 'em from him, David."

Rain began to spit and David was out of beer. He now had two excuses to leave, so he grabbed the bike he'd won on a dare and said, "Bobby, I'm outta here."

"No!" Bobby begged. "Don't leave me!"

David left anyway, not looking back once, letting the sound of Bobby's weeping fade away with each push of the pedal.

The next day, David learned that Bobby was found dead, laying in the mud under the giant cyclone slide in Neihardt Park's playground.

The community was stunned. Everyone knew Bobby wasn't a partier or a risk taker. The boy always had a book with him and read everywhere he went. He seemed most content when living in the world of words.

Many assumed that the constant harassment Bobby Harmon received from his peers finally wore him down, and that he took his life by poisoning himself with alcohol. An autopsy determined the boy had passed out on his back and choked to death on his own vomit.

Kids at St. Cecilia's were genuinely upset and grieved at the loss of one of their own. Guilt swept over most everyone, even those not directly involved in teasing and bullying Bobby, because they could have stopped it instead of looking the other way. It was ironic, David thought, that the acceptance Bobby longed for came only after he was gone.

After Bobby's funeral, David was weighed down by remorse and shame so heavy that all he wanted to do was escape. This harmless boy who just wanted to be liked would haunt David forever. Instead of a catharsis, the incident was the impetus for a long, steady descent into the dark world of drugs and alcohol.

Not a soul learned of David's presence in the park that night. He knew others suspected he was somehow involved, but he told no one – not even Father Anthony during confession. Eventually, David stopped going for fear that one day he would yield to the temptation of unburdening his guilt. He was deathly afraid of being found out. He trusted no one.

Tires screeched in the church's parking lot. David snapped his head around, away from the rectory door, to see where the sound was coming from. Although he saw nothing, David knew the speeding vehicle was headed his way. Seconds later, a cherry-red Jeep Cherokee appeared and rounded the corner near the entrance of the pastor's residence, nipping the high curb bordering the parking lot. This threw the Jeep in the opposite direction, heading directly for David's Honda Civic. He braced himself for what appeared to be a certain collision. At the last second, the driver of the Jeep slammed on the brakes, causing the vehicle to skid to a stop, inches away from yet another dent in the Honda's worn, rusted body.

The Cherokee came to rest at an odd angle between two parking stalls, overshooting its mark. The driver side's front tire smothered two feet of freshly-cut grass.

The car door swung open and Father Anthony McFarland, all six feet four and 275 pounds of him, lumbered out, stepping right onto a neatly-arranged bed of purple, yellow, and red mums.

"Holy shit, for the love of God!" Father Anthony said with a noticeable slur. "Sister's going to have my tail." He sighed. "Oh well, it won't be the first time. Let's see if I can't fix these little buggers."

"Hello, Father Anthony," David said softly.

The elder priest was bent over, absorbed in a vain attempt to right the crushed mums, leaning one against another for support so that he could escape Sister's wrath.

"Father Anthony," David said in a louder voice. "Hi."

Father Anthony looked up and broke out in a warm, friendly smile. Standing and stumbling a few steps, he trampled the remaining upright flowers and said, "David...I mean, Father Cooper, welcome!"

He walked over to David, teetering one way then another, opened his arms and gave David a long, tight hug. He instantly recognized the hug. Father Anthony was famous for it, and it was the same type of hug that all the boys and girls had loved when David was a young boy growing up in St. Cecilia's parish nearly twenty years ago. David automatically stiffened; he was no longer comfortable with hugs.

Father Anthony's breath bore the familiar scent of alcohol – David's one-time friend.

"You look well, my boy," Father Anthony said. "Please forgive me for being late. I was at Dr. Peck's house for our weekly cribbage game. We haven't missed a game in over fifteen years. It may take me another fifteen years to square the match with that son-of-a-gun, but I've got a big lead in the Guinness Stout department."

"That's okay, Father. I just got here anyway."

"It's been a long time since you've been back to St. Cecilia's, David." He draped a massive arm around the younger priest's shoulders. "You'll find that as much as life changes, many things stay the same. St. Cecilia's is one of them. I'm glad you're back, even if you were a pain in the ass as a kid. But I knew you were a good boy at heart."

"It's good to be back...I think."

"Oh, you'll do just fine. People have short memories," Father Anthony said with a wave and a laugh. "Don't worry, you'll be part of the St. Cecilia's family again in no time. Come on, let's get you settled in."

David went to the Honda, and with a pound of his fist, popped open the hatchback. He retrieved a well-traveled duffel bag that held all his possessions. There weren't many. David had learned it was best to travel light when one didn't have a place to hang his hat. The three years he was about to spend at St. Cecilia's as associate pastor would be, next to the seminary, the longest time spent in one place since leaving home at age seventeen.

Entering the rectory, the first thing David noticed was an almost life-sized painting of Jesus on the cross. David had seen portraits of the Crucifixion many times, but this one was different. The head was bowed in the familiar position with the crown of thorns and nails brutally goring His scalp, hands, and feet. But His eyes, instead of being closed or looking down, were open, gently looking upward. His gaze mesmerized David.

"Powerful, isn't it?" Father Anthony said, startling David. "Larry Peck discovered it on a trip to Italy and donated it to the parish. It's my favorite picture of the Crucifixion. You seem intrigued. What do you see?"

David set down his duffel bag and walked over to the painting. Only inches away, he took off his silver wire-rimmed glasses. "It's His eyes. Jesus doesn't look like He's suffering. It's like He's content, at peace, totally okay with what's happening. His eyes are saying, 'Don't worry, I know.'"

"Hmm..." Father Anthony stroked his beard and nodded his head. "Yes, very good. Most people are drawn only to the pain and suffering. They aren't able to look long enough to see the beauty and serenity in His eyes. Ah, but when they do, they see the mirror to His soul. The eyes, my boy. If in doubt, the eyes will always tell you the truth."

Father Anthony smiled and then quickly turned to face David who was still staring at the portrait, seemingly unable to look away. "You must be thirsty. I'll show you to your room. You can unpack and I'll grab us a couple of cold drinks, then a full tour of your new home."

Jostled out of his trance, David managed to say, "Great." He looked back at the portrait as he followed Father Anthony down the dark tiled hallway, their footsteps echoing off the stone walls. David felt as if he just passed some kind of test.

His room was spacious enough – one big chamber with a small closet, but no bathroom. He would have to use the facilities down the hall.

"Well," David mumbled. "I'm used to taking a crap and sharing the showers with a bunch of seminarians. At least I'm prepared for this much. I don't know about the rest."

Two windows occupied the wall opposite the room's door. David opened the long drapes that hung to the floor and looked out to a view of the sports fields and, in the distance, St. Cecilia's school. A group of children were playing tackle football in the dusk on this September evening. He wondered if one of them was Christopher. David hadn't seen his godson in nearly six months, the last time Christopher visited David at the seminary.

The single bed under the windows looked comfortable: a dull brass headboard and a frame that held a thick mattress. A colorful patch-pattern quilt covered the top of the bed, providing the only visually stimulating colors to the room, even though it was faded and worn.

There was little dresser space, not that David needed much – four medium-size drawers built inside a small fat dresser next to the bed. A nightstand on the other side held a tall, skinny lamp with an aged yellow lampshade. These two furnishings were made of dark wood that looked antique but were probably just old, cheap furniture. At most all of the pastor's residences David had visited over the years everything seemed donated – old and worn and out of place, sort of like misfit stuff people couldn't even give away after their garage sales.

On the wall opposite the bed was a porcelain sink. Above that, a mirror with a curving crack running from side to side. He attempted to open the mirror and almost pulled it from the wall; it wasn't the opening kind.

He turned the sink's brass handle with an "H" branded on it to wash off the grit and grime that had accumulated on his hands and face from the long drive. He was greeted by water so cold it hurt. He then realized that hot meant cold and cold meant hot. This was okay with him, but he preferred to know the rules ahead of time. Finding them out by trial and error was always a drag, but that's how life seemed to unfold most of the time.

With the palms of his hands resting on the sink, David lifted his head and looked into the mirror. He had to stand on the tips of his toes to see his reflection. This was easy for his athletic five-foot-six inch frame. He thought sarcastically, I'll probably have to use the damn phone book, but in a town this small I still won't be able to see the top of my head. His short brown hair was covered by the football cap he'd put on before leaving the seminary to return to his hometown of Willa. He took it off and swore he had a few more gray hairs than he had before he left.

"Thirty-four and already going gray. Well, maybe the parishioners will think I'm wise beyond my years."

David had driven straight through from St. Louis to Willa in a little over nine hours. His hazel-colored eyes were streaked red with swollen blood vessels. He was beat.

―――――――

Father Anthony came back with a Guinness and a Coca Cola Classic in an old style bottle.

David smiled with amusement. "I can't believe they still make those things."

Father Anthony handed David the soda and abruptly said, "How long's it been now?"

"About a year and a half." David was embarrassed. He gathered himself by guzzling down some of the soda.

"How'd you know I slipped?" David wiped his lips with the back of his hand.

"Secrets are few in this community or in the community of priests. Get used to it. Watch what you say to folks – fellow priests included." Father Anthony stopped and took a long draw from his beer bottle, then said, "Father Tom at the seminary is an old friend of mine. I've kept up with you. I asked the archbishop to assign you here after you were ordained."

"Why me?" David said. "I wanted to ask you this the last couple of times we spoke on the phone, but thought it'd be better if I waited until we were face to face. I mean, everyone in town knows my past here. I'm sure they're all just thrilled to have the town delinquent return home to be their new associate pastor. Father Tom mentioned you and your friendship many times and I know you go way back with the archbishop. I'm sure you could have had your pick of the litter."

Father Anthony smiled and chuckled, then turned serious. "David, let's face it, you've had trouble staying sober since high school. You were almost kicked out of the seminary when you slipped, as you so neatly put it. There's not a lot of slack left in your rope. I know it's unusual for a priest to return to the parish he grew up in right out of the chute, but sooner or later you'd be back here. I know the baggage you're carrying, more of it than you think. But that's okay, we all bring something with us."

David smiled half-heartedly and bowed his head, looking at the floor.

"Listen, you're a caring, sensitive young man and I believe you've got what it takes to be a great priest. The archbishop made the final decision to appoint you to St. Cecilia's. He was hesitant, and I'll be honest with you, I had to sell him hard on the idea. In the end, we both felt that the sooner you came back and faced your past head-on, the sooner you'd find out if you could handle being a priest –

straight and sober. I don't want to lose another young priest; Lord knows we're shorthanded as it is."

Memories of David's seventeen years growing up in Willa attempted to bubble to the surface, but he wouldn't let them. He had spent many years learning how to suppress them; he hated the thoughts and feelings that came with the memories. Coming home after being away such a long time, seeing Father Anthony again and envisioning the difficult journey ahead was all too much. The emotions began to seep through like a slow leak in a tire. David felt lightheaded, a familiar sense of fear crept over him.

"I've always been fond of you. And I've admired how you've handled yourself in spite of all the crap that happened when you were growing up. In my forty-two years as a priest, I've seen how devastating and destructive the effects of drugs and alcohol – and abuse – can be. Too many times, I've watched these things tear families apart and ruin good kids before they even had a chance to live life. I don't want to see that happen to you."

David said, "But how can I be a good priest here? I'm so wet behind the ears they're dripping. I've got no credibility." He struggled to stay composed, wondering if Father Anthony knew everything about his past. "I can't even help myself half the time, how am I going to help others? And how do I start repairing the damage I've done here?"

Father Anthony put his beer down on the dresser and walked over to David. He put both giant paws on the young priest's shoulders and said, "You are qualified to be a priest. You know why? Because you've experienced hurt and suffering, you've struggled and you've had to overcome problems. That, my boy, is life in a nutshell. We see more pain and suffering than we do happiness and joy in this calling. People come to us during the dire times in their lives for strength and peace of mind, but what most are desperately seeking are answers to unanswerable questions.

You know what they're thinking and feeling because you've been there. When people come to you, you'll know what to say. You've asked those questions, haven't you?" David nodded. "Then you know they can't be fully answered, only explained the best that you can so that others are able to find comfort and peace in their faith.

"Now, as far as repairing any damage, just let things take care of themselves. Let your deeds and actions speak for you. It'll take time; it won't happen overnight. But if you really believe in yourself and your calling, you'll remain patient and find a way to succeed."

David felt the tears coming; it took all he had to hold them back. Everything was happening so suddenly, and it was all so overwhelming. His throat tightened with each breath. After a moment, he said with a restrained tremble in his voice, "Father Anthony, I'm scared. What if I can't do this? What if I fail? I desperately want to be a priest – a good one. I truly believe it's my calling…what God wants me to do with my life."

Father Anthony looked David straight in the eye. He felt strength and trust radiating from the wise, old priest's eyes; the kind of strength and trust a child feels as he jumps into the water for the first time, knowing his dad will be there to help him if anything goes wrong.

"Remember David, you're not alone. I'll be here for you. Anytime, day or night. More importantly, you always have your faith. When you need to, lean on Him, ask Him for help and guidance. If your faith is strong, He'll come through. Now, it's been a long and eventful day. You look exhausted. Let's take that tour tomorrow after morning Mass. Okay?"

David rubbed his watery eyes. "Yeah, I'm ready to call it a day."

"My room is down the hall. If you need anything, just knock."

"Father Anthony?"

"Yes?"

"Thanks."

"Anytime. Day or night," Father Anthony said, walking toward the door.

"Don't forget your beer."

Father Anthony smiled and winked. "Take care of it for me, would you? Good night. Sleep well."

David poured the remaining beer into the sink, appreciating Father Anthony's trust, but hating the temptation he left behind.

David woke early to get ready for 6:30 a.m. Mass, his first at his new parish. He was refreshed but anxious, like an athlete who had trained years for an event. Thanks to his preparation at the seminary, David was ready to go. He also knew he was just assisting Father Anthony and that helped tame some of the jitters. After a shower, David looked into the mirror and decided a change was in order. Out of his three-day old growth he shaved the outline of a goatee. He walked down the hall and saw a light. In the kitchen, Father Anthony was already sipping coffee from one of the multi-colored mugs that must have been made and given to him by the little ones in the parish. A large bowl with only a few spoonfuls of oatmeal left was pushed off to the side.

The room was cold and drafty. It smelled like an old cafe. The floor was covered with worn white and gray tiles. The kitchen table and four matching chairs were an off-white color, one step in quality above a folding table and chair set. All the appliances were different brands and colors. Probably all donated, David thought. Money's always an issue in a Catholic parish.

"Good morning," David burst out cheerfully, feeling as if he had to make up for his emotional display the previous evening. In the shower, he convinced himself that when he was lacking confidence about any of his new duties, and he knew he would, he would mask it. "Fake it 'till you make it" was one of the few things he could remember his father telling him. Over the years, David discovered this was pretty good advice. It was the only sound advice his father ever bothered to pass along.

"Sleep well?" Father Anthony said, still groggy from lack of sleep and too much Guinness.

"Like a rock." David's first lie to his mentor.

"I've never been good about getting up this early," Father Anthony said with a yawn. "An occupational hazard, I guess. There's coffee ready. Watch out, I tend to make it strong, especially since it's about the only thing we can have this close to Mass time."

"Dang," David muttered under his breath. He wanted a bagel but was reminded that he couldn't eat solid food an hour before Mass. The coffee was as black as a moonless night and poured like syrup, so he only filled his mug half full. An intense caffeine buzz was the last thing he needed this morning.

He sat down opposite Father Anthony who was studying the local sports section of the Saturday morning newspaper. "About last night—"

"Forget it." Father Anthony continued leafing through the paper. "Big football game today. The Crusaders better be ready for Silver Grove's defense, otherwise it's going to be a long day. I can't remember having a game this early in the season when we were playing the number one team in the state. I'll tell you, it doesn't get any better than this."

David had forgotten all about St. Cecilia Crusaders high school football – a sin for a native son.

"Larry and I had planned on going to the game," Father Anthony said. "Silver Grove's only about an hour away, but we need someone here just in case. I hope you don't mind staying behind."

"Not at all," David said, remembering the excitement of game day in Willa.

"Corey Hansen's also coming with us." Father Anthony neatly folded the paper and put it on the table. With a look of concern, he continued. "He's one of Larry's patients. You'll meet him soon enough. He's a pretty troubled child who spends a lot of time in the office at school. He's gotten worse lately and Larry feels an outing like this might help build more trust in their relationship."

"What exactly does Dr. Peck do?"

"A psychiatrist. Kids mostly. Real nasty stuff. But he's great with 'em. Larry's worked wonders with children others have left out to rot. He does it all; writing, speaking, counseling. We're lucky to have him in Willa. He could pull up stakes, go to a bigger city and make one hell of a living."

Intrigued, David said, "What keeps him here?"

Father Anthony sipped his coffee and set it down. Slowly stroking his beard, he said, "Larry's never been married and doesn't have any kids. He's totally devoted to his work and those he treats. After graduating from medical school, he came back home to Willa to set up his practice. He's always said it's the quality of work he's interested in, not the quantity. Money doesn't drive him, although he's far from destitute. Unfortunately, sexual abuse is everywhere, even in our own little town. Willa's his home and he's said several times that he has no intention of pulling up roots now, not at forty-seven. He earned his degrees on the east coast – Columbia University, if I'm not mistaken – so he's experienced big city life. He's a small town guy at heart. Always will be."

"Sounds like a good man."

"That he is," Father Anthony said. "He's a good friend, and a good friend to the town and to St. Cecilia's."

"I'd like to meet him sometime."

"I'll introduce you to him this morning." Father Anthony got up to pour more sludge into his cup. "He's a regular every morning at six-thirty Mass."

"Great," David said.

"Oh, by the way, we're taking off for Silver Grove around ten o'clock. I imagine you remember how deserted it can get during an away game. It'll probably be standing room only at the game, so it should be pretty quiet around here. You've got the whole day to unwind and get settled in. The plan is to officially welcome you back to St. Cecilia's at noon Mass tomorrow. We'll have a reception afterwards."

"Boy, I'll bet that'll just be jam-packed," David said sarcastically.

Father Anthony smiled and dismissed the comment with a slap to David's back. "Relax. Come on, let's clean up and get over to the church."

As they were cleaning the kitchen, Father Anthony said with a sly grin, "You trying to disguise yourself?"

"What?"

Father Anthony put his fingers to his bearded chin and playfully stroked it.

Now it was David's turn to smile. "Oh that." He touched the whiskers on his chin and upper lip. "Yeah, I'm incognito."

David had forgotten what the eighty-year-old church looked like. As a kid he didn't see the elaborate and detailed architecture, he just looked at it. But now, like a serious art lover, he studied the stained glass that was built into the walls and the buttresses that swept from the ceiling. St. Cecilia's wasn't a modern church with cozy carpet, padded pews, and heated holy water. David disliked those kinds of churches; they had no character, no history. St. Cecilia's was a giant structure made of light-colored stone and dark-speckled marble tile. From the outside it looked like a castle.

Inside, the tile and stone amplified even the smallest noise. As a young boy, he remembered going to confession once and being extra careful to talk quietly. But the priest, Father Anthony, kept telling David to speak up. At the time, he was horrified, thinking all the kids waiting in line could hear how he had peeked up Mary Farley's skirt with a small mirror taped to the top of his shoe. When he left the confessional that day, he didn't look up from the floor; the guilt was still too fresh to let go. And, he was sure that others would be shaking their heads in disgust, while all the girls tightly clamped their skirts to their legs as he walked by.

David continued to scan the church and was instantly drawn to the row upon row of stained glass windows. They had deep rich colors that he imagined would have been difficult to recreate. The young priest thought, these must have been made by someone with a gift, with a passion for God and craft.

The windows on the two sidewalls were especially breathtaking. At least six-feet wide, they started about twenty feet up from the floor and rose another fifteen feet. Each one depicted a defining moment in the life of Jesus: His birth in the stable, raising Lazarus from the dead, the Last Supper, Pontius Pilate's judgment, the Crucifixion and many other scenes. They were spectacular, and the pride of the parish. As a nine year old, David had learned this the hard way when a rock intended for a pine cone that dangled from one of the many pine trees surrounding the church bounced off a branch and crashed right through a window during twelve o'clock Sunday Mass. Unfortunately for David, his mother was there that day – one of the rare occasions she was sober enough to attend Mass. She quickly realized he hadn't come back from the bathroom yet and knew exactly where the rock had come from. David couldn't sit down for two days without intense pain searing through him, which was just as well because sitting wasn't required as he scrubbed every inch of the church floor on his knees for his punishment. His mom couldn't walk a straight line most of the time, but she could wield a belt with uncanny accuracy.

The rows of pews on both sides of the center aisle were made from dark, hard wood. The only modern accommodation made to the church was to the kneelers. They were padded, but only after the parents and Father Anthony got fed up with the collective moans and groans that came every time the kids kneeled during Mass.

The sanctuary was the heart and soul of the church. In it sat the altar, which was crafted from white marble with shades of gray streaked in a random pattern. Father Anthony called the surface on which he broke bread and blessed wine his holy workbench. Right behind the altar was the tabernacle. It was simple in design and bright gold in color, the type of gold that sparkled in just the right light. This was where the consecrated hosts, sacramentally changed during Mass into the Body and Blood of Christ, were placed.

As the two entered the sacristy to get ready for Mass, David said, "You know, this church has always had a special feel about it, a real spiritual one."

"I wish I could add to that today," Father Anthony said while stretching his arms. "But I don't think I'm gonna knock anyone's spiritual socks off this morning."

"What do you mean?"

"My boy, here's lesson number one in the life of a priest." Father Anthony rubbed his hands together, his droopy eyes started to show sparks of life. "It's called winging it. I must admit I had a few too many last night and didn't properly prepare for my homily. So it's time to let the Holy Spirit take over. He's batting a thousand at six-thirty Mass on Saturday morning."

"You don't know what you're going to say?" David said, dumbfounded.

Laughing, Father Anthony said, "With all the things we have to do and the demands on our time, you have to let someone else drive every once in awhile. When I first started, I put a lot of late night preparation into every homily. Eventually, you have to learn to trust and let go, but it's hard. You know, most of my best sermons have come when I've totally surrendered and put my trust in the Holy Spirit."

"Well, I don't think I'm gonna give up the wheel anytime soon," David said, already beginning to sweat just thinking about doing Mass solo.

"Would you get the hosts and wine and take them out to the server's table for me?" Father Anthony said while slipping an alb over his head. "I'm sure you remember where they're kept."

"Now you know I wasn't the only altar boy to sneak a couple of hosts every now and then. I never touched the wine, though."

"Ah huh. Remember you're in the house of God. No bullshitting allowed."

David chuckled and his nerves began to fade. He went to the same upper cabinet where the hosts and wine were kept when he was a kid. And, just like when he was a young altar boy, David couldn't reach the handle. So he jumped. On his third attempt, he managed to grab the handle and open the cabinet door. Sure enough they were still stored there, and still well beyond his reach.

Father Anthony was watching this display with amusement. "Why don't you go get the stool you all used to get up there."

David looked at Father Anthony out of the corner of his eye. "In the closet?"

"Yep." Father Anthony walked out the sacristy door to finish his preparations.

It was the perfect first Mass: a light turnout. And, there was no one in attendance that David recognized from his childhood. He didn't want to hassle with that just yet; it would happen soon enough. Mass was short, as early ones tend to be, and his responsibilities were few.

To David, it was obvious at the start that Father Anthony was going through the motions. However, he began to gather energy and momentum as Mass progressed, peaking during the homily. David was amazed and mesmerized at Father Anthony's passion and presence during his sermon. He appeared to grow in stature, and the crowd of about thirty people, which seemed small because they were scattered throughout the humongous church, was totally enraptured. All seemed on the edges of their pews, spellbound, absorbed in Father Anthony's message. They nodded their heads in agreement, grimaced when he spoke of Christ's pain and sacrifices and laughed at the old priest's humor. Father Anthony's oratorical abilities were like an expert conductor effortlessly leading an orchestra. And, like the musicians, the parishioners were drained but deeply satisfied at the end.

David was proud to be associated with a holy messenger as fervent and skilled as Father Anthony, but he also felt totally inept. His heart told him that he too could become a great messenger; his head told him that it would take a great deal of time and effort. That was fine with David. Even though patience wasn't exactly a virtue of his, David was willing to pay the price.

When Mass ended, Father Anthony's flock went to the back of the church, lined up and patiently waited for him. Most thanked him for his words of inspiration; some wanted to update him on those who were gravely ill or those who were getting better. Others simply wanted to complain about inane, inconsequential things, like a decision made by the athletic committee or school board, while a few asked advice on how to cope and make it through another day. Through it all, Father Anthony remained upbeat and positive. He patiently listened to each person, then offered advice, words of encouragement or a consoling hug.

David watched and heard most of this as he cleared the altar and extinguished the candles. Unsure of what to do when finished, he headed to the sacristy. Before walking through the door, David noticed one man in a pew toward the middle of the church. He was kneeling and his head was bowed in silent prayer. Slowly, he lifted his head, made the sign of the cross and got up to leave. Genuflecting to pay adoration to Christ in the tabernacle, he spotted David, smiled and enthusiastically raised his hand to signal "Hello." Right away, David knew who this was. He gave the man an awkward wave and a quick smile before disappearing into the sacristy.

David was elated. These simple gestures were his first contact with a parishioner, and they weren't the sneers or looks of contempt that he had visualized and braced himself for. Deep down, David felt he had another ally. Hey, it was only a wave and a smile, David thought. But, hell, I'll take anything I can get.

He noticed some spare offertory envelopes sitting on the sacristy counter. It was then David saw the small black safe – the very one that he had been responsible for. David grew ashamed as he sat down recalling the incident that was the impetus for him to leave Willa.

The summer after his high school graduation, David had been deep in debt to a dealer who sold David the weed he got high on every day and the psychedelic mushrooms he tripped on nightly. The dealer refused to sell David any more drugs until his four hundred dollar tab was paid in full. Already fired from two jobs that summer because of his inability to show up on a regular basis, David was unemployed and broke. For a few weeks, he had lived off the good will of his buddies, but that had dried up fast.

Desperate to feed his addictions, David snuck into St. Cecilia's on Easter Sunday, while Father Anthony was busy hosting the annual Easter egg hunt and picnic that immediately followed noon Mass. Once in the sacristy,

David went to the drawer that he knew from his altar boy days held the offertory money. In it, he found a wad of cash, all ten and twenty dollar bills bundled together with a rubber band, sitting on top of a thick leather satchel tattooed with "Willa Bank and Trust." David set the stack of money aside and peeked inside the bag; it was loaded with cash, change and unopened envelopes.

"I can't take all this," David whispered. He put the satchel back in the drawer and picked up the rubber-banded cash. A quick count gave him over two thousand dollars. More than enough, David thought. Satisfied everything had been put back exactly the way he found it, David stuffed the money down the front of his jeans and left.

Over the next two weeks, the parish was in an uproar about the theft. The money, raised through a special collection, was to be given to the winner of the annual Spittler Award, which was presented to a high school senior to assist him or her with college expenses. The award winner was the one whom Father Anthony and other members of the church and school felt best exemplified leadership in the classroom, in the community and on the sports field — and the student who had the greatest need for financial support. Erik Patten had won the award and was crushed when he learned of the heist. College and law school always had been his goal and David's best friend was counting on the money; without it, Erik might never realize his dream.

During this time, David was on a binge. His debt paid off and plenty of pot and mushrooms to stay high on for a while, David also purchased a Chevy Impala for seven hundred dollars from Tom Meyer, the self-appointed handyman for the church.

"The body needs some work," Tom said to David when he had handed over cash at the sale. "But, I rebuilt the engine myself. It's good for another hundred thousand miles. I'll even throw in some nice rims for three hundred bucks; they're worth twice that." David agreed and drove off in his first car.

It was two days later when the police pulled him over.

"Got a tail light that's acting up," Chief Gardner said, while gnawing on a toothpick. He peered inside the car window and did a quick sweep. "New car, Cooper?"

"A friend's."

"Ain't what I heard."

Looking away, David said, "You heard wrong."

Chief Gardner smiled, rolled the toothpick around in his mouth with his tongue and spat the sliver of wood to the ground. "Get out of the car you lying shit." David complied. The Chief continued, "Tom Meyer said you came by a couple of days ago and bought this piece of crap, said you had a fist full of cash." The Chief pulled another toothpick from his shirt pocket and slipped it into his mouth, "Where you working these days?"

"Here and there." David looked up and around, refusing to give the man any eye contact.

Chief Gardner grabbed hold of David's shirt and pushed him hard against the car. "Listen, cowboy, you want me to search this fucking thing? Do you think I'll only find a spent roach in the ashtray? My money says there's a lot more where that came from."

David's eyes grew wide; there was a quarter pound of marijuana in the trunk he had intended on selling to make money, but he never got around to it. Instead, it had turned into his personal stash. David's eyes narrowed and his jaw muscles grew tight. "Whatta you want from me?"

"That's more like it," Chief Gardner said, letting go of David's shirt, then smoothing out the wrinkles. "Tell you what, I won't search the car if you come clean about the money."

David stayed silent, weighing his options.

Chief Gardner snickered at David's indecision, spread his arms wide and said, "You want to fuck with me or take your chances with Father Anthony? You can be guaranteed that I'll rip you to pieces. Hey, I've got an idea: Let's open up the trunk, maybe I can help you fix that tail light."

David dropped his head and said, "I'll pay it back."

Much to the dismay of Chief Gardner and many of the parishioners, Father Anthony had insisted that charges not be pressed as long as David agree to repay the money and publicly apologize to the parish. David had accepted the terms. However, within four hours of making that promise, David was on the road, leaving Willa for good.

He had always intended on keeping his word, at least most of it. A year and a half later, David had mailed Father Anthony a short letter of apology and the two thousand dollars he took – plus a couple hundred more – with his winnings from a hot pool stick. A short time later, David had received a post card; it read: "You're forgiven. Be safe."

Father Anthony burst through the sacristy door, snapping David from his thoughts. Following Father Anthony was the man David had spotted at Mass. The elder priest said, "Janet Manelli is an absolute pain in the ass!" He whipped his alb over his head and threw it on a chair. "In the scheme of life, will it really matter if we purchase single-loop bike racks or double-loop bike racks for the school? That woman is hell bent on creating waves with every decision made by every committee in this parish."

"Well, Anthony, the parish is important to her," the man counseled. "Not being able to have children has been devastating to her. She treats the parish as if it was her child. I'll tell you what though, I wouldn't want to be one of her kids."

Father Anthony laughed, the frustration and tension of dealing with an unreasonable parishioner began to dissipate. "Yeah, I know you're right. How about sending her over to you next time? You're much more patient and understanding with people like her than I'll ever be."

"What a salesman," the man said with a large grin and easy laugh. "No thanks. She's all yours. I've got enough nuts to crack."

He then turned to David, offered his right hand and said, "You must be Father David. Welcome back to St. Cecilia's! I'm Larry Peck. I've heard all sorts of great things about you from Anthony."

"They couldn't have all been great, unless Father Anthony left out some minor details. But thanks. I'm glad to meet you, Dr. Peck. Father Anthony speaks very fondly of you."

"Larry. Please, call me Larry. The only ones who call me doctor – along with other names I won't reveal – are my patients, and that's usually when they're ticked off at me, which seems to be happening with greater regularity these days. I'm blaming it on the change of season; it's a viable reason that keeps my ego and sanity intact."

David smiled and laughed; he couldn't help it. Larry naturally invited people to laugh along with him. He was a tall man, about six-foot-two, tall by David's standards anyway. The doctor was thin but not skinny; kind of wiry, like a basketball player. When he moved it was graceful and without effort. It was obvious Larry kept in shape. He had a high forehead and his hair was thick and curly, not a wisp of gray could be seen in the sandy-brown color. David looked deeply into the blue-gray color of Larry's eyes; they were comforting, affable, enchanting.

"I hear you do great work with some tough kids."

"I'm not sure about great," Larry said. "It can be a tough profession, but it also can be very rewarding. Just like what you do."

"Oh, he's being modest," Father Anthony interjected. "It's a habit I'm trying to break him of."

Just then, the black pager attached to the psychiatrist's belt began beeping. He quickly pressed a button to stop the noise and adjusted the pager so he could clearly see the phone number displayed on the small screen.

"Damn. Not on game day. I have to leave for a bit. This shouldn't take long, Anthony. Would you mind picking up Corey and I'll meet you both at the rectory around ten fifteen?"

"You bet." Father Anthony nodded toward the pager. "Problems?"

"Nah, this is my Janet Manelli. I'll tell the patient to listen to the game on the radio as part of therapy." All three men laughed.

"What a great idea," Father Anthony said. "I'm gonna have to use that one with Janet."

Larry turned to David. "It was nice to meet you. If there's anything I can do to help you get adjusted, let me know. After the game, Anthony, Corey and I are cooking out at my place. Please come and join us."

"I'd love to."

"We'll swing by and pick you up after the game. See you all later." Larry rushed out the door.

"Have any plans today?" Father Anthony said while hanging up his chasuble. "I hate leaving you here alone so soon after you've arrived."

"Don't worry about me. I thought I'd stop by and see the Pattens. Maybe I'll catch some of the game on the radio over there. Lizzy made me promise to come over as soon as I got back in town. I haven't seen the three of them together in a long time."

"You and Erik, now there's trouble," Father Anthony cracked. "Frick and Frack back together again."

CHAPTER 2

David was feeling pretty good, better than he had in a long time. His first Mass was over and that was a huge relief. Also, Father Anthony made him feel welcome and confident that this whole thing was going to work out just fine. Now he could jump in with both feet and do what he longed to do: minister.

The day was stunning, one of those rare Midwestern autumn days sandwiched between the sweltering, humid days of summer and the frigid, snowy days of winter. There was an abundance of warm sunshine, cloudless blue skies, and comfortable temperatures. It was shorts and T-shirt weather, even for David who shunned his "blacks" and white collar. After all, he was off the clock.

With a couple of hours to kill before the game, he hopped into the Honda and decided to explore his hometown, see what had changed and what had stayed the same. He rolled down the car windows and propped open the broken sunroof with a small ice scraper. In the new CD player he had received from Erik and Lizzy as an ordination gift, David loaded a Bruce Springsteen CD. Lizzy was the one who had presented the CD player to him; Erik had been too busy with work to make an appearance. Both friends shared David's love and taste for music – rock-and-roll – and he loved the gift. He was sure it was worth more than the old car.

As he debated where to venture first, he thought about what Father Anthony said before Mass and decided to let the Holy Spirit do the driving, taking David wherever He willed.

"At this point, I'd rather have You drive my car than my sermons," David joked out loud, while raising his eyes skyward. "No offense. I gotta start somewhere."

He found himself traveling through the downtown area. Not much had changed but even the familiar was disorienting. The same clay-colored brick buildings filled with many of the same small businesses passed down from generation to generation appeared untouched. The main road through the heart of downtown was still bricked and uneven. It was also very narrow. So narrow that David questioned whether to stick his arm out the window to signal he was turning left or right, fearing his arm might get ripped off by an oncoming car or semitrailer truck. He hadn't gotten around to changing the burned out light bulbs in the car's rear blinkers.

David remembered the huge trailer trucks constantly rumbling up and down this path, tying up traffic and causing the ground to shake, as they headed for the grain yards or stockyards located on the outskirts of town. Today, there wasn't a truck in sight. He didn't have to visit the yards to know they were vacant and empty. Farming was dwindling as the primary livelihood of Willa residents.

As he clattered along the old road toward the end of the downtown district, he came upon Baumm Drug. Memories of Erik and his other buddies came surging back like a splash of cold water on a tired face. This old drugstore used to be their hangout: A place where they ate hot fudge sundaes after baseball games, plotted their next scam, fought and argued, talked about girls and sports and what they wanted to be when they were older. It was a special place. David was drawn to stop and peek inside.

When he walked into the store, he was immediately taken back in time. As he was looking around, a high-pitched, perky voice behind him said, "Can I help you?"

David turned and was face to face with Mr. Baumm. He, like the rest of the store, remained frozen in time, just as David remembered.

"Well look what the cat dragged in!" the storeowner said, extending his small, chubby right hand to David. Mr. Baumm had a strong grip for a man a couple inches shorter than David and, at least, thirty years his elder.

"David Cooper. I heard you were coming back to town," Mr. Baumm said, amidst a bite of a Mars chocolate bar. "How the hell are you?"

"I'm fine," David said, somewhat shocked by the pleasant reception. "Boy, the store hasn't changed a bit."

Mr. Baumm beamed. "I always figured if it ain't broke why fix it." He reached up and pushed back a few straggling pieces of thin, greasy-black hair. The man was still trying to cover up a balding scalp by combing the few remaining strands of hair he had left over to one side. The problem was the sparse locks kept falling back in front of his eyes or onto the horn-rimmed bifocals that set on the end of his pudgy nose.

"Man, this place brings back some great memories," the young priest said, looking around. The soda counter remained in the back of the store; the pharmacy center was much larger but right where it was fourteen years ago. And the aisles and items on the shelves appeared to be exactly where he remembered.

"I also have some memories of you and your friends, not all pleasant though." Mr. Baumm arched his eyebrows over his bifocals and peered at David.

Groping, David managed, "I know we were …rambunctious."

"Rambunctious! You guys could be real troublemakers. But not in my store. Not after I kicked all you guys out for a month for pouring laxative into Mr. Brillman's milk shake."

"That was a stupid and mean-spirited thing to do." Part of David was ashamed, while another part of him desperately wanted to laugh out loud at the memory of Mr. Brillman running back and forth to the bathroom, totally baffled about what was happening. Only Erik's guilty giggles had given them away. "I hope you can forgive me for all those juvenile pranks. It was a long time ago, and I'm sorry for any headaches I caused you."

Mr. Baumm boomed out a hearty laugh. "Actually, John Brillman was a dope. Never paid his bills on time. He was an arrogant, demanding son-of-a-bitch. When everyone cleared out that day, my wife and I laughed our butts off. He passed a few years back, a jerk to the end."

"Well, I'm truly sorry for all that stuff."

"Water under the bridge. I always liked you guys, you reminded me of myself when I was young." He slapped David on the back, throwing him off balance. "I was simply smarter than you knuckleheads – I never got caught! Christ, your ass always seemed to be in a sling."

"Well, we were just stupid kids." Embarrassed, David changed the subject. "You still make a mean hot fudge sundae? Boy, did I look forward to those."

"You betcha. As good as ever." Mr. Baumm's face lit up. He winked at David and said, "How about one for the prodigal son returning home? On the house."

"I can't pass that up," David said, politely laughing at the remark. Actually, he was thrilled at how well things were going. Maybe time does heal all wounds, he thought.

He followed the old man back to the soda counter. Even Mr. Baumm's walk was the same: He waddled back and forth, like a penguin. His powder-blue polyester pants and white pharmacy coat were a little too snug, contributing to the stiffness in his walk.

David took a seat on the only red vinyl stool cushion that didn't have gray duct tape covering a rip. The soda counter was large and constructed in a U-shaped design. It sat twelve people with plenty of room between each of the stools, which were bolted directly into the worn pea-green colored linoleum floor. As far as he could tell, the Formica counter top was the only new addition. It was bright green and clashed with the stool cushion's red color, giving the area a year-round Christmas look.

Mr. Baumm was busy making two hot fudge sundaes, babbling about someone's depression and medication, when two people entered the store and headed for the prescription counter.

An incessant talker, Mr. Baumm rarely let an opportunity to gossip slip by. As a pharmacist, he knew everyone's medical secrets. When discussing a person's condition, he tried to keep it confidential, but it didn't take a genius to realize who he was talking about. Actually, if you waited long enough and didn't interrupt, he would usually slip and say the person's name, then swear you to secrecy. It got him into trouble every once in a while but he couldn't help himself. Plus, many people loved to gossip and Mr. Baumm was the man with the news. He was always forgiven; everyone knew that it wasn't malicious.

Mr. Baumm set down the two sundaes. "My son Ron...you remember Ron, don't you?"

"Yeah, he graduated a couple years ahead me." David was eying the sundae in front of him, a huge creation of ice cream and hot fudge, all expertly crammed into a tall old fashion ice cream glass.

"Ron works here with me. He's also a pharmacist. Gonna take over the business some day," Mr. Baumm said with pride. "He's on his way to the game. We switch off: one of us goes, while the other stays behind to mind the store. Today was his turn. Shitty luck, huh? The boy wouldn't even trade with his old man. Can you believe that? Oh well, I'd have probably done the same thing. When it comes to Crusaders football, there's no sympathy. Go ahead and dig in. I'll be right back."

The storeowner merrily waddled off to help the elderly couple. Handshakes and pleasantries were exchanged; it was evident they were long-term customers. Soon enough, the three were huddled together. The pharmacist was holding court and the couple listened intently as he whispered juicy morsels of scuttlebutt.

David dove straight into the sundae. It was even better than he remembered. No low-fat ice cream or yogurt in this work of art. This was all real ice cream and chocolate fudge, calories and fat included. He slowed down to savor each bite, losing himself in pleasant childhood memories.

"David Cooper?" a raspy, trembling voice said behind him.

Startled from his daydreaming, David stopped in mid-bite and quickly spun around. Unfortunately, this particular stool's ball bearings must have retained its grease well, because it raced around so fast that he had to flail out an arm to keep from being thrown to the floor. He didn't stop spinning until he was back facing the counter again. In the process, his arm knocked over both sundaes, splattering them all over the counter and onto the floor. He felt blood rush to his face. Within seconds, it was bright red with embarrassment. His first instinct was to look over and gauge Mr. Baumm's reaction. He was standing with the older man; both looked amused, but also concerned.

"David Cooper?" the female voice demanded.

"Uhh, yes. That's me." He turned around more slowly this time, acting as if nothing unusual had just happened. "Why, Mrs. Greene. Hello."

"Father Anthony said you were going to come crawling back," she spit out with venom. It was hard for David to look into her gray eyes; they were like two sharp rods piercing his eye sockets. "I don't care what the archbishop says, it's asinine for you to come back. You're not wanted here."

David took a deep breath to compose himself. This was the kind of reception he was waiting for, but still he wasn't prepared for this.

Agnes Greene had it out for him ever since her German shepherd, Buddy, died. David was in eighth grade, and the street Mrs. Greene lived on was the quickest route to and from St. Cecilia's school for him and many others kids. Everyday Buddy terrorized anyone who ventured down the street, either side. The dog would corner a horror-struck child, bare his giant yellow fangs and bark loudly and ferociously. Whoever the poor kid was that Buddy chose as his victim was frozen in panic until Mrs. Greene came to get the beast. David swore she got a kick out of the whole thing. The old lady seemed to wait a tad longer than she should to call the hound off, and she was always smiling as she dragged Buddy away with foam spewing from his snapping jaws.

One day Buddy went after David and Lizzy on their way to school. Fleeing for their lives, they climbed a tree. On the way up Lizzy's new school uniform was ripped and the dog bit her on the calf, resulting in eleven stitches. She also had to endure rabies shots because Mrs. Greene refused to tell Lizzy's mother if Buddy had been vaccinated. The old witch insisted the two little kids were taunting the poor ninety-pound beast and deserved what they got.

After school that same day David was returning home from baseball practice, bat and glove in tow. Again, Buddy came tearing around the side of the house, crossed the street, and headed straight for David. He remembered the odd feeling of calmness as he dropped his glove, raised his bat and, with a perfectly timed swing, blasted Buddy in the jaw.

David sprinted home, leaving the scene – and his ball glove – as fast as he could. Mrs. Greene accused him of killing her precious pooch but she couldn't prove it. Of course, David denied any involvement. The one person who knew the truth was Father Anthony, but only after he coerced it out of David during confession. Father Anthony was good at that when he needed to know something.

Exhaling quietly, David stayed in control. Mrs. Greene was still a mean, spiteful woman, and he knew there was nothing he could do or say to change that. So he thought of a quick prayer and summoned his seminary school training to deal with this woman.

"Well, Mrs. Greene, I'm glad to be back and hope we can start with a clean slate."

She grimaced her wrinkled, leathery face and said, "Clean slate! I'll never forget what you did to my Buddy. You...you...dog murderer!"

"I'm sorry about what happened to your dog," David said. It was a no-win situation and he wasn't about to let it go any further. "How's Mr. Greene?"

"What do you care?" she said, clearly irritated David wasn't going to take the bait and defend himself. "I can't believe that they let you become a priest. Of all people!"

David conjured up fond memories of his old baseball bat, but quickly wiped those thoughts from his head. Instead, he turned to something Mrs. Greene could relate to: religion.

"As you know, God forgives those who sincerely mean it. I hope to do my best when serving the people of St. Cecilia's."

"You won't serve me! A sinner like you shouldn't be part of the Church. Like I told Father Anthony, I don't want you here and I'll do whatever it takes to get you out!"

David rested his elbows on the counter and folded his hands so that his fingertips were lightly touching each other as if in prayer. Gently he said, "As the Bible says in John chapter eight, verse seven, 'He that is without sin among you, let him first cast a stone.'" It really wasn't a fair fight. If there was one thing that was fresh in David's mind, it was scripture.

The words hit Mrs. Greene like a slap in the face: Her mouth was open, moving, trying to respond but nothing came out. Her eyes moved wildly back and forth searching for something to say. Finally, she managed, "Don't...don't you dare hide behind that collar. I know what you are, and you can rest assured that others will too!"

She spun around on her black-heeled shoes and stomped back to the pharmacy counter. Mr. Greene and Mr. Baumm quickly looked back at each other and started a conversation, acting as if they didn't hear or see a thing.

"Arnie, let's get out of here!"

"But our prescription isn't ready yet, dear."

"I don't care! We'll go to Walgreens and get it filled. I will not remain in this place with that fraud for one more second. We're leaving!" As she turned to go, Mr. Greene looked at Mr. Baumm and David and shrugged his shoulders as if to signal, "Sorry, I'm not in control here," and slinked out the door behind her.

Mr. Baumm trudged back to the soda counter and quietly began cleaning up the spilled sundaes. David sat on the stool blankly staring at the door the old couple had just exited. He felt like shit.

"Pay no attention to her." Mr. Baumm was on his knees wiping up the ice cream that was flung to the floor. "She's as cold as dead fish on ice. Poor Arnie, he has to deal with that witch everyday."

"Maybe she's right. Maybe I shouldn't have come back."

Mr. Baumm looked over his shoulder while wringing out a towel in the sink and said, "Absolutely not! Everyone deserves a second chance. She's had hers and many more. You, on the other hand, haven't had yours yet. Not everyone in town is like her. Believe me, she is one of a kind, thank God. She's high and mighty; a holy roller who rarely practices what she preaches. Everyone knows what she's about. She shouts but no one listens anymore."

"Thanks for the pep talk." David began to get up and said with a forced laugh, "I should probably head out. Don't want you to lose any more business."

"Sit your butt down," Mr. Baumm said, wagging and pointing his finger toward the stool. "I promised you a hot fudge sundae, and a sundae you shall have. Listen, I don't need her business, and I'm sick and tired of her bullying people around. Although, just to be on the safe side, I'd better call Otis over at Walgreens and warn him she's on the war path and headed his way."

Both men grinned at each other. Mr. Baumm made two more sundaes, all the while talking endlessly about this and that, filling David in on the happenings of the town over the years and the people in it. He learned who had stayed in Willa and who had left; who was still alive and who had died; who was struggling and who was doing well.

The place remained empty and David lost track of time. He was thoroughly enjoying himself. Also, he knew the information would come in handy later, even if it was gossip. Mr. Baumm was a terrific and entertaining chatterbox.

Almost two hours and a banana split later, Mr. Baumm said, "Oh my gosh, it's almost kickoff!" He dashed over to the radio and turned it on. "God, I wish I was there. I hate listening to big games on the radio. I just get too jazzed up."

"I'd better get going." With a thin white paper napkin, David wiped whipped cream from the corner of his mouth. "I was supposed to be over at Erik and Lizzy Patten's house by now."

"You're welcome to stay and listen to some of the game here," Mr. Baumm said, clearly hoping David would.

"Thanks, but I promised them I'd come over as soon as I got back in town."

"I enjoyed seeing you again. Don't be a stranger. And don't let hypocrites like Mrs. Greene get to you. I, for one, am looking forward to the breath of fresh air you'll bring to St. Cecilia's. Hey, ruffling some of those old feathers will do them good."

"I don't intend on doing that. Survival is my plan," David laughed nervously. "But thanks for the kind words, and thanks for the goodies. They were outstanding. When it comes to ice cream, you're an artist."

"Years of practice," Mr. Baumm said, grandly rubbing his large stomach. "Take care."

"I will."

As he opened the door to leave, David heard Mr. Baumm yell at the radio, "Goddammit, tackle that son-of-a-bitch!"

As Father Anthony had predicted, the town and its roads were almost deserted; not many were about. David tuned the car radio to the game in time to hear that Silver Grove had kicked a field goal and was now leading three to zero. He decided to take his time driving to the Patten's house. He wasn't in that much of a hurry; after all, the Holy Spirit was leading the way.

The only major upgrade to the town that David could discern was a small strip mall right off of Highway 6, directly across from Lewis and Clark High School. It was a place where a person was able to get a flavored coffee or a video rental after shopping at the supermarket or searching for clothes. David imagined that it was a mad house when the public school was dismissed during the weekday afternoons. He had Baumm Drugs years ago; today, kids had malls.

Cruising at a comfortable pace, and now only a few miles from Erik and Lizzy's home, David came across Neihardt Park. It, too, was empty. This was another gathering place from his youth: The place where he played when he was a child, where he later took his first drink and toked from his first joint, where he lost his virginity. And the place where the joy of his youth was stripped from him.

Deeply buried memories began to percolate as he stopped to look at the place where his life had changed forever. Anger and bitterness swelled in his belly and swiftly rose upward until he felt he would choke. For most of David's childhood and adolescent years Neihardt Park was a fond and beloved area, but in one moment, it was transformed into ugly, haunted grounds.

"Touchdown, Crusaders!" the radio announcer roared, awakening David from his thoughts.

David stepped on the gas pedal much harder than he intended and the car screeched and lurched forward. He wanted to distance himself from this place as fast as he could, before the memories and pain broke through the barrier he had built up over the years.

After traveling ten or fifteen minutes on Highway 6 – all the while wrestling to keep the demons boxed up or, at least, at bay a while longer – he drove up a newly blacktopped road and arrived at the Patten's home.

When he pulled into the circular driveway, his head and body were throbbing. It was the same soreness he felt in his muscles and joints after an intense physical workout. But now, there was no sense of accomplishment like there was after having jogged a couple of miles or having played a few games of basketball, only the dread of knowing that the memories would arise again, unannounced and unwelcome.

David grew concerned. Since his return home, these ominous recollections were emerging with greater frequency. He knew there would be many more triggers, like seeing Neihardt Park for the first time, and he wondered how long he could keep himself together. He also knew it was unhealthy to keep it all inside – hell, even he counseled people against it. It was at that moment when David acknowledged that he probably was going to have to face his past soon or he would go crazy or, worse, start drinking again.

What a choice, David thought with a sense of doom, because to him they were one and the same.

———

"Uncle David's here! Mom! He's here!"

Christopher Patten came running down from the newly built house, clearly thrilled to see his godfather. Christopher was David's only godson so he spoiled the boy rotten. No gift was too big or too hard to find. More importantly, when David was with the boy, nothing else got in the way. Over the years, their relationship blossomed into the kind of intimacy shared between brothers of a wide age gap. David would do anything for Christopher.

"Hey, buddy, how ya doin'?" All of David's demons scattered.

"Great, now that you're here!" Christopher leaped into David's outstretched arms. This was the one hug he never minded giving or getting.

Christopher was not cute or handsome; he was striking. His blonde hair was a mop on top and tapered shorter on the sides. It sat lightly on his head and looked better mussed up than combed or brushed. His frame was slender, yet strong, though he seemed thinner than David remembered. But what always caught a person's attention were the boy's doe-like eyes. They were large, slightly almond shaped, and colored blue like the sky on a cloudless day. They were the focal point on his face, the feature you were first drawn to – and they took your breath away. Strangers and friends felt compelled to comment on them, not out of jealousy or envy; it was more a declaration of wonder.

Putting the ten-year-old boy down, David teased, "I've got something for you. I may have missed your birthday party last month, but I didn't forget about it."

"I knew you'd remember! You always remember. Dad was working and didn't even come to my party. He forgot all about it until him and mom got into a big fight the next day."

"Well, I'm sure your dad felt real bad. I know he loves you very much."

Frowning, the boy said, "He just loves work."

David noticed that the brightness in Christopher's eyes had dimmed and that his head and shoulders sagged slightly when he spoke about Erik. Something was up.

"Hey, do you want your present or not?" David said, holding his hands out to his sides.

"Yeah!"

Reaching into the back seat of the car, David pulled out a standard-size manila envelope.

Christopher, not wearing his disappointment well – presents at his age were judged by size – took the envelope and opened it. "Brett Favre!" His eyes almost popped out of his head as he stared at the photograph. "It even has my name on it! 'To Christopher, Happy Birthday, Brett Favre.' Awesome! Do you know him or something?"

"No," David chuckled, thoroughly pleased with the boy's reaction. "He played a football game against the St. Louis Rams. Afterwards, he came to the parish I was working at in East St. Louis and talked with some inner-city kids about the importance of staying in school. When he was done we had a chance to talk. I told him you were a big fan of his and mentioned that your birthday was coming up. About a week later, I got this in the mail. I didn't even ask him. He just sent it."

"Wow! Thanks, Uncle David."

"You're welcome."

The boy ran over and gave David another hug. "You're the best! I know just where I'm going to hang it in my room."

They started for the house. David looked out over the eighteen acres of land the Pattens owned, some of it open fields and some wooded forest. "How do you like living out here?"

"It was kinda neat at first," Christopher said, as they walked up the winding brick steps that led to the front door. "But there's nobody around here to play with. At our old house, it was great because I could ride my bike over to the park and play with my friends whenever I wanted. It sucks not having any friends around."

David was taken aback by Christopher's harsh language. "Hey, bud, you supposed to be saying words like that?"

Christopher skipped up the final two steps, grabbed the brass handle that opened the front door and, as he disappeared to go hang the picture in his room, said, "Mom and dad don't give a shit."

David felt like he was just kicked in the gut. All his instincts told him something was very wrong. He thought he might know the reason behind Christopher's uncharacteristic language, but determined he should tread lightly and make sure before saying anything to Erik and Lizzy. David's antenna was up.

Lizzy came dashing down the bleached oak floor in the hallway to greet him. She still looked like the head cheerleader and prom queen from high school. No make-up or curlers for her hair; she had a natural beauty and needed nothing artificial to maintain it. Her tousled brown hair cascaded down to her shoulders and bordered on the fine line between appearing unkempt and spending hours just to get it that way. Christopher had inherited his mother's eye shape but not her color. Hers were emerald green, and they sparkled. She was about an inch or two taller than David and still had a fit figure. Knowing Lizzy, she worked hard at it. She was proud of her looks, but not in a conceited way.

"You made it," Lizzy said, bouncing up and down. David thought she might do a back flip right then and there – she probably still could.

They embraced. She held on a little longer than David expected.

"I'm so glad to see you." She said this with enthusiasm but also with what David interpreted as relief. "How are you?"

"Good. Real good," David said, nodding his head up and down, trying to convince himself it was true.

"Come on, David, you can't fool me." She locked eyes with him and wrapped her left arm around his right. "Let's go listen to the game and you can fill me in on what's going on."

"All right, mother."

"Hey, we've got to look out for each other," Lizzy said, leading him down the hallway. "Oh! You've got to see the house. I can't believe it's finally done. There were so many delays and problems. But I love how it came out. Come on, I'll show you around. Halftime's almost over, so let's hurry."

"What's the score?" The fervor for St. Cecilia's football was already flowing through David's veins. It didn't take long to become a fanatic again.

"Crusaders are ahead ten to three. It's a great game so far."

"Erik's not here?" It was more a statement than a question.

Sighing and forcing a smile, Lizzy said, "No, he's busy at the law firm. They just made him a partner about six months ago. He's the youngest one so he says he needs to earn his keep or prove his worth or something macho like that. He's promised to back off but it won't be for a while. We'll see." Lizzy stared out a large window that overlooked a full-size basketball court and a small pond in the distance. Her brow was furrowed and her arms hugged her upper body.

After a few seconds of silence, David said, "Is everything okay?" He didn't want to push her. He knew her well enough to know that she would talk only when she was ready. He simply wanted to give her an invitation.

Quickly turning to David, she flashed her best cheerleader smile and said, "Of course. Now, let's show you around."

She guided David through the basement and main floor, followed by the upstairs bedrooms with walk-in closets bigger than his room at the rectory and, finally, the heated three-car garage. No expense had been spared in any room; Erik was obviously doing well at work. Lizzy's personality radiated throughout the house. It was comfortable in many areas and classy in others, while not appearing pretentious. Even though it was a large, expensive home, David felt like it was okay to put his feet up or put his drink down without having to search for a coaster.

"Wow," David said when they finished. "And you did all the decorating yourself?"

"Yeah. And it's been great for me. With Erik gone so much over the last couple of years, I've kept myself busy with the house. It's made not having him around a little easier. Plus, it's been a chance for me to put my interior design degree to work."

"It's a wonderful home."

"Thank you." Lizzy seemed reinvigorated by the tour. "It's so good to have you back after all these years. I can't believe you're finally here."

"Me neither," David said with a feigned grimace.

Lizzy laughed. "Oh, come on. It's going to be great. Now, instead of us coming to visit you a couple times a year, we can see each other all the time. Although, Christopher will miss visiting you in St. Louis."

Smiling, David said, "I'm sure he's gonna miss the Cardinals baseball games even more."

"Stop that." Lizzy playfully slugged David's shoulder. "Christopher and I have loved making those trips. I just wish Erik would have gone more often." Lizzy paused. "Hey, you're here now and that's all that matters."

David turned serious. "Lizzy, I've never thanked you guys for all the visits, phone calls, and letters. Your support and friendship have meant so much to me over the years. After I first left town, I know I was terrible about calling or writing back, but I was going through —"

"I know," Lizzy said gently. "I know. David, lifelong friendships like ours are special, and they don't wither away because we haven't seen or talked to each other in a while. We just pick up where we left off – time and place mean nothing." Lizzy leaned over and kissed David on the cheek. "Come on, let's go listen to the second half."

They entered a new room. It appeared to be a shrine to Crusaders football, complete with the team's primary color. A couch was upholstered red, the wood trim was painted red, pictures and drawings of Crusaders lore hung on every wall and tacky Crusaders football memorabilia was scattered all over. Even the felt on the snooker table was red. There was a big screen TV that the room centered on. This was a St. Cecilia's football fanatic's dream room.

"I was not involved here." Lizzy raised her hands in mock self-defense. "This was Erik's only contribution to the decorating, and you can see why. He's still a Crusaders football nut." She looked away and crossed her arms. "But we haven't been to a game together as a family in a long time. Erik's usually got something to do at work, or he'll go with a client from town. 'Good business,' he says. Poor Christopher's dying to go to a game with his dad."

David said, "I'll take Christopher." He sat down on the couch and sank into the soft cushions. He wondered if he was going to be able to get out. "I haven't been to a game in years."

"No." Lizzy said sternly. "That's Erik's responsibility."

Here it comes, David thought. It never took Lizzy long to get whatever was bothering her off her chest. All he had to do was nudge her a little more and she would pop like a cork from a wine bottle. The radio announced that St. Cecilia's was kicking off to Silver Grove. David thought this was going to be a very interesting second half, in more ways than one.

"It sounds like Erik's really caught up in the firm," he said cautiously.

Lizzy took a deep, long breath, sat back and looked up at the ceiling. "You know he's always been driven. Growing up poor left a lot of scars. I mean, when his dad killed himself after the bankruptcy, it had a profound effect on Erik and how he views money. It had to, especially at twelve years old. But his obsession with money has got to stop. We have enough stashed away to retire comfortably right now.

"We go round and round about how his job interferes with our relationship, and how it's starting to affect Christopher. There's only so much I can give him. Christopher wants to shoot baskets, play catch, wrestle around on the floor – all those things he sees other kids doing with their dads. I get so frustrated because Erik doesn't see that Christopher's growing up, and I mean emotionally, without a father – just like Erik did. Christopher has every material thing a kid could want, but that's not what he really wants. He just wants his daddy."

David expected tears, but there were none. Instead, she seemed numb, like someone who was defeated and had given up.

"Maybe Erik doesn't know how to be a father," David said.

"His idea of a father is someone who is the breadwinner, period."

"That's understandable. Erik didn't have anyone to show him that there is so much more to being a good father than bringing home a paycheck. I know it would be tough for me to be a father. After my dad left us, I hated him and everyone who had a dad. I guess that's one of the reasons why Erik and I became such good friends. We had that common bond."

The game was now background noise.

"Do not defend him."

Retreating, David said, "Lizzy, don't take what I said the wrong way. I'm not justifying Erik's actions, just trying to understand what's going on with him. I don't know what you guys have been through lately, so it's not fair for me to pass judgments or draw any conclusions. I'm sorry if I offended you. I want to help, that's all."

They both looked away from each other. David thought, You idiot! Slow down, don't try so hard.

"Shit!" Lizzy said.

David snapped his head around to face her. He said, "I'm sorry, I really had no right to—"

"No, no, no." She grinned. "Silver Grove just ran a fumble back for a touchdown and tied the game."

David chuckled. They looked at each other and burst into laughter; it was the same kind of infectious laughter that used to overtake them as kids during all-school Mass. Some inane, silly thing would set it off and, the next thing they knew, the giggles held them hostage. They would stop, then start up again merely by looking at each other. The tension between the two instantly disappeared.

Gasping for a breath, Lizzy said, "God, I haven't laughed like that in a long time. I'm sorry I snapped at you. It's just that this isn't something I feel comfortable talking to my friends about, so it's been bottled up for a while. I really didn't mean to bitch at you."

"Hey, that's what friends are for. Bitch away – it's good for you."

"Well...okay then. I'm sick and tired of arguing with Erik over and over about the same thing. He doesn't see any problems. I mean, he's absolutely blind to what's going on in his own home, because he's never here. He doesn't see how disappointed Christopher is when he breaks his promises, like being a no-show at Christopher's ball games or canceling an outing at the last minute because of work. It crushes Christopher. And now he's starting to act out. It seems like the only time Erik interacts with Christopher anymore is when he's in trouble."

"So, is Christopher acting up, trying to get his dad's attention?"

"Yeah," she said slowly, as if a question was answered, but not fully understood. "Why is that?"

"I've seen it many times." David was grateful that his training and experience could finally provide insight for someone. "Kids crave attention from their parents, both parents. And when they get it in the right way, they usually grow up healthy and happy. If the people they love are ignoring them, kids can get very creative in going after the attention they desire, including getting into trouble. I guess kids would rather have negative attention than no attention at all."

Lizzy was nodding her head in agreement. "That makes a lot of sense. Christopher's done so well in school in the past and has always been well behaved, until the last year or so. Maybe we've grown so accustomed to him being such a good kid that we've taken it for granted and don't pat him on the back for it anymore. I know I'm guilty of that, and Lord knows Erik is too. But what can we do? Erik and I can't agree on anything lately and he doesn't think, or want to admit, that anything is wrong with his son."

The picture was now clear to David: Erik and Lizzy needed to rally around their son's problems, both for Christopher and for their marriage. He had a good idea what needed to be said next, but he sat silent listening to the end of the game with Lizzy, weighing the risks, calculating if it was worth it.

There were fifty-four seconds left in the game and the score was tied. St. Cecilia's was at their own forty-two yard line. It was fourth down and they needed two yards for a first down. The Crusaders called a time out to discuss whether to go for the first down or punt. Suddenly, the offense sprinted onto the field to the thunderous approval of the crowd. This was it: make it, they have a chance to win, be stopped and they probably lose. At that moment, David realized that the chance of possibly helping Lizzy, Erik and Christopher through this tough time far outweighed any risk of hard feelings or damage to their friendship.

I can't let my fear of losing keep me from trying, David thought.

They both sat on the edge of the couch, listening intently as the Crusaders quarterback ran an option play to the short side of the field. Just as he was about to be hit for a loss, he flipped the ball to the running back who was trailing him. The field was wide open and he was finally tackled at Silver Grove's seven-yard line. The radio erupted with the sounds of frenzied celebration.

David and Lizzy jumped up and cheered wildly. Christopher sped into the room and joined in on the fun. Everyone forgot their problems for a moment and high-fived and hugged each other. Two plays later St. Cecilia's scored a touchdown and won the football game seventeen to ten. The whole game came down to one decision, one gamble, and it paid off.

Once the excitement wore down, Christopher ran off to his room to call a friend. It was time for David to say what he had to say. He knew the hazards and possible consequences, but he loved these people too much not to take the chance.

Lizzy and David sat on the couch for a few moments basking in the Crusaders thrilling victory, when he said, "Lizzy, if you think it would help, I'll talk with Erik."

Lizzy pursed her lips and looked hard at David. After a moment, she said "No...I don't think it's a good idea to put you in that position. Erik's agreed to go with me to visit with Father Anthony next Thursday. It's a start. We'll see how it goes."

"The offer's always there," David said, both relieved and disappointed. "And if you ever need anyone to talk to—"

"Now that I'll take you up on."

David looked at his watch. "I'd better get going."

"Oh, stay for dinner. I'm sure Erik will be home soon, and Christopher would love it."

"Can I take you up on the offer another time? I promised Father Anthony and Larry Peck I'd join them for dinner."

"You're always welcome here. You know that."

David said good-bye to Christopher, who was still on the phone discussing the game and bragging about his Brett Farve autographed picture. Lizzy gave David another hug and kiss on the cheek. It was good to be among friends. He regretted having to leave. As he drove away, David couldn't help but feel sad thinking that a couple once so in love with each other were currently at odds. God, please bring them together again, David prayed.

CHAPTER 3

When David returned to the rectory, there was a message on the answering machine from Father Anthony. Apparently, the revelry after the game had caused the three to run late. He asked David to meet them over at Larry's house and left detailed directions on how to get there. His home was located on a remote piece of land south of town.

Unaware of how and where things were organized in the rectory, it took David several minutes to locate a pen and piece of paper that he could use to scribble down Father Anthony's route, and even more time learning how to replay the answering machine. The mixture of shouts of joy, good-spirited honking of car horns and the loud, irritating static from Larry's car phone made deciphering Father Anthony's garbled message a challenge.

Father Anthony also instructed David to bring some beer and soda from the rectory's pantry. This irked him. Was this another test? Was Father Anthony being insensitive? Was it just a simple request? David went on the assumption it was the latter.

"Sometimes a cigar is just a cigar," he muttered. "Lord knows I'm going to be around drinking while I'm living with Father Anthony, so I'd better get used to it."

David trudged off to the kitchen and grabbed a twelve-pack of Diet Coke and three bottles of beer from the refrigerator. After a thorough search of the large walk-in pantry, he realized he'd have to stop on the way and get more beer. The alcoholic in him couldn't fathom that a few beers would be enough for anyone. He sacked up the beverages, grabbed his notes and headed out.

The pace of the town was beginning to pick up as people trickled back from the game. Overjoyed fans were still sparked by the thrilling outcome. In the cars and on the streets, people were holding up their index finger and chanting to anyone and everyone, "We're number one! We're number one!" Willa was alive, upbeat, and happy.

Except for Agnes Greene, David thought devilishly. She'd find something to bitch about.

Community spirit was soaring and that's what David remembered most about Crusader football. It was a factory, producing winning seasons year after year, but never a state championship. St. Cecilia's football was a common bond among all those in town. In victory or defeat, people were unified in celebration or mourning.

He felt invisible driving the streets of Willa, so he pulled over to watch the festivities.

"Cooper, got yourself a new ride, huh?" David looked out his open window, searching for the familiar voice; his heart skipped a beat, then began to pound. He furrowed his brow and his jaw muscles stiffened.

"Shit," David grumbled, as he spotted a blue uniform approaching.

Chief Gardner walked with the same robust stride that David remembered from his younger days. Pushing seventy years old, the man looked more like fifty: His barrel chest stuck out leading the way, and his biceps bulged beneath tight shirtsleeves. He set a tanned, beefy hand and Popeye-like forearm on David's window. Smiling smugly, the Chief peered into David's car and quickly snooped around with his eyes before settling them on David.

"Heard you were back."

"Yep." David crossed his arms and locked onto the police chief's eyes. He wasn't going to shy away this time.

"How's Father Anthony?"

Before David had a chance to think, he said, "Ask him." Immediately, he regretted it, but this man brought out the worst in David.

Smirking, the Chief said, "Slow down, cowboy. I'm just trying to bury the hatchet here."

"Consider it buried." David slipped the idling car into gear. Chief Gardner gripped David's shoulder; he quickly moved it back and dislodged the Chief's hand.

"What's the hurry? Why don't you stay and chat; we got a lot of catching up to do."

David put the car back in park and glared at the Chief. "Yes?"

The big cop grabbed a toothpick from his shirt pocket and slipped it into his mouth. "Just wanted to know how the good people of St. Cecilia's are treating their new priest."

"Great."

"Really?" Chief Gardner said in mock surprise. "Boy, with all the shit you pulled, I thought it'd take quite a while for them to warm up to you."

David stayed silent, not looking away. He figured it was best to keep his mouth shut before he said something really stupid.

Chief Gardner continued, "After the stunt you pulled at graduation, I didn't think anyone wanted to see your face around here ever again. I mean, chaining up the church doors and setting off the fire alarm at noon Mass was a little over the top, even for a senior prank...don't you think?"

' and managed to say, "Long time ago, Chief. Lots happened since then."

"I'll bet." Chief Gardner rolled the toothpick in his mouth. "You know, there's one thing I was always curious about: Who pulled the alarm?"

David's eyes grew narrow. Following the incident, no one had ever asked him this question.

The Chief chuckled, "What? You think I'm stupid? How the hell could you have locked the doors from the outside and pulled the alarm on the inside?" He grinned and said, "Come on, Padre, it'll be our little secret."

David couldn't take it anymore. "You weren't interested back then, why should I tell you anything now?"

Smile gone, the Chief said, "What are you talking about?"

"You think I'm stupid? You never asked me about another person because you finally had someone to hang: me. Put all the blame on one kid and you don't have to interrogate a bunch of parishioners' kids — wouldn't have been prudent with your re-election only days away, would it? Listen, I told you everything you asked me back then. I took responsibility for a senior prank that I admit crossed over the line, and I accepted my punishment. If you think I'm going to get into this shit again, you're wrong."

Chief Gardner snapped the toothpick in half with his teeth and the pieces hit the car door. "Once an asshole, always an asshole."

David stared at Chief Gardner, and said, "I couldn't agree more." He put the car into gear and sped away.

David was about to leave the city limits when he remembered to stop and get Father Anthony's liquid cheer. A block and a half ahead, David saw a sign that read *Harmon Liquor*. He already felt uneasy about going to buy beer, let alone at this place. But he was running late and didn't want to travel back into town. Pulling into the gravel parking lot, David thought hopefully, Maybe the ownership's changed hands.

As he sat in the car, David realized this was a mistake. He desperately wanted to turn around and get the hell out of there. But he couldn't. The remorse was too overwhelming. He sat still, staring at the name flashing on the sign, helpless as the painful memory washed over him once again, taking control of his mind and body. He felt paralyzed. With the car idling, David slumped in his seat looking at nothing, lost in the disturbing reminisce of Bobby.

Closing his eyes, David took a deep breath and, in an attempt to regain his composure, began to pray. The dreadful events that led to Bobby's death had been shut off from David's consciousness for so long that he had never thought about what to do to make things right. He realized that the truth behind Bobby's death needed to be told: It was an awful, tragic accident and not a suicide. David had to face this reality straight on, regardless of the damage it caused him personally, as much for Bobby's memory as for his own sanity.

But how do I do this, Lord? David prayed.

He sat up when he heard the sound of tires crunching on gravel. A rusted, brown pickup truck pulled into the lot and parked on the side of the building. A weathered old man got out, straightened his faded-green John Deere baseball cap and sauntered over to the entrance. He stopped momentarily to light a cigarette from the nearly spent one he was puffing on seconds before. He flicked the old butt onto the gravel surface, stomped on it with his cowboy boot, and disappeared into the store.

David gathered himself and decided he would go into the store and talk with Mr. Harmon, if he was still the owner. The young priest wasn't exactly sure what he was going to say, or even what good it would do, but he felt compelled to talk to the man and tell him what he knew of his son's death. It just seemed to be the right thing to do and, selfishly, perhaps it would help cleanse his mind and soul.

After a few minutes, David realized that the old man in the green cap wasn't coming out anytime soon. He got out of the Honda and walked to the store's front door, as if danger lurked on the other side. He figured by entering the store, the old man might leave. If not, then...well, David would play it by ear.

It took his eyes several seconds to adjust to the darkness. Neon lights flashing the colorful names and logos of Budweiser Light and Miller Genuine Draft were crammed into the store's only two windowsills, blocking the sunlight from penetrating inside. The store was cold and damp, and the stale scent of beer and cigarettes hanging in the air stirred up memories of bars that David used to frequent.

He saw the old man at the cash register with a twelve-pack of Budweiser. A cigarette magically dangled from his mouth when he talked; an opened beer was in his hand.

David walked to the back cooler that housed the many different brands of beer and located the Guinness Stout. As he opened the glass door, he looked back to get a glimpse of who the old fart was talking to and if he was ever going to leave. Unfortunately, he had popped open a second bottle of beer and was puffing on another freshly lit cigarette.

"The guy's a chimney," David mumbled to himself, irritated that the man wasn't on his way by now.

He grabbed two six-packs from the top rack of the cooler, but only after a loud buzz indicating that the door had been open too long jolted him into action. He was so startled that he almost dropped the beer on the peeling gray cement floor. The old man took notice but quickly returned to his conversation.

Walking down a couple of aisles, David pretended to be looking for a particular beverage. He was killing time, hoping that the smoking machine would leave so he could talk to Bobby's father alone. While studying the inventory, it was clear that this was not a liquor store for the connoisseur. Jack Daniels, Jim Beam, Stolichnaya, and other brands of popular hard liquor crowded the shelves, along with any kind of domestic beer known to man. David was surprised that Guinness was even in stock, although he surmised it was on hand specifically due to Father

Anthony's fondness for the beverage. A few token bottles of wine were stacked off in one corner, dusty and untouched for ages.

David snuck another peek. The old man took a long, deep swig from his Bud bottle and set it down. He said something to someone behind the counter; a male voice laughed a wicked, croaky rasp followed by a hacking cough, as if he was trying to catch his breath. A large hand appeared from behind the counter and snatched an empty bottle. The sound of breaking glass ensued as the bottle was tossed into the trash along with other spent ones. David got a quick look at the hand: It appeared arthritic, claw-like, gnarled.

He couldn't see who was behind the counter because it was built into the back corner of the building and had a windowless wall and door that blocked the view of the rest of the store. David had never set foot in this place, and he now understood how easy it must have been for Bobby to snatch booze.

The old man opened up a brown paper bag that held his beer; the ugly hand reappeared and tossed in a carton of Camel cigarettes. Finally, the man in the John Deere cap turned and began walking toward the front door. When he exited the building, he was attempting to hold onto the sack and light another Camel at the same time.

David lingered a minute or two, pretending to examine the cheap wine, all the while praying for the courage to face Bobby's dad. After taking a deep breath, the young priest reluctantly headed to the counter. As he neared it, David grew calm and relaxed. Even though he knew this would be painful, he was confident that he was doing the right thing.

David strode to the counter. He set the two six-packs on the flimsy wood countertop and looked up, only to be disappointed. No one was there. It was a narrow but long enclosure with three doors; two of the doors faced the inside of the store, the other was built straight back into the far wall. David knew that one door led out to the store area, and he surmised that one of the others lead to a cellar where inventory was stored. He had no idea where the third door could lead.

He's probably down in the cellar, David thought, after patiently waiting for what seemed like an hour but was really closer to a minute. "Hello!" he said in a voice loud enough to reach someone down in the basement.

"Keep your pants on!" an irritated voice shot back from behind the far door. "I ain't deaf. I'll be right there."

After a few more seconds, there was a flushing sound where the voice had come from. David immediately felt stupid for shouting so loud. He strained to hear the muffled speech that continued behind the closed door, but could only make out, "Jesus, a man can't even take a shit in peace..."

The door flew open and he knew the store hadn't changed hands; it was unmistakably Mr. Harmon. What gave him away was the tattered red cap that sat on his head. It was inscribed with "Crusaders #13" over the bill. David remembered that Bobby's dad had worn this cap everywhere, even in church – when he went, which wasn't often.

Mr. Harmon's claim to fame was quarterbackering the Crusaders football team to its only appearance in the finals of the state championship, a narrow loss. Over the years, his stories of superior athletic prowess and incredible exploits on the football field grew, as did his bitterness and drinking habits.

The man's thick gray hair shot out of the ball cap in all directions and reached down past his shoulders – unusually long for a man his age. Must be in his mid-fifties now, David thought. Strangely, even with the cap on, Mr. Harmon's hair looked unkempt. The rest of him, which there was an abundance of, also looked disheveled: from his soiled, once white high-top tennis shoes to his stained, gray sweat pants to his tight, dirty-yellowed tank top that squeezed out a few too many inches of his large hairy belly. He had a good-sized tattoo on his upper left arm of a devil-like figure holding a football, and a thick growth of whiskers that would take a lawnmower to trim covering his bloated face.

He plodded over to the counter. Suppressing a belch, Mr. Harmon said, "Jesus, boy, what the hell's your hurry?"

"Sorry. I thought you were down in the cellar."

Reaching under the counter, Mr. Harmon grabbed a large coffee mug. He took a quick slug of the contents and scrunched up his face like someone who had unexpectedly swallowed sour milk.

"Why the hell would I be down there?" He took another shot from the mug.

"I thought you might be busy with inventory or something."

The man bellowed the same nasty, bitter laugh David had heard earlier and said rudely, as if David was stupid and should have known, "What you see up here is all I got. That's my castle down there."

This astounded David. He always assumed Bobby had lived in a house like all the other boys and girls. But he hadn't. Realizing the boy had grown up in the bowels of a ratty liquor store, David felt pangs of pity and sorrow. With all the time he had spent with Bobby that summer, David knew next to nothing about him. The only thing David really knew was that this broken down man standing before him physically and emotionally damaged his only child.

After another belt, Mr. Harmon put the cup on the counter. "That it?"

"Yeah," David said, paying for the beer, unsure of how to begin. So, he just blurted out, "Are you Mr. Harmon?"

"Who wants to know?" Immediately, the man behind the counter became defensive and suspicious. He nonchalantly tried to sneak the cup back under the counter.

"My name's David Cooper. Umm, actually, it's Father David Cooper now. I'm the new associate pastor at St. Cecilia's."

"Whatta you want?" Mr. Harmon said, appearing relieved that David wasn't an undercover cop or liquor inspector. He took out a half-filled bottle of vodka and the mug from under the counter. While looking defiantly at David, he filled it to the brim. He put the bottle back in its hiding place and smugly sipped from his cup, all the time his turbulent, bloodshot eyes remained fixed on David.

"I...I grew up in Willa and knew your son," David said, waiting for an angry outburst. But there wasn't one, just silence followed by a long, remorseful sigh from the large man.

Drooping his head and emptily staring at the floor, Mr. Harmon went to take a drink from the mug, but hesitated and set it down on the counter.

"You knew my Bobby, huh?" He looked up, took off his cap and brushed back his greasy, matted down hair. Ache filled the man's eyes. From a stray box on the counter, Mr. Harmon took out a Marlboro and lit it. The first drag off the butt was long and powerful; it was like he was trying to suck in all the hurt and blow it away with the exhaled smoke.

"I went to school with him. We hung out some together. He was a good kid."

"Yeah, he was..." Mr. Harmon's voice was saturated with pain and regret. He snatched his mug again, spilling some vodka on the counter and slammed down a giant gulp of the colorless liquid. The attempt to regain his composure didn't seem to work because he looked confused and surprised, like a master whose old, trusted hound had turned on him.

David wondered if this man even knew that his cruel treatment of Bobby helped kill the boy. David thought, Should he know? Should he know that, instead of adding to the abuse, he should have helped his son battle the taunting and bullying from other kids. For a moment, David wavered.

I'm sure he's suffered enough, David thought at last. I know I have.

The silence between the two was uncomfortable and interminable. David couldn't stand the quiet tension anymore. So to balance the shock, he said slowly and calmly, "I was with Bobby the night he died."

"What?"

"It's true. I was with him." Unexpectedly, David felt serene, and an exhilarating freedom washed over him. He was finally releasing one of the monsters that had danced a perverted dance within his mind, teasing him, mocking him. "It was an accident. Bobby didn't do it on purpose."

His hand shaking, Mr. Harmon set the mug down. In a whisper, he said, "An accident? How the fuck do you know that?"

"We drank together that night." David hesitated, thinking about how much of the story to tell. He decided just enough to give this old man some solace. "When I left Bobby, he was pretty drunk, but okay. I know it was the first time he had drank. I'd never seen him do it before. But he was drinking so fast, and being so small, well, it must have poisoned his body. He wasn't trying to hurt himself, I'm sure of that. He just didn't know what he was doing."

Mr. Harmon plopped down hard on the padded stool behind him, dazed like a boxer in a fog after a surprisingly vicious punch. David didn't say anything. He was thankful he had come clean.

Mr. Harmon seemed to gather himself. "Why the fuck didn't you say something back then?"

David wasn't prepared for this question. Foolishly, he thought telling the man his son didn't kill himself would be all the comfort he would need. But it was only logical he would have questions. "I...I don't know," David said. "My life was pretty messed up back then. I was just a kid – and I was scared."

Mr. Harmon began to seethe; he also began to look like a man who just received a get-out-of-jail-for-free card. Seizing David's well-intentioned gesture of honesty, Mr. Harmon desperately said, as if trying to convince himself, "You, you little shit. You killed him. You killed Bobby."

As the words rolled off his tongue, the man gained momentum and grew more confident in his accusation. David knew it would be useless to defend himself, so he remained quiet. He readied himself for the assault, and in a strange way welcomed it.

"You murdered my son!" Mr. Harmon shouted with more intensity. He was now convinced this was fact, and he leapt at the opportunity to wash his hands of any participation in Bobby's death.

"I'm sorry."

"Shut the fuck up! Take your goddamn beer and get the hell out of my store." He grabbed the mug and took a shot.

David paused, wanting to explain that Bobby's death was not one person's fault. Rather, it was everyone's fault. And any blame lay not only with the two of them, but also with others who refused to accept Bobby for who he was.

"I said get out. Leave now, before I step around the counter and throw your ass through the door."

David picked up the beer and gave Mr. Harmon a long, piercing stare. David wanted Mr. Harmon to understand that he knew what horrible, awful things Mr. Harmon had done to Bobby. The old man got the message. He tried to maintain eye contact with David, but after a few seconds turned away. In a subdued voice, Mr. Harmon said, "Leave…please leave."

David was in no hurry to get to Larry's house; he needed time to recover. The encounter with Mr. Harmon was an unsettling and humbling experience. But as David recreated the situation again in his mind, he wouldn't have changed a thing. He believed he did what was right, and casting off some baggage helped him feel lighter, healthier, cleaner.

He wasn't troubled much by Mr. Harmon's accusation, to a certain extent David was guilty. By telling Mr. Harmon what he knew, David felt he had finally taken responsibility for his part that night. He did wonder if Mr. Harmon's distorting of David's admission of the truth would be publicly aired. But that was something out of his control now and David did his best to let it go, which had never been an easy thing for him to do.

Larry's house was located about twenty-five minutes from the rectory. Most of the ride was on highways dominated by views of rolling fields fenced off with rusted, twisted barbed wire and filled with corn and soy beans and other crops that David recognized but couldn't name. There were farmhouses and barns huddled tightly together every so often along the road. Only one looked inhabited, the rest appeared abandoned, rundown, dilapidated. These once thriving homes were now litter on the land.

David spotted Larry's mailbox and turned off the highway. The service road was covered with a thick layer of gravel and wound up a large, steep bluff densely inhabited with trees and untamed bush. The changing colors of the autumn leaves on the giant trees formed a dazzling tunnel all the way to Larry's home. Out of the corner of his eye, David caught glimpses of wildlife.

Larry's house sat majestically atop the bluff's peak and was completely surrounded by trees of all sizes, along with thick, dense undergrowth. His two-story home was built from redwood that had weathered naturally, enabling it to blend in with the nearby countryside. On both levels, large windows – six-feet tall and three-feet wide – were evenly distributed on every side of the house, allowing one to see in while also providing an open view of the woods from the inside.

As David stood on the blacktopped driveway, whirls of smoke rose from the back of the house and lazily drifted his way on a gentle breeze. He tentatively sniffed the air and took in bigger and bigger gulps once he recognized the pleasant aroma of mesquite from a charcoal grill. David loved anything on the grill, and he was hungry. It was after six in the evening and he hadn't eaten since his ice cream binge at Baumm Drug.

Instead of knocking on the front door, David decided to follow his nose and go around to the back of the house. He grabbed the drinks and followed a stone path. As he got closer to the back of the house, he heard voices. Once there, he came upon steps that led up to a huge redwood deck.

As he climbed the stairs, David said, "Hello?"

"Hey, come on up," Larry welcomed.

Once on the deck, David took one look and said, "Wow." The deck was connected to the second story of the house and positioned so that there was nothing blocking the view. A natural break in the trees allowed for a spectacular sight: acres and acres of forest and flat plains. There also was a huge redwood hot tub filled with bubbling water sitting at one end of the deck. A boy was splashing around, oblivious to the scenery or those around him.

"Incredible view."

"I'm glad you like it." Larry smiled and turned toward the landscape. "I built the house around it."

"How were my directions?" Father Anthony said. "I thought you might have gotten lost."

"Fine. I just got tied up in football traffic." David didn't want to get into his meeting with Mr. Harmon in front of Larry. He planned to talk with Father Anthony about it later in private – and this time also in confession. "Everyone's pretty fired up."

Larry grinned and said, "That was the best Crusader game I've ever seen. And I've been going to games for thirteen years. The place was rocking."

Larry reached out for the brown paper sack in David's hands. "Here, let me take that."

As the doctor was opening the sliding glass door to the kitchen, he said, "Anthony, Guinness?"

Father Anthony winked mischievously. "Why don't you bring out two. I got some catchin' up to do."

Larry laughed. "David?"

"Diet Coke would be fine."

"Corey!" Larry shouted to the boy.

"What?" Corey said, somewhat peeved, as he stopped somersaulting and came up for air. His long, jet-black hair was drenched and hung over his eyes. In order to see, he had to brush the wet bangs aside. His face was plump and his body was chunky, a typical pre-teen boy ready to shed his baby fat.

"I want you to meet Father David Cooper. You'll be seeing lots of him. He's the new priest at St. Cecilia's."

Squinting skeptically at David, Corey finally said, "What's up?"

"Nice to meet you, Corey. Have a good time at the game?"

"It was okay."

"Aw, come on Corey, you loved it," Larry said playfully. There also was a hint of authority in his voice.

Corey smiled and said to Larry, "Yeah, it was fun." The boy then took a huge breath and disappeared under the water to continue his somersaults.

Larry brought out a tray filled with appetizers, along with everyone's drink. Sipping on iced tea, Larry manned an enormous grill. On the menu were large T-bones for the adults and a cheeseburger for Corey.

There was a long history between Father Anthony and Larry so there were more than a few tales to tell. They had David in stitches as he listened to the stories that they had probably told a hundred times before. They ate on the deck. David kept returning to the view, awed by the brilliant change of colors as the sun set before them. The steaks, corn-on-the-cob – fresh from a neighbor's field – and Caesar salad were delicious.

Corey sat next to Larry, content to gobble down his meal without a word. As soon as he was done, he got up and disappeared into the house. Through the sliding glass door, David could see him playing a video game on a large television screen. Corey seemed to know his way around Larry's home and appeared very comfortable, going wherever he pleased.

"This also is my office," Larry said to David, picking up on his thoughts. "Corey's been here many times for his sessions."

David nodded.

Father Anthony said, "Larry, and I agree with him, believes that the key to helping people is to first build a strong relationship. He treats patients here because, as they become more and more comfortable, they're more willing to open up and talk about their problems. It's the same thing with St. Cecilia's: The church and rectory are like second homes to many parishioners, so they feel at ease telling us their sins during confession or what's bothering them during counseling."

"This is so true with treating physically and sexually abused kids," Larry said. "They don't trust adults anymore – and can you blame them? The only way for these kids to get better is to open up and trust again; it's kind of like someone who's had a stroke and must relearn how to walk and talk. Most of the time, it takes months before even the slightest hint of trust is established. It seems to speed up the whole process if I'm not in some sterile office environment. Hey, it's also a great tax write-off."

All three men laughed, then quieted down when Corey came outside and announced, "That fucking VCR ain't workin' again!"

This startled David. Father Anthony sighed deeply. Larry, however, stood up and calmly said, "I understand it can be upsetting and frustrating trying to get the VCR to work, but swearing isn't acceptable here at this time. You follow me?"

Corey clenched his fists and his jaw tightened. After a few tense moments, he took a deep breath and said in a shaking voice, "It just came out."

"That's the way to keep yourself together," Larry praised immediately. "Why don't you take a couple more deep breaths and calm yourself down."

Slowly, Corey took two more deep breaths and unsuccessfully tried to suppress a grin. He was proud of himself, but didn't want to show it.

"Fantastic job of controlling your anger. I knew you could do it. Now let's take a look at the VCR." Larry lightly patted Corey on the shoulder as the two headed into the house.

"That," Father Anthony said, "was brilliance at work. With any other person, Corey would have flown off the handle: cursed, thrown things, gotten physical, you name it. I've seen that look before, been on the opposite end of it a few times and, trust me, it can get ugly. Most of the time, his anger comes out in school.

"It's taken Larry over a year to help Corey recognize when he is about to blow and how to calm himself down. Right now, it only seems to work with Larry. He said the next step is for Corey to learn how to do this with others in different settings, like teachers at school. He's a tough nut to crack, but Larry refuses to give up on the boy. Many other therapists would, and have."

David's curiosity was piqued. "Not that it's any of my business, but what's Corey's history like? Who abused him?"

"Actually, it is your business. Corey and his family are our parishioners, and there are certain things you'll need to know. We're a team, David. I'll bounce things off you from time to time to get your perspective and I hope you'll feel comfortable doing the same. Of course we'll have to maintain complete confidentiality, but we each need to know what's going on."

David gave a nod affirming that he understood and was in total agreement.

"I'm not exactly sure of Corey's situation, and I haven't asked Larry about it. I don't want to put him in an awkward position. But I do have my suspicions. The boy doesn't know who his father is and I doubt his mother, Rhonda, does either. She's never been married, but has had many live-in boyfriends. Down deep, I think she's a decent woman, but she's promiscuous and very insecure.

"It seems she's drawn to the rough type of guy: hard drinker, drug user, bully – you name it. Maybe she doesn't think she deserves better. Anyway, she's come to me on occasion for guidance, but it's very difficult for her to let go of these losers. Bruises, cuts, even broken bones aren't enough to convince her."

"You think any of these guys abused Corey?"

"Probably more than one. Whether it's physical or sexual abuse I don't know. These men usually are violent toward Rhonda and I doubt a young boy would be off limits. As a matter of fact, a particularly disturbing man is currently living with them. You may remember him: Reggie Cempak."

David's eyes opened wide. "How could I forget that thug! The guy scared the hell out of everyone in town, even Chief Gardner. When I was growing up, nobody, and I mean nobody, messed with Reggie. I was always careful to steer clear of him, so he didn't hassle me much. I would have thought he'd be in jail by now."

"Well, he's been back in town for a while," Father Anthony said. "About all I know about him is that he's working as a mechanic. Corey's been acting out quite a bit lately, so I have my suspicions about Reggie."

"Isn't there something we can do?" David was drawn to help this boy who had been damaged at the hands of adults. He knew full well how devastating the consequences could be to Corey if nothing was done.

"At this point, no," Father Anthony said. "Corey's been in trouble with the law so the courts are involved. He's required to attend therapy. Thank goodness Larry was gracious enough to take on Corey for free. Otherwise, I doubt he'd be getting any help at all. Rhonda and Corey aren't talking about Reggie. Rhonda hasn't been to Mass since she met him, so I haven't had a chance to talk with her. I've called, but she seems cautious, like she's being monitored. It's so damn frustrating that we can't do anything about these situations until the shit hits the fan and someone gets hurt."

They fell into a troubled silence; both men looked up at the moon and stars as they began to emerge for the night. David had forgotten what a wondrous sight the clusters of stars were at night. The polluted lights of the big city had made them invisible.

Larry came out from the house with a cordless telephone. "Anthony, you've got a call. Janet Manelli's on hold and insists on talking to you. Says it's an emergency. Something about the playground committee meeting this morning."

"I can't believe she tracked me down. Tell her I'm busy giving last rights to a dying animal in the forest."

"I think you already used that one." Smiling, Larry handed the phone to Father Anthony. Larry turned to David and said, "I just got a call from a colleague regarding one of her patients and I need to fax some information right away. I'll be down in my office for twenty minutes or so."

"Don't worry about me. I'll go visit with Corey. I'm a pretty mean Nintendo player."

Laughing, Larry said, "Great, he'll like that. Corey, like a lot of kids, judges others on their video game prowess. I've spent hours trying to play those damn games and haven't gotten any better; at least the kids see that I'm trying. I'll be back in a flash."

As the two men entered the house, David heard Father Anthony say with forced politeness, "Janet, dear, what seems to be the problem? No, I didn't know the meeting was this morning."

Corey was absorbed in a game of video football and didn't hear David enter the living room. So he sat down on the plush, cream-colored couch and watched Corey play. His brow was furrowed in deep concentration as he sat on his knees, back erect, just a few feet from the TV screen. Furiously, Corey moved his fingers across the many buttons on the controller, expertly guiding his offense up and down the field. He was good, but also intense and serious. David wondered if the boy was even enjoying the game.

"Shit," Corey said, as a pass was intercepted. "That guy sucks."

"He usually doesn't throw many interceptions in this game," David said.

Corey whipped his head around and shot an angry look at David. "What're you doing here?"

"Just appreciating an expert at work. You're very good."

Corey allowed a quick smile, then quickly said, "Ahh, whatta you know." Turning around, Corey hit the reset button and began a new game.

"Hey, I love Madden Football. How about a game?"

Corey turned around and said, "You're kiddin', right?"

"Not at all. Let's give it a go." David smiled. "Unless, of course, you're chicken."

Now smirking, Corey said, "All right, but you're in for an ass-kickin'." He tossed the other controller to David.

"We'll see. I'll be the 49ers."

"That's my team!"

"No problem," David said, seeing how easily Corey could anger. "Give me the Rams."

The game was competitive and exciting, and went right down to the wire. There was some friendly trash-talking that grew as the game progressed. Corey seemed to be having fun. In the end, with time running out, he made a short field goal to win by two points.

"You're not bad," Corey admitted. "Where'd you learn to play?"

"At the seminary. We played almost every night. Last year I went undefeated, won two hundred six straight games. This is my first loss in a long, long time."

"No shit?" Corey cautiously looked around. "I mean, no kidding." He was proud that he beat David, as he knew the boy would be. The victor turned and looked directly at David, giving him full attention. The earlier disdain had melted and was now replaced with respect. It's amazing how respect is earned in the world of kids, David thought.

"How about another one? I need to start a new winning streak."

Corey laughed. It was short and quick, as if he forgot how to do it, or would get in trouble if he continued too long. "Let's go!"

Just as they began the second game, Father Anthony came into the room. He looked bothered. "David, I've got to go talk with Janet and settle her down. She's all bent out of shape about the meeting this morning. Apparently, the committee didn't go with the equipment company she wanted, so now she's threatening to sabotage the project. I've got to go nip this thing in the bud."

"A pastor's job is never done."

"Very funny. Where's Larry?"

"He's in his office faxing some information to a colleague."

"Well, my boy, I've got to get going pretty quick here," Father Anthony said, stroking his beard. "Why don't I drop Corey off at home on the way—"

"Yeah," Corey interrupted, almost too eager at the opportunity to leave. "I gotta get home."

Father Anthony looked at Corey quizzically, then said to David, "Would you wait for Larry and let him know what's going on?"

"No problem," David said. "Hey, Corey, I've got a Nintendo machine and some games in my bag at the rectory. We can play any time, if that's okay with Father Anthony."

Father Anthony gave David a surprised, but pleased look. "You bet. Maybe I'll learn how to play and give you young guns a run for your money."

"Cool," the boy said.

"Let's hit the road, Corey." Father Anthony patted his pockets in search of his keys.

"See you later," Corey said to David.

"Good game. But next time, no mercy." David walked over and held out his hand. Corey slapped him a high-five, then grabbed his coat and hustled toward the door. As the boy and elder priest were walking out of the room, Father Anthony turned to David, smiled and nodded in approval.

David stayed in the living room waiting for Larry. He killed time by perusing Larry's collection of black and white abstract art that hung on the walls throughout the large room. There were eight images done by the same artist.

Each piece was presented differently, yet all were related in a way David couldn't quite grasp. To him they all appeared to be large inkblots. He pictured Larry asking patients, "What do you see in this picture?" though he doubted Larry used that kind of therapy.

The brilliant evening sky was too good to pass up so David made his way back out to the deck. He sat down and inhaled a deep dose of the cool, refreshing country air. As the stars continued to sparkle above, David pondered Corey's situation. He was definitely a troubled and angry young boy, but David liked him. Their childhoods were somewhat similar, and he could empathize with the turmoil Corey was experiencing.

As the silhouettes of dark, ominous thunderheads appeared on the horizon, David sank into the memory of the dreaded afternoon twenty-two years ago in Neihardt Park when he had been sexually molested. He shuddered at the memory, promising himself that he would pay special attention to Corey. With Larry, the boy seemed to be in extremely capable hands, but David also believed that his assistance could be valuable.

David had never sought any help, nor had he ever said a word to anyone about that terrible day. Over the years, the horror of staying silent and trying to resolve the issue on his own had taken its toll. Returning home only intensified the vile memories, and they were beginning to dominate his consciousness once again. He knew that sometime soon, very soon, he would have to confront the incident and work through it, once and for all.

Suddenly, he began to feel panicky. Tomorrow, he would be officially installed as the new associate pastor at St. Cecilia's. As he sat there, David questioned his ability to be effective and helpful to others while his own wounds still festered. His heart pounded, his thoughts started to race and he felt lightheaded and detached like he was floating out of his body. He knew these sensations too well and he was weary of battling them. David felt like he couldn't keep them under control anymore. And he didn't want to. He simply wanted the torment to stop.

"Sorry it took so long." Larry surprised David who quickly blinked his eyes several times in an attempt to clear his head. "Where did everyone…?"

The fast moving clouds were still a considerable distance away, so the bright moon and stars provided Larry with enough light to see the agony written all over David's face. It was as white as the moon itself; his eyes were welled-up, looking as if they were ready to float out of his head.

"David, what's wrong? Is everything okay?"

The first thought that came to David's mind was, God works in mysterious ways. He'd heard that adage over and over again throughout his life, and he'd told others the same thing many times. He believed it to be true. Perhaps God was at work right now: Here he was with a respected therapist and a leading authority on treating sexual abuse. This wasn't happening simply due to chance. No, he had to trust his instincts and beliefs. This was God's doing. God was providing him an opportunity and a vehicle to unload his burden.

The fog began to lift in David's mind and he heard Larry say, "What's wrong? You look like you've seen a ghost."

David remembered the liberation he felt after talking with Mr. Harmon and gained some confidence from that thought. "Hum…Larry, can I talk with you about something very personal?"

"Of course." He grabbed a patio chair and sat down directly across from David. Larry moved a small table to the side so that there was nothing between them. "Whenever you feel comfortable, tell me what's on your mind."

Larry's soothing voice and relaxed posture made David feel more at ease. "I don't know how much you know about my past. Father Anthony said you moved back to Willa a few years before I left. I'm not exactly the prodigal son returning home."

"I remember a little about you, and Anthony has told me quite a bit about your history and your current situation. Please don't be upset with him. Anthony's very fond of you and has taken great interest in your well-being as a person and your success as a priest. We're very good friends and he was speaking in the strictest of confidence."

"I guess I'm kind of relieved that you know something about me," David said. "I won't have to start from scratch. In the two days since I've returned home, some memories have come flooding back; memories that I've put tremendous effort into trying to forget. It's been a constant struggle, one that I feel I'm starting to lose. I'm full of anxiety and shame about my past. Some events in my life I want to make up for, while others I just want to stash somewhere and never have to think about again."

"David, we all have skeletons in our closets. Each of us has something that we're not proud of and want to bury. That's normal. Experience has shown me it's imperative that we come to terms with what's occurred and forgive ourselves. Everyone goes about this process differently and it can help tremendously if there's someone who's skilled to guide you, whether that's someone like me, or a clergy member like yourself or a wise, trusted friend. The important thing is to get it out in the open so we can let go of the past and move on. Suppressing unpleasant feelings only allows them to quietly gather strength and momentum, like a snowball rolling down hill getting bigger and bigger until it's out of control."

"My snowball's getting pretty big," David said.

Larry smiled politely. "People are forgiving, David, and I'll bet most of those in town have already forgotten your childhood antics. They'll chalk it up to typical adolescent behavior."

"It's more than that," David said quietly, his voice trembling. He wasn't able to look at Larry.

After a few moments, Larry said, "It's okay, David. Go on."

The brakes slammed in David's mind and everything came to a screeching halt. What the hell is going on? David asked himself. What am I doing talking to a man I just met? I barely know Larry, and I'm about to tell him my most private thoughts? This is crazy. I should stop, excuse myself and go home...or just tell Larry never mind, and keep on trying to forget the whole damn thing. This is all a terrible mistake.

David heard a sweet, enticing voice in his head beckoning him back to the warm cocoon of familiarity and caution. But David knew freedom would come only after a period of awkwardness and pain. The voice whispering in his head had run its course and could no longer protect him. It was time to say goodbye to this old friend.

"I was sexually abused," David spat out quickly, as if the words burned his tongue.

The silence was deafening. David barely noticed the wind rustling through the leaves in the large trees surrounding the deck, or the owl announcing its emergence for the night. All he heard was the withering cry of the voice dying in his mind. David felt sad, like a piece of him was gone forever.

"Would you like to tell me about it?"

"Yes."

David didn't know where to begin. He had never put it all together in a logical, coherent order. This was the first time he really had to think about how and why it happened.

"It was only one time." David felt like someone else was talking from a distance. "I was twelve years old and my dad had died about six months after he left my mom and me. He was never much of a father. If he wasn't working, he was drinking. We did have some good times though. He loved card games, any kind of game, and he was good at them all. We played a lot and he always let me win. Anyway, there was a new associate pastor at St. Cecilia's, Father Emery. He came right after my dad had passed away – a car accident. Dad was drunk and went right through a train crossing. They said he probably didn't even feel the impact.

"My mom wasn't much better in the drinking department and she just drank more and more after dad died. I don't have any brothers or sisters, so I was pretty lonely back then. I did have some close friends, but no one wanted to talk about what happened to dad. Hell, I don't blame them; we were just too young. Everyone kept telling me how brave I was, and how I was the man of the house now. So I acted like nothing happened and kept it all to myself, even though it was killing me.

"Father Emery was nice to mom and me during that time. He'd come over to the house and try to help mom, but she didn't want any part of it. She just kept on drinking. I suppose that was her way of coping. Father Emery took me fishing a lot at Neihardt Park, and we talked about dad and mom and how I felt about it all. It helped, and I was thrilled that an adult actually cared about me. I'd never had that before. I felt special and important and loved." David stopped and adjusted his glasses.

"I know this is hard," Larry said. "You're doing great."

David continued. "One summer day, Father Emery brought me to one of the park's remote lakes. After fishing for a while, he suggested we go for a swim. It was real hot that afternoon and no one was around, so he said we could skinny-dip. I was embarrassed and didn't want to do it, but he kept telling me it was no big deal. I finally agreed. We were splashing and laughing and having fun. At one point, I remember looking up to the sky and watching a small plane in the distance spraying someone's field when…when I felt a hand on my…on me. I never turned around to face him as it happened. I just froze. I didn't know what to do. He told me to do the same thing to him. I should've known I had a choice. But it felt like a command. I remember feeling sick and wanting to throw up. I didn't turn around or move."

Gently, Larry said, "David, you were only twelve. You didn't know what you were doing, don't blame yourself for what that asshole did to you."

David sighed, then continued. "He told me he wouldn't be able to do things with me anymore, like take me fishing, unless I showed him I cared about him. I was so afraid of being alone I did what he wanted... God, I was just a lonely little kid. When it was over, I got out of the lake, grabbed my clothes and ran into the woods. I heard him call for me, but I hid. I stayed in the park that entire night. I got home before my mom woke up, which was in the afternoon most of the time.

"For the next two weeks, I didn't go to school or church. I hated that monster for what he did to me. I wanted him to die. I faked sick for a week. The next week, I just wandered around. Mom was out of it most of the time and hardly ever answered the phone, so Father Anthony finally came to our house and told mom I wasn't at school. She made me go back the next week. I'll never forget how terrified I was...I was frightened that he might try to do something to me again. If he did, I was going to kill him. I was so full of hate that there's no doubt in my mind I would have done it. Before going back to school, I even put a hunting knife in my backpack."

David glanced at Larry. He was nodding his head and his eyes remained fixed on David's.

"When I got to school that Monday, I didn't see him anywhere. Later in the day, I heard some kids talking. Apparently, he had been transferred the previous week. It happened real quick. No one seemed to know why he had left or where he went. People asked questions, but it was all hush-hush. I didn't care. All I remember was the relief of knowing that he wasn't going to be around anymore. I've never seen or heard anything about him since.

"You know, it's odd. One of the reasons I had such a strong desire to join the priesthood was because of what happened. That bastard took advantage of a fragile little kid who trusted and believed that priests were holy, wise and safe. Now, one of the highest priorities in my ministry is to make sure that every child who needs help gets it."

David stopped. He didn't have anything left to say. It surprised him how clearly the facts had come back to him, like it happened just yesterday.

He wiped away the wetness he felt rolling down his cheeks. That's strange, he thought. Why am I crying? He didn't feel upset and was sure his voice never wavered or cracked.

He looked over at Larry but had trouble seeing out his glasses. They were covered with moisture, and for the first time David realized it was raining. He was so engrossed in recounting the tale he didn't know the storm clouds had moved in and rain was now drenching them both. Nevertheless, the cool raindrops were soothing and helped numb the pain. David didn't make any attempt to move out of the rain, he simply let it wash over him.

Larry sat unruffled, soaked, intently listening.

"It's raining," David said in a drained, feeble voice. "Shouldn't we go inside?"

"It's up to you. A little rain never hurt anyone."

After a few more moments, David began to come out of his stupor and gather his bearings. The rain started to come down in heavier drops. There were loud claps of thunder and sharp flashes of lightning that were getting closer by the minute.

After lightning struck across the field, Larry said, "We'd better get inside." He got up and grabbed some dinner dishes.

"I'm sorry, let me help," David said, now fully alert.

Over the pounding rain and booming thunder, Larry said loudly, "Everything will be fine. Let's get inside." They both made a dash for the sliding glass door.

Once inside, Larry said, "It took a lot of courage for you to talk about what happened. That's the first step in the healing process. If you'd like, I'd be happy to help you work though this."

"Yeah, I think I would."

Larry grabbed two kitchen towels and tossed one to David. "Listen," he said. "You've had a tough evening and look absolutely exhausted. I think you've done enough talking for one night. These things take time. If you feel comfortable, you're welcome to stay in one of my guest rooms tonight. It's a bitch driving out of here in the rain, especially in a storm this bad. I'd feel much better if you didn't drive back to the rectory tonight."

David looked at his sopping wet clothes, then at Larry's and said, "Hey, I'm sorry I kept you tonight. I shouldn't have—"

"Absolutely not," Larry said. "I know you would have done the same thing for me or someone else. It's what we do, David. I'm honored that you trusted me enough to tell me about Father Emery. You took a giant stride tonight, and you should be proud of yourself. If it's acceptable to you, I'd like to meet with you once a week and keep this positive momentum going."

"Thanks," David said with hesitation. "You know, I am tired. I think I'll take you up on your invitation. Are you sure I won't be imposing?"

"Not at all. Let me get you some dry clothes and I'll show you to your room. I can toss your clothes in the dryer so they're ready to go in the morning. I'll call Father Anthony and let him know you'll be back first thing tomorrow."

"Please don't say anything to him about this," David said. "I don't want him to know, not yet. He was the pastor when Father Emery was here, and I don't want him to blame himself or worry about me. He's got enough to deal with."

"Absolutely. If that's what you want, it'll stay between us."

Later that night, there were low rumblings of thunder and occasional flashes of lightning as the storm began to fade into the distance. The melodious sound of a steady rainfall filled David's room. He lay in bed thinking about the day's events. Two of his darkest secrets were no longer dormant; they were out in the open for David to see and deal with. They didn't look so daunting now, especially knowing that he didn't have to go it alone anymore. He didn't kid himself. There was a lot of hard, painful work to be done; however, the most difficult battle was over. He was still apprehensive about his future at St. Cecilia's, but he was more at peace with himself than he had been for as long as he could remember. And for the first time since he returned home, David allowed himself to think that he had what it took to be a good priest.

CHAPTER 4

David woke early Sunday morning to the chatter of birds merrily gathering worms who had climbed out of the mud to breathe. The storms had cleared, giving way to sunshine and clear skies. It was a beautiful day.

Lounging in bed, David felt rested. He had slept without waking through the entire night, something he hadn't done in years. Before nodding off, he thought he'd wake with a start, feeling jumpy and anxious about noon Mass. But he wasn't nervous at all. The events of the prior day had set in motion the healing process, and he thanked God for Larry's invitation to help.

At 7 a.m., David reluctantly rolled out of bed. He purposefully waited until this time so he wouldn't disturb Larry, in case he liked to sleep in on Sundays. After making the bed, David quietly opened the door to search for the laundry room and his clothes. To his surprise, they were newly-washed and folded outside his door. A note sat on top.

David,
I went biking and won't be back for a couple of hours. Help yourself to anything in the kitchen. I'll see you at noon Mass or afterwards at your reception.
Good luck,
Larry

P.S. I know it wasn't easy talking about your past last night. I hope you can find comfort in knowing I'm here to help you, and that your life will only get better by facing this straight on. Congrats.

Folding the note, David smiled. He felt the need to save it, a tangible reminder of the difficult decision he had made last evening. Pain and struggle lay ahead, he knew that. Still, David thought, I'm ready to finally fight this battle.

He wasn't hungry enough to go rummaging through Larry's kitchen, so he got dressed and headed out to his car. The temperature outside was chilly and David could have used a light jacket and long pants instead of his T-shirt and shorts. Trees shaded the Honda, allowing a light layer of frost to form on its windows. To his chagrin, the ice scraper was nowhere to be found; it must a have been jarred loose during yesterday's drive. He started the car and cranked up the heater. Knowing it would take more than a few minutes for his old ride to begin spitting out enough heat to defrost the windows, he went back into the house to warm up.

Larry hadn't given David a full tour of the house, so he decided to look around. He was familiar with the main floor where he had slept and the upstairs that contained, among other rooms, the living room, kitchen, and sliding glass door that led out to the deck.

He decided to quickly peek into the basement. Larry's office must have been located there and David was curious to see it. After all, he reasoned, I'm going to be spending some time there.

When first entering the basement, he saw all sorts of toys and games in the main area. There was another big screen television, exactly like the one in the living room, that had another Nintendo plugged into it; at least a dozen game cartridges were strewn around the video machine. Two beanbag chairs sat in front of the TV. A VCR also was connected to the television. Next to it, a bookcase held a gigantic library of kid's movies. There was a foosball table in one corner of the room, a pool table in the middle, and a pinball machine in another corner. The walls were decorated with posters of sports stars.

A nerf basketball hoop was secured to a wall; there were markings on the carpet mimicking a three-point line and a free throw line. The ceiling was high, and David imagined that this would allow for a spirited game of nerf basketball.

A large table held board games, cards, colors and other items that kids of all ages could play with. However, David noticed there were no dolls or kitchen sets or other playthings little girls tended to be interested in. All in all, it was a boy's dream room.

"So, this is how Larry works his magic with kids," David said. "He plays with them. Pretty simple, but that's the same way I try to build trust with kids." David nodded his head while looking around. "Makes sense."

He opened one of the three doors in the main area and saw the furnace, water heater, washer and dryer, piles of boxes and other items neatly stacked in the dark storage room.

The next door was slightly ajar and he looked inside. It was Larry's office. The room was light and snug. It contained a large desk loaded with files and papers and other important looking stuff; a bookshelf overflowing with, what appeared to be, material pertinent to the field of psychology; two cozy-looking chairs sat facing each other with a table that held a bowl of peanut M & Ms on it between the chairs; and, of course, a long leather couch. Soft, cute pictures of exotic animals, the kind displayed in *National Geographic*, adorned the walls.

Figuring the car windows were defrosted by now, he started for the stairs. When he touched the first step, David thought he heard sounds coming from behind the third door. He walked over to it. The sounds were barely audible and impossible to discern. Maybe a TV or radio had been left on, David thought. He grabbed the door handle to go in and shut off whatever was making the noise. He banged into the door; it was locked. The sounds, David noticed, were no longer there.

"Hearing things," David said with a chuckle, as he bounded up the stairs two at a time. "Man, that's all I need right now."

Father Anthony wasn't around when David returned to the rectory. He figured his mentor was busy with morning Masses. After being formally introduced and welcomed, David was to assist at noon Mass and begin leading services on Monday. With four Masses scheduled, Father Anthony had a busy morning.

David showered and changed into his blacks and white collar. He was starving. As he approached the kitchen, he heard someone rummaging through the refrigerator.

"Good morning, Father Anthony," he said, stepping into the kitchen.

"Wrong."

Startled, David said, "What are you doing here?"

"Came to finish our game," Corey said casually, between bites of a cherry Pop Tart. "Father Anthony said I could wait for you."

"Does your mom know you're here?"

Corey slurped from a glass of chocolate milk. "She's sleepin' and won't get up 'till lunch time. As long as I'm back before dark, she don't care where I go."

David wasn't sure whether or not to believe Corey. Until proven otherwise, David thought, I'll give the boy the benefit of the doubt.

"Okay, you're on," David said, rubbing his hands together. "First, let me grab some grub, then we'll set up the game."

The only television he could find was in the den. It was an older model that wasn't cable ready. Luckily, neither were the TVs at the seminary, so David had all the necessary hookups and gadgets to get the machine rigged up.

The two played a couple of football games, splitting victories, then moved on to some of David's other games. Corey was awed by David's wide selection of video games, and even more impressed by his command of them all.

David was busy teaching Corey the finer points, shortcuts and secrets of the latest *Super Mario Brothers* game when Father Anthony laughed behind them. "Well, well, what do we have here? The two video junkies are at it again."

"What's up?" Corey said pleasantly.

"I had an early visitor this morning," David said. "Apparently, Corey enjoyed beating me so much he came back to pile it on."

Corey swiveled his head to face Father Anthony. The boy was smiling broadly and his cheerful expression caught Father Anthony off guard. It had replaced, at least for now, the perpetual mask of toughness and nastiness that Corey had used over the years to keep people at bay.

"Nah, he's pretty good. And, man, he's got all these sweet games." Corey looked back at the TV just in time to aim a cannon that was to shoot Mario into another imaginary world.

Father Anthony nodded his head toward David, indicating he wanted to talk in private.

"I'll be right back," David said to Corey.

The boy continued playing, frantically attempting to maneuver Mario through the traps and goblins of the newly discovered underwater world.

Once they were out of earshot, David said, "I'm sorry. I had no idea he was coming over. He was sitting at the kitchen table when I—"

Father Anthony slapped David on the back. "I don't know what you did or how you did it, but that little boy likes you. That was the first time I've seen him smile a genuinely happy smile at someone other than Larry for…well, I can't even remember the last time."

"I haven't done anything special." David shrugged his shoulders and tried to suppress a grin. "We've just played some video games and I've made sure to focus on the things he likes to talk about. We both enjoy playing Nintendo, and I think that connection helps. I don't know what all the fuss is about with him. He's rough around the edges, I'll give you that, but I dealt with a hell of a lot worse when I interned at that inner-city parish in St. Louis."

Father Anthony paused, then gave David a look of respect. "You can't fool a fool, especially an old one. You know exactly what you're doing with Corey. From now on, we'll let you deal with all the tough little buggers."

"Gladly. But only if they're all like Corey." David said, smiling. "I hope you don't mind that we're sitting here playing video games. You've got to feel swamped this morning. Anything I can do to help out?"

"Nope. It's all under control. I've run the parish solo for the last two months, so what's another twenty-four hours. You'll be busy enough come tomorrow." Father Anthony looked at his watch. "I'm going to head back for ten-thirty Mass. Why don't you come on over in about an hour and we can prep for noon Mass. Hey, you got your homily ready to go?"

Jerking his head upward, David stared at Father Anthony. The young priest looked like a rabbit caught in the middle of the road.

"I'm just kidding," Father Anthony teased. "You're still assisting. Remember though, you've got six-thirty Mass all week. It's always a small turnout that early on the weekdays, so it'll be a nice way for you to get to your feet wet. Plus, I need to catch up on my sleep."

David gave a short, facetious laugh. "Holy smokes, you about gave me a heart attack. I'll be ready to go tomorrow."

"Relax, my boy. Everything'll turn out fine. See you in about an hour. In the meantime, go ahead and spend some more time with Corey." Father Anthony tugged at his beard. "You know, he likes you because you don't have any preconceived notions about him. Everyone else – including myself, I must admit – has labeled Corey a bad kid. And that blinds us to anything other than what we expect to see. You bring a fresh pair of eyes. Hmm...believe it or not, David, you're already making a tremendous contribution here. Keep it up."

David maintained an even keel on the outside; inside he was dancing. "Father Anthony, I wanted to check with you on something. Corey said that his mom doesn't care if he's here, or anywhere as far as I can tell, as long as he's back by dark. I'd like to believe him, but I've been burned by trusting kids before I got to know them and their situations better. What do you think? Should I have him call his mom or not?"

Father Anthony said, "On this one, I'd be inclined to believe the boy. Have him call anyway; better safe than sorry. I know you like the kid, but I want to caution you: He's got a long history of making up stories and crying wolf. So be careful about believing everything he tells you. Larry says the lying and storytelling are ways of getting attention from adults, and it's worked extremely well for Corey.

"In fact, Larry asked me to instruct Corey's teachers to start ignoring the stories. In the past, they would come to me worried about every tale he told. I'd follow up – you know, spend time talking to him and to the teachers. Larry said all we were doing was reinforcing the dishonesty by giving it so much attention. I guarantee he'll try to suck you in, so keep your guard up."

"Okay."

"I'd better get going. Gotta go save some souls." David watched as Father Anthony left.

Over the next hour, David noticed that Corey was more talkative and less focused on the games. Nothing of substance was discussed, but enough that their relationship seemed to be unfolding naturally.

David looked at the grandfather clock loudly ticking away in the corner of the den, and said, "I've got to get over to the church. You're welcome to stay here or come to Mass. I'm gonna be introduced and welcomed to the parish, so I'm kinda nervous. I could use a friendly face in the crowd. There's also a reception afterwards and, if your mom doesn't mind, you can come to that to. I'll bet there will be lots of great food."

Corey thought for a few seconds. "Sure, I'll help you out. Mom won't care. I'll bet your good at doing Church stuff too."

Chuckling, David said, "I sure hope so. Let's call your mom and let her know what's going on."

Corey glared at David. However, the boy's intimidating expression faded as David held the boy's gaze, signaling to him that this wasn't open for debate.

"Fine." Corey swung around and stomped off to the phone.

David was fourth in the procession line. In front of him were two altar boys. One led the procession with a tall, skinny crucifix, while the other slogged along behind, obviously bummed-out that he wasn't chosen to lead the pack. Behind him, the lector – an elderly lady – lugged a large leather Lectionary. It was so heavy that the poor woman kept shifting it back and forth in her frail arms so she wouldn't drop it. Father Anthony anchored the rear.

The boys walked at what David thought was a snail's pace. Father Anthony was belting out the processional hymn while smiling and nodding to various members of his admiring flock. This was his stage, and he reveled in the moment. David stared straight ahead, not daring to make eye contact with anyone in the pews. Still, he knew all eyes were on him. He felt naked.

After what seemed like an eternity to David, the group made their way to the altar and the members of the processional party took their traditional places. Father Anthony sat in a huge, elegantly designed chair reserved for the priest leading the service. The chair was so big that it engulfed even a man of Father Anthony's size.

After bowing his head in a short, silent prayer, the elder priest rose and greeted the congregation. "Before we begin today's celebration, I would like to make a very special announcement. St. Cecilia's is lucky to be adding a new member to our family. I'm proud to introduce Father David Cooper as our new associate pastor. As many of you know, Father Cooper is a native son returning home. He was born and raised in Willa and attended St. Cecilia's school and Church. He's a wonderful priest and we're extremely fortunate to have been assigned such a capable young man. Immediately following Mass, there will be a reception in the church basement. You're all invited to meet and welcome Father Cooper."

To David, the silence was deafening – not that he expected a wild outbreak of applause. But this wasn't a typical church silence; it was heavier, thicker. Even though it was standing room only, no one made a sound. No coughing, no rustling about, not a single baby was crying or even fussing. Hostility permeated the air and, for the first time since Mass began, David looked out at the sea of faces that packed the pews. They were all centered on him, judging him, sizing him up. He had never felt so self-conscious and uncomfortable in his life. It was like he was giving a speech and realizing halfway through that his zipper was down. Should he stop and zip it up or go on, pretending that he knew and was perfectly comfortable with it? David decided the latter would be the best option. So, he stood next to Father Anthony's chair, hands folded together in reverence, and forced a light, confident smile.

Screw'em, David thought. At that time, he truly did not care what everyone thought of him. He was called to serve God and that meant serving His people, these people. It wouldn't be easy. But David felt that he could do it as long as he trusted in God and stayed true to his faith. The Lord was the only one he had to answer to when it was all said and done; He was David's sole judge and jury, not the people and faces before him.

"Let us pray," Father Anthony said to the crowd. And with that, David's first official Mass as an ordained priest at St. Cecilia's was under way.

As the service progressed, he felt more at ease. This was his domain and David focused all thoughts and feelings into the sacred ceremony. In concelebrating the Eucharist, he joined Father Anthony in the priestly role of consecrating bread and wine into the Body and Blood of Christ. Then, Father Anthony went to distribute Holy Communion to the gathering, while David served the lector, the choir and the disabled and elderly that sat in the first row of pews. He then took up station in the middle aisle next to Father Anthony.

By the time David joined Father Anthony, the elder priest's communion line was jam-packed. It wove down the middle aisle to the back of the church and around to the side aisle. David's line remained empty; no one made an immediate move to come over. He anticipated that people would be more comfortable going to Father Anthony, but David also expected some folks to move over just to speed things up.

David stood strong, determined not to retreat until all the parishioners were served. He hid his embarrassment and discomfort as best he could. Father Anthony was clearly rattled and did what he could, through glances and head nods, to encourage others to move to David's line.

After a few agonizing seconds, which felt more like hours to David, a lone figure rose from the other side of the aisle, crossed through the crowd waiting for Father Anthony and strolled up the empty line. It was Corey. As he passed by, some parishioners in Father Anthony's line scowled at the boy like he had just committed a crime. But Corey remained undaunted. Upon arriving, he smiled at David before he gently placed the light wafer in Corey's hands.

When he turned to go back to his seat, David looked up – there was Larry, followed by Christopher, Lizzy, Erik, Mr. Baumm and his wife, Ronald Baumm and a smattering of other parishioners that David didn't know or recognize. As he placed the host in the hands or on the tongue of each person, David's hand trembled, and his voice cracked with emotion each time he said, "Body of Christ."

Following Mass, Father Anthony said, "I'm so sorry." He yanked off his alb. "I can't believe those people. Here we preach the virtues of forgiveness and acceptance and, when it comes time to put the rubber to the road, they act like idiots. I've never been so disappointed with them in all my years here."

"Forget about it," David said. "People will be skeptical about me until I prove them wrong, and I'm okay with that. If I was in their shoes, I'd probably be leery too."

Still miffed, Father Anthony said, "You've got a good head on your shoulders, my boy. I don't think I would be as understanding as you are at this moment. We're a community, a family. I expected them to respond differently. My God, people never cease to amaze me."

"Talk about amazing, how about Corey. I was absolutely flabbergasted. God was at work there."

Father Anthony grinned. "I guess I'm looking at the forest instead of the trees. Yeah, that was something. You've obviously made quite an impression on that boy for him to take a risk like that. You and Larry are right: Corey probably does have a good heart in there somewhere. I just wish we could see it more often, but that's probably our fault. Perhaps some good did come out of this today."

"I think so. One thing I know for sure is that it's going to be a small reception. But, hey, that's more food for us."

Laughing, Father Anthony said, "That's just fine with me." Then, he added seriously, "I'm proud of the way you handled yourself out there. It takes a man of great faith to find the good during bad times. That's what separates the great priests from the good ones. And today you demonstrated you've got the right stuff. I knew you did. Well done."

The reception room was huge, but also sparse and dreary. Several religious paintings were randomly hung on the faded beige-colored walls. Old green tile, ten or fifteen years old, covered the floor. The only furniture in the room was several stacks of folding chairs and tables that varied in kind and color. A few were set up in the middle of the room.

David was right-on with his assessment: It was a light turn out. As a matter of fact, only a few people from his communion line showed up. The Baumm's were already eating, and they gobbled down their food as if it was going to be taken from them any minute. This, however, was highly unlikely. One of the tables was loaded with a smorgasbord of food that could have fed a party of forty. Various members of the parish provided it all. Some parishioners, David speculated, believed that supplying food was their duty and enough to welcome him.

Larry and Lizzy were sitting at a table immersed in a serious conversation. Christopher and Corey were hovering over the portion of the table that held cookies, cakes, pies and other homemade treats. Erik was nowhere in sight. David wasn't surprised, but he was disappointed. He hadn't spoken with his best friend since arriving home and was looking forward to catching up with him.

Father Anthony wasted no time grabbing a plate of food and joining the Baumm's. David immediately went over to Corey, who was now standing alone slyly poking a finger into a pie for a quick sample.

"What kind is it?"

Corey jumped backwards. "Man, don't be sneakin' up on me like that." He was more embarrassed than angry. "It's strawberry or cherry. Patten said there was a rhubarb pie in here somewhere. Those things suck. I think he's bullshitting me, haven't found one yet."

"Grab whatever you want," David said. "You deserve it. Most people don't have the guts to do what you did today. It means a lot to me."

"Wasn't no big thing," Corey said, eyes filling with life.

David could tell the young boy felt good about what he did, but David also knew Corey would never admit it. David thought it was best to not gush over the boy; that would only annoy him. It would mean more if David showed his gratitude slowly over time.

"Let's get a plate before the Baumm's get all the good stuff," David whispered. They both snickered.

All nine people eventually loaded up their plates and sat at one table, opting to squish together rather than spread out to other tables. The feast was delicious. Father Anthony was holding court and had everyone, including Corey, laughing hysterically at his silly jokes and funny stories.

They all sat a little straighter and walked over to the food table for seconds and thirds with a lighter bounce in their step. There was a bond between them; they were proud of themselves and each other for standing up to the parish hypocrites. David sat back and looked around the table – he wished Erik were there – and promised himself that he wouldn't disappoint or let any of these people down.

An hour and a half later, the party had run its course and people began to clear out. Father Anthony was the first to leave. He had a pre-marriage counseling session with a young couple and, as usual, remembered the appointment at the last minute. He dashed back to the rectory.

Father Anthony was everyone's common link, the person they all identified with. When he left, there was a noticeable void. The uncomfortable, awkward silences grew longer and multiplied. Larry tried to fill in but it wasn't the same. David spared the gathering any more clumsy moments and thanked them for coming and, especially, for their support at Mass. He said, as a reward for their valiant actions, he would do all the clean up. The Baumm's didn't hesitate at the offer and practically bolted for the door. However, with Lizzy and Larry, David had to insist that he really wanted to do this as a way of showing his gratitude. Eventually, the two relented.

As Larry was putting on his suit coat, he said to David, "Can I talk to you for a minute?"

"You bet."

They waved goodbye to Lizzy and Christopher who were opening the heavy metal door that lead upstairs to the church parking lot. Corey had already retreated to the rectory for a fill of video games. David told his new buddy he would join him later.

"Would you still like to meet?" Larry said once everyone departed.

Without hesitation, David said, "Yes. I would. Now that it's out, I'm not going to bury it."

"I'm glad to hear that. If your schedule is even remotely close to Father Anthony's, I would suggest a time when the parish is supposedly quiet. How about after six-thirty Mass on Saturday mornings?"

"I don't want to put you out on the weekend."

"No, no. Actually, it would be a great time for me," Larry said. "Do you like to bike?"

"Yeah, but it's been a while, and I don't have one," David said, puzzled.

"Not to worry. I've got a couple of road bikes. Let's meet at my place about seven-thirty next Saturday and we can take our session on the road, if you're comfortable with that."

"Darn," David said, snapping his fingers. "That means no couch."

"Well, you can always strap one on your back."

David laughed. "I think I'll pass. But I'll be there Saturday morning bright and early."

"Outstanding." Larry turned to leave, then stopped, and turned back around to face David. "Oh, one more thing. About Corey: It's plain to see he's already grown fond of you. Since he's been my patient, I haven't observed anything close to what he did for you today. It took a tremendous amount of courage on his part. I honestly wasn't sure if he was capable of doing something like that. He's so turned off by adults that, up to this point, he has only shown disdain and disrespect for them, and I mean all adults. I would have expected him to enjoy seeing you in the awful position you were in. To take charge and lead the way is a tremendous stride forward for him.

"Also, I want to give you some insight so you know whom you're dealing with. Has Father Anthony told you anything about Corey and his home environment?"

"Yeah, a little. Mostly about his mom's drinking and drug use."

"Those addictions have helped to create a very damaged little boy. In order to feed her cravings, she maintains relationships with some real seedy characters. These men produce a lot of confusion and disorder in Corey's life. More than one of these miscreants have physically abused Corey – slapped him, punched him. A while back, Corey ended up in the emergency room after one of her boyfriends beat him senseless – black eye, two cracked ribs, broken wrist. It was ugly."

"Why does Corey's mom allow this to happen? And can't the police or social services get involved?"

"Good question," Larry said, shaking his head. "Her addictions blind her to reality, which is typical of people who are using. Somehow, she can rationalize it all away in her alcoholic mind. As a matter of fact, the explanation she gave the police and social services for Corey's injuries that day at the hospital was that he fell off the garage roof while getting a baseball out of the gutter. Well, that was a pack of lies. He isn't into sports, and he sure as hell wasn't playing catch with her boyfriend. She covered it all up."

"Why does Corey keep quiet?" David said.

"Like most all of us, he loves his mother – faults and all. And, he doesn't want to go live with foster parents or in some other placement. Home will always be home to him, no matter how bad we perceive it to be. I also believe he wants to protect her from the idiots that she chooses to live with. Basically, he's become the adult in that relationship.

"There's a lot I know about Corey's history, and it's taken me a long time to earn his trust and confidence. But, as much as I know, there's still a lot I don't know. One thing I have learned over time, unfortunately through trial and error, is that Corey is a compulsive liar. And he can be extremely believable and convincing. On more than one occasion, he's even sucked me in, and I've worked with many, many kids who've used the same tactic."

David pursed his lips and slowly shook his head. "Boy, I haven't seen any of that from him."

"David, I'm giving you this information so you're prepared. Be attentive. Corey's a master manipulator and his fabrications serve a purpose: He gets what he wants, he gets out of trouble, or he avoids something he doesn't want to do or face. Trust me on this one: He will begin to disclose some pretty wild things to you if your relationship continues to develop, and after today I'm convinced that it will, if you allow it to. My advice is to listen to what he has to say, but take it at face value. Don't hesitate to talk to me or give me a call. I'd be glad to help you decipher the truth from the bull. Believe me, I've had lots of practice at it.

"My goal in therapy is to get him out of the world of lies and make-believe so he's able to see his life as it really is. Believe it or not, it's safer and less painful for Corey to remain living behind the walls he's built around himself – heck, he's had to in order to survive."

There was a sense of urgency in Larry's words, like he was trying to convince David of something. It was odd, and David couldn't quite put a finger on what or why. Perhaps, it was simply Larry's strong desire to use all his resources to help Corey.

David said, "I appreciate the heads up. Father Anthony also advised me to be cautious."

"I knew you'd understand." Larry turned to look at the large, round clock hanging high on the basement wall. For a split second, he had his back to David. That's when he noticed that Larry took a deep breath and his shoulders, previously tense, relaxed. He seemed relieved, as if he was concerned the conversation might have turned out differently.

"See you Saturday." With that, Larry was on his way.

Returning to the rectory, David went to the den to spend some more time with Corey. David wasn't too fired up about playing video games all day; after all, his first solo Mass was early the next morning and he wanted to get to a head start on his homily. He had to read the Gospel, reflect on the scripture, write down his message and practice his presentation. There was no way he could just let it fly like Father Anthony.

To his relief, he found Corey curled up on a sofa sitting outside the den. The boy's slow, deep breaths indicated that he was fast asleep. David decided not to wake him. Instead, he took the opportunity to begin preparing for Mass.

As David turned to go hunt down some paper and a pencil, he noticed two awkward bulges sticking out of the white athletic tube socks that Corey wore under his haggard Levis. David made the shapes out to be two video cartridges. After checking the number of cartridges lying around the machine, he confirmed that two were missing. David grew confused and angry. Corey knew he was welcome to the games any time he wanted; there was no need to steal them.

Disappointed, David thought, I guess they were right; he's not to be trusted. The young priest shrugged it off and chose to deal with the boy later, after he woke up.

David went into the den and sat down at a desk. The first drawer he opened held pens and pencils, and a couple of legal pads. He grabbed the *Ordo* from the shelf behind him and got down to business.

Excited, David thumbed through the *Ordo* until he found Monday's date. This scripture would be the heart of his Mass and homily. It was from Matthew 7:1-5 and read:

> "Do not judge, so that you may not be judged. For with the judgment you make you will be judged, and the measure you give will be the measure you get. Why do you see the speck in your neighbor's eye, but do not notice the log in your own eye? Or how can you say to your neighbor, 'Let me take that speck out of your eye,' while the log is in your own eye? You hypocrite, first take the log out of your own eye, and then you will see clearly to take the speck out of your neighbor's eye."

"Shit!" David said. "How can I possibly preach about not judging others after all that's happened over the last two days? Surely, the parishioners will think I'm being vindictive; that I'm using the word of God against them for my own purpose."

David slumped back into the chair. "This is no way to begin gaining the confidence of the people at St. Cecilia's."

The excitement of his first Mass and homily quickly faded. How am I going to swing this one? David thought frantically. He couldn't choose a different passage; the Church mandated that he use the scripture listed in the *Ordo* for that day.

"Father David," Corey said, as he stretched and yawned in the doorway. "I gotta split."

"Sure you don't want to hang out and play a game or two?" David was now anxious to take his mind off his new predicament and this would buy a few moments of delay.

"Nah, mom cooks a dinner on Sundays. It's the only time the butthead is out of the house. He goes to play poker and shoot pool. So mom and me eat dinner and watch a movie or something."

"That's great." David was genuinely pleased Corey was getting some semblance of a normal mother-son relationship, even if it was only once a week. "See you at school tomorrow. I'm teaching religion so you'll be in one of my classes." He was sure Corey cut classes, and David said this as a way to get the boy to school.

"Umm…yeah," Corey said. "See you in class."

He left the den and David returned to his dilemma.

Within a few seconds, Corey returned. "Hey Father, I almost left with these." He was holding the two video cartridges. David had forgotten all about them.

"I had to show these to Christopher. He didn't believe me when I told him you had 'em. Nobody's got 'em yet. Sucker owes me five bucks. I bet he never pays up though."

Corey set the two cartridges down next to the machine. "Catch you later."

David was stunned. He didn't say a thing as the boy left again. Slowly, however, feelings of joy and relief swept over David. He was now confident that he could stand and deliver a homily about not judging others.

CHAPTER 5

The loud static blasting from David's clock radio was a rude awakening. He had forgotten to tune the music alarm to a local station before he went to bed, so the dial was still set to his favorite St. Louis station. He preferred waking to music, rather than the piercing beeps of an alarm, but this was even worse.

He stayed in bed, too tired to get up and shut off the annoying noise. The glowing red-colored numerals read 5:33 a.m. At two o'clock in the morning, he had finally called it quits, putting down his homily and religion class preparations. Normally, three and a half hours of sleep would have made for one hell of a long day, but adrenaline began to flow as David's thoughts drifted toward Mass and his first day of teaching. Within minutes, he was wide-awake. He hopped out of bed, went over to the radio and passed over the country and western stations that dominated the FM dial before he found a fairly static-free, rock-and-roll oldies station.

"This'll have to do," he muttered.

After a quick shower, David skipped breakfast to allow himself extra time to set up for Mass and get acquainted with where everything was located in the sanctuary. Also, he wanted to slip in a practice at the lectern.

By six-fifteen, he was all set. That's when the nerves kicked in. Up to that point, he had been busy preparing and didn't have time to think of all the things that could go wrong, but probably would not. So, David did what always worked when he was nervous, scared or upset: He knelt down and prayed. Selfishly he prayed for the strength and courage to make it through the service without embarrassing himself by tripping or fainting or forgetting how to read. Mainly, though, he prayed for the Holy Spirit to guide and work through him by granting him the words and the enthusasm to motivate, invigorate and heal those that needed and depended on him.

The church bell tolled six times, signaling that Mass was to begin. On the last toll, David rose from his knees, made the sign of the cross, took a deep breath and walked out the door. Being so jacked-up, he feared that he would speed through the service at record pace. So he made a conscious effort to be unhurried. Continuing to breath deeply, David slowly made the walk from the sacristy door, past the tabernacle and over to the same majestic chair Father Anthony had occupied the day before. On the way, David snuck a peak at the crowd. It was small, maybe ten or twelve people. However, that was no comfort; it might as well have been a packed house. The only person he recognized was Larry, who sat alone in the first row of pews.

As tradition dictated, David made the sign of the cross then bowed his head. After finishing a short prayer, he panicked, thinking it was too quick. So he allowed a few moments to pass before he raised his head to start Mass. During this time his face remained serious and grim, as if he were discussing important matters with the Almighty Himself. In reality the only thought that passed through his mind was that he felt like vomiting.

David heard a women's forced cough and took it to mean, "Enough is enough, get on with it." He stood up and gracefully spread out his arms in a welcoming gesture and said, "Let us pray."

He went to read the first scripture. The small, snake-like lamp attached to the lectern wasn't turned on, and David had no idea where the on/off switch was located. It was still dark outside, but the two towering candles burning on each side of the lectern shed enough light to read by. So he stopped fumbling around trying to find the switch and made a mental note to ask Father Anthony where the stupid thing was located.

Reading wasn't a problem – David didn't forget how – but the microphone was. Like the lamp, he forgot to turn it on while practicing. He couldn't believe he had neglected to check how these two, now critical, components on the lectern worked. Shit! He thought, What an idiot.

Unlike Father Anthony, whose voice could reach every nook and cranny in the church without effort, David's voice didn't boom. He needed the amplified help of a microphone. Nonchalantly, he began to search for the button or switch that turned it on. The microphone's slim chrome neck was smooth; nothing protruded from it indicating a way to get the mike revved up. He glanced up at the crowd. They were beginning to rustle about at the delay. That's when he saw Larry subtly pointing his finger downward. David gave a slight head nod, reached under the top of the lectern and found a switch. He flipped it up; a short, piercing crackle resonated from the church's speakers. David gathered himself and began the first piece of scripture.

David was not an extemporaneous preacher like Father Anthony. Rather, his strength was as a compelling reader of scripture. He always read unhurriedly and carefully, helping others to comprehend the message of passages that many times could be as confusing as a physics equation. A homily, he believed, could only be inspiring if he was able to hold the congregation's attention during the readings.

After the first reading and the psalm came the Gospel. When practicing before Mass, David worked at finding the best way to read it. He wanted to convey this particular passage with thoughtfulness and reverence. He didn't want to sound righteous; that would make it appear personal.

After the reading, David raised the leather-covered Bible over his head and said, "The Gospel of the Lord."

"Praise to You Lord Jesus Christ," the early morning crowd responded in a tired mumble.

Out of nervous anticipation David cleared his throat. Unfortunately, it was too loud; scratchy feedback from the mike and speakers shot through the church.

After crumbling up several versions of his homily the night before, he finally came to his senses and heeded the advice of one his favorite teachers at the seminary: "When in doubt, keep it short and simple." This was an early Mass so quality was overshadowed by brevity; most people had places to go.

David began. "'People in glass houses shouldn't throw stones.' Who here has ever used this expression when defending themselves? Probably most of us at one time or another. I know I have. It's a common phrase in today's world that nicely sums up this morning's readings. When others judge or criticize us, we tend to say things like this to our accusers, especially when it's unjust or untrue. No one likes it when people jump to conclusions or condemn them for the things they do or say. But the fact is there's no escaping these things; they're part of human nature and ingrained in our society. It happens all the time: at home, at work, and with friends. Sometimes, people misinterpret our intentions by a wide margin; other times, they hit the mark dead on. Either way it can be painful.

"How do we deal with this? Today's Gospel reading tells us. First, and perhaps most important, the scripture says to not judge or condemn others, simply stay away from it. If you choose not to do this, then don't be surprised if it comes back to haunt you. How many of you know a person who is the first to judge or condemn others when they err? Aren't these very same people instantly attacked when they blunder? How about those who, instead, remain silent – or better yet – choose to help and encourage? When misfortune or hurt strikes them, aren't they the ones that receive help and comfort from others without asking? In today's words, the first part of the Gospel might read: 'What goes around comes around.'

"The second message of today's Gospel says that we should only look inside of ourselves and not at others. We are God's children and He doesn't expect us to be perfect. All of us have shortcomings and faults, and no one – not a single one of us – is immune. It's called being human. The Word of the Lord tells us to look inward and recognize our own weaknesses, while also accepting the flaws of our neighbors.

"The last part of the Gospel teaches us that once we look inward and accept our faults, then and only then, can we begin the mending process. Because we will always be imperfect in some way, working on our shortcomings will be a life-long task. This makes our world and lives challenging enough. Why then would we choose to concentrate any of our time or energy toward trying to fix the faults of others?" David paused for a moment to let those in attendance ponder the question. "When we have help and support, life's aches, pains and struggles are made easier to bear. All of us can experience the love that others bring into our lives, if we learn to accept people as they are, and lend support – a helping hand – when needed, despite our differences. When our focus is first and always on bettering ourselves, we're able to experience and share with others the peace, joy and harmony that life brings."

As David went to sit down, he thought, there, it's over. Short, simple, and to the point.

It wasn't a rousing homily, but he thought it accomplished what he wanted: To interpret the day's scripture in simple words that everyone could understand; an added bonus was that he didn't faint in front of everyone. David didn't feel like it was his best effort. However, he believed that as he got to know the people of St. Cecilia's better, and gained more confidence in his own abilities, he could take some risks. But not today; not this time.

The remainder of Mass went without a hitch. Although David suffered some trepidation when it came time for communion, to his relief, there was no hesitation from parishioners to receive Holy Communion from him. Led by Larry, they all lined up to receive the blessed host, the Body of Christ. Perhaps some came forward willingly because they were embarrassed by their behavior on Sunday, or maybe the absence of a large crowd with all its pressures allowed others to do what they thought was right. David wanted to believe it was their faith and belief in God that led them up the center aisle, but he knew it was more complicated than that.

At the end of Mass, he rose from the giant chair, walked to the middle of the sanctuary and said, "Mass has ended, go in peace to love and serve the Lord."

David left the sanctuary and walked down the steps to the center aisle so that he was even with the first row of pews. His hope was that people would feel more comfortable coming to him here. Many considered the sanctuary holy territory and off limits to anyone except a priest; David wanted to be on common and equal ground. His hands clasped behind his back, David put on his most amiable, welcoming face. However, the parishioners blasted out of the church like kids on the last day of school.

This didn't surprise him; early Masses were like that. He understood people had to get to work or hurry back home to get their kids ready for school or hustle to make a tee time. Still, he was disappointed that no one came to him. To David, that would be the ultimate sign of acceptance.

"Be patient," a familiar voice said. Larry rose from the kneeler, gathered his mini umbrella and tattered Bible and made his way to the aisle. David was so busy anxiously watching the last few people exit the church that he didn't notice Larry had remained behind. He was smiling broadly.

"You looked like an old pro up there." He gave David a light slap on the back.

"Thanks. But it could've been a lot better if—"

"Whoa, stop right there young man. Don't discount what you just accomplished. Frankly, with all the circumstances leading up to this Mass, I was impressed with your poise. You were wonderful. You appear natural and comfortable and that's how your Mass feels. I loved it."

"Okay, you're right," David said, as if this had just occurred to him, which it did. "I guess I did pretty darn good for my first time out."

"Now you're talkin'." Another slap on David's back, this one with more vigor. Larry looked at his watch. "I'm off. Got a conference call coming in around eight."

"Thanks for setting me straight. I would have beat myself up all day. Oh, and thanks for the help with the microphone."

"No problem. Try not to be too hard on yourself. Just let things unfold naturally." Larry gave the smiling priest a quick wink and began the long walk to the church door.

David joked, "Remember, I'm playing here all week, same time. Come on back."

"Wouldn't miss it. See you tomorrow."

As Larry walked out the door, David's heart swelled with pride, and he was overcome with thankfulness that such a kind person had entered his life.

After picking up and putting the sanctuary and sacristy in order, David made the short walk over to St. Cecilia's school. It was a giant, old brick building with three floors. The grade school and high school students were both housed here. Entering the front door, he immediately recognized the pebble-colored tile floor. The white-painted walls and ceilings were faded and peeling in many spots. All in all, it was the same building that David remembered, just older and a little more ragged – much like himself.

He had no problem finding the administrative offices. David wanted to introduce himself to the principal, Penny Heins. Her office door was halfway open so he knocked. A high-pitched, perky voice said, "Come on in. I'll be right with you."

He sat down in one of the heavy wooden chairs that faced her desk. The principal's back was to David. She was on the phone politely placating, what he guessed, was an upset parent. When Ms. Heins turned around and saw him, she broke out in a huge, surprised smile and gave him an excited, welcoming wave. It was contagious; he smiled and waved back. Right away, he liked her and knew they would get along fine.

There was a masculine look about her: She was small, no more than five-foot three or four, with a stocky build – not plump, but solid. Her burnt-orange hair was styled in a short boyish-looking bob. She looked young for a principal – under thirty, easily. Her eyes were large, like an insect, and blue-green in color. And they danced. They were filled with youthful enthusiasm and energy. In the tough world of teaching and working with kids, she was obviously a pup.

She hung up the phone. "You must be Father Cooper! Welcome." She stuck out a small, stubby hand. As they shook hands, she continued, "I'm Penny Heins, please call me Penny. I'm not used to people calling me Ms. Heins yet. This is my first year as principal here and the minute you go from a being a teacher to an administrator, you lose your first name. I'll bet the same thing happened to you once you were ordained. We're so excited to have you here. Father Anthony speaks highly of you. You'll just love the kids. Oh, I forgot, you grew up here. I'll bet the building hasn't changed much. It needs a face-lift badly but we don't have the money. I'm planning some kind of fund-raiser for this summer. If you have any ideas, let me know." She spit all this out so fast and with such vivacity that David had a tough time following it. He couldn't help but smile, and did his best not to laugh out loud. "Oh, listen to me, I'm running on again. Come on, I'll bet you're eager to see your classroom."

"That'd be great," he said, still reeling from the barrage of words.

Before they went to his classroom, she gave David a fast tour of the school. He enjoyed listening to her so much that he didn't have the heart to remind her he already knew every inch of the building. He was pretty sure she knew nothing about his past. If she did, she didn't show it – or didn't care.

As they walked through the hallways, Penny introduced him to all the teachers. After leaving each classroom, she provided him with a thorough synopsis of the teacher, ranging anywhere from hobbies to rumors of dating habits. She kept David engrossed, and he was amazed at the amount of scoop she already had on each teacher. Between Penny and Mr. Baumm, David now felt like he had a good grasp on the lives of most everyone in town.

When they finally arrived at his classroom, Penny scurried around straightening chairs, desks and books, all the while chattering away. "Boy, am I glad you're here. These first few weeks have been unbelievably hectic. On top of my responsibilities as principal, I've also had to take over many of Father Anthony's religion classes, even though I'm not certified to teach the subject. There wasn't anyone else qualified or available, so I had no choice but to assign myself. I thought it would just be an occasional substitution. Was I ever wrong! Almost everyday, Father Anthony has some kind of emergency. I never realized how busy priests are until now. I'm Catholic, but I must admit I've felt like a fish out of water trying to teach religion."

David was almost sure she had said all this without taking a breath. This time he couldn't contain himself and he let out a short laugh. "I'm sure you did fine, Penny."

She smiled warmly. "Let me show you where everything is located, and what I was working on with the older and younger students."

They spent about twenty minutes reviewing the curriculum. As they were winding things down, a voice exploded over the intercom that almost caused them to fall out of their chairs. "Ms. Heins to the office! Ms. Heins to the office!"

"I don't think I'll ever get used to that thing," Penny said, dramatically clutching her chest. "The volume's broken on that darn intercom system and it's stuck on the loudest setting. It's too expensive to get fixed. As a matter of fact, it's so old that it would cost about the same to get a whole new system than to repair it. Hopefully, we can get it into next year's budget.

"It also doesn't help that Mrs. Loeber, our school's secretary, is hard of hearing. Seventy-three years old and she refuses to wear her hearing aid. Poor dear doesn't realize she's yelling into the microphone. She keeps this place running. I don't know what I'd do without her. Fifty-one years here and still passionate about her job. Amazing.

"Well, I'd better get going before she rocks the building again. I've learned that I've got about three minutes to get to the office before she pages me again. Let me know if there is anything you need." And she was gone.

David stood still, gathering his bearings, like after a wild roller coaster ride. Penny had bombarded him with so much information in such a short time that his head was spinning trying to process it all. A buzz rang out over the intercom; it was time for the first class of the day to begin. David got himself and his teaching materials together as students began to fill the classroom.

LITTLE VOICES

At St. Cecilia's, every student was required to attend religion class. David was to teach six classes throughout the school day: three with the grade school kids and three with the high school kids. The curriculum Penny had taught was basic, mostly busy work to keep the students from getting bored. Last evening, he had mapped out what he intended to teach the rest of the semester, but that would have to wait until tomorrow.

When David was at the inner-city Catholic school in East St. Louis, he apprenticed under Mr. Terrence Jordan. David had learned many valuable lessons from this wise teacher. What he remembered foremost was the importance of developing and building a positive learning environment in the classroom. Mr. Jordan believed that, in order for the students to learn and the teachers to teach, the first thing to do was to inform the students exactly what behaviors would be accepted and what would not be accepted, and what the consequences were for both. He always began the first class at the start of each semester, or each day for the occasional rowdy class, pre-teaching the students these things.

He had said more than once to David, "Letting kids know, right up front, what they can and can't do in the classroom sets them up for success. They learn exactly what's expected of them and what the consequences are, both positive and negative. So, it becomes their decision whether or not to be a member of an enjoyable class or get their asses kicked around all day."

While in St. Louis, David had witnessed many hard-hearted and troubled inner-city youth, who were holy-terrors in other classes, transform into enthusiastic, productive students in Mr. Jordan's class. Kids viewed him as a fair and consistent teacher who never wavered from his philosophy.

So, David spent each class the same way: Pleasantly, but firmly, informing the students of his expectations and what the resulting consequences would likely be. Instead of a boring or threatening lecture, David made it into an interactive process. Together he and the students made up a list of class rules and, when appropriate, some possible consequences. This, according to Mr. Jordan, was the key because it empowered the students, making it much more likely that they would follow the classroom rules and accept the consequences. Also, David previewed the upcoming curriculum. By the end of the last class, he guessed this was going to be much easier than St. Louis, and that was just fine with him.

"One of the perks of the job, my boy!" Father Anthony said, drumming his hands on his stomach.

It was around 5:30 p.m., and David had just walked in from school. He had stayed late rearranging his classroom. He preferred that the desks were setup in a half-circle; this was more conducive to promoting discussions.

On the kitchen table sat a steaming lasagna; warm garlic bread smothered with melted butter; a salad of lettuce, tomatoes, cucumber and broccoli; and a pitcher of iced tea. It was all homemade and, according to Father Anthony, anonymously delivered. As usual, the food could have easily fed ten or more people, and it covered most of the kitchen table. The two hungry priests chose to eat in the den.

As he piled huge helpings onto his plate, Father Anthony said, "Someone was feeling mighty guilty about what happened yesterday. They all know the way to my heart is through my stomach, but it's not me they should be sucking up to. I'm sure whoever brought this over intended it as a peace offering to you."

"So that's what it takes to get a decent meal around here, huh?"

"I'm glad to see you haven't lost your sense of humor."

As he loaded his plate, David said, "Ancient history."

Father Anthony led David into the den and sat on the couch, while David hunkered down at the desk.

"How was your first day on the job?"

"I'll stick around for one more day," David cracked, in-between bites of garlic bread.

Father Anthony laughed, spattering bits of lettuce onto his beard. "Larry said you did an excellent job at Mass this morning; 'an old pro' were the words he used."

"Yeah, it went pretty good," David said with his best poker face. He was determined to show his mentor he could handle all that was being thrown at him, even if he wasn't sure yet. "I met Penny Heins today. Talk about energy. I can't even remember half of what she told me. Seems like a neat lady."

"A ball of fire, isn't she? I just hope she stays around for a while. I've been spoiled rotten. Charlie Feller was the principal when I got here. He was on the job for over thirty years, an outstanding principal right up to the end. After his wife passed last year, he retired and moved to Arizona to be closer to family."

"I remember him," David said, going back through his hazy memory. "All the kids thought he was a pretty good guy."

"He taught me quite a bit about working with and managing people. Charlie believed in hiring the best teachers and then getting the hell out of their way. 'Just let 'em do their jobs,' he would say. Good advice for anyone who manages people, methinks."

"It is," David said. "Seems like few pastors do it that way, though."

"You're right." Father Anthony stopped to gobble down a couple of large forkfuls of lasagna. "Too many pastors want total control over every aspect of the parish, even though they know nothing about half the crap that's going on. Their micromanaging just creates an atmosphere of distrust and causes people to distance themselves from the Church. Not a good way to build community spirit."

The rotary dial telephone rang, interrupting Father Anthony. David wasn't sure if he should let the phone ring or answer it.

Father Anthony said, "Why don't you see who's got a problem. We get very few calls from people telling us everything's going great and we're doing a bang-up job."

"Hello?" David braced himself for his first crisis.

"Hi ya, buddy. It's Erik." His voice was upbeat, but laced with a hint of weariness. It sounded like he was talking from the inside of a tin can. He's probably on a speakerphone, David thought. God, I hate those things.

"Well, hello stranger," David said, happy to finally hear from his friend but somewhat disappointed that his first crisis would have to wait. He mouthed "Erik" to Father Anthony, who wiped his forehead with the back of his hand in mock relief, then dug back into his meal.

"Sorry about the reception yesterday. I had a shit load of work that had to be finished by this morning. I won't bore you with all the details, except to say that it was for some clients who pour a ton of money into the firm."

"Don't worry about it. Thanks for your support at Mass. I really appreciate what you all did."

"Ahh, screw those guys," Erik said. "It's par for the course for those holier-than-thou blue hairs. The whole thing was so hypocritical it made me sick. Lizzy tells me it's only a few people who start that kind of crap, but they influence the others who don't have minds of their own. Hell, most of those people act like a bunch of sheep being led to slaughter. But, hey, with your charm and good looks, you'll have them eating out of your hands in no time."

"Yeah, right. I hear congratulations are in order – a partner, pretty impressive."

Erik said, "You bet. And I worked my ass off for a long time to get it. Youngest partner in the firm; hell of a nice raise too. Now, I'm busier than shit. I'm in charge of some pretty big clients, so it keeps me hoppin'. If I'm not in Omaha or Minneapolis or Kansas City or some other damn place, I'm at the office. It pays the bills, though, and that's what I gotta do. Heard you came out and saw the house. What'd you think? Pretty nice, huh?"

With effort, Father Anthony rose from the sofa and left the room, empty plate in hand. It didn't take him long to wolf down his meal and he was headed back to the kitchen for seconds.

"It's fantastic." David wanted to test the waters and see how tuned in Erik was to the problems at home. "How are Lizzy and Christopher handling your new job? You know, with all the travel and long hours?"

"They're real troopers." There was a pause. "It can be hard on all of us sometimes. I only want the best for them."

"Erik, I'd like to talk to you about something."

"Sure, what's up?"

"It's about Lizzy and Christopher—"

Erik interrupted, "Whoops, I've got another call, been waiting for this guy to call me back all friggin day."

David was getting ready to respond when he heard music. He was on hold. While waiting, he took the opportunity to think of the best way to broach this delicate subject. A couple of minutes went by before Erik returned. "Sorry buddy, but I've got to take this call. Listen, why don't we get together for lunch real soon. Call me. If I'm not around, schedule something with Norma, my secretary. It's great to have you back." With a click, the line went dead.

"Shit."

"Everything okay?" Father Anthony said as he came back into the room.

For a split second, David thought about not discussing the Patten's problems with Father Anthony and dealing with them on his own. However, David quickly realized that consultation with this talented and experienced priest might help.

"No. There's a problem." For the next ten minutes, David summarized his conversations with Lizzy, her concerns about Erik, and how it all was affecting Christopher. Father Anthony stopped eating and gave David his full attention. The old priest stroked his beard faster and faster as David got deeper and deeper into his account of the Patten's troubles.

Once finished, both men sat in silence, taking it all in. Sadness hung in the air, and Father Anthony seemed to lose his appetite as he pushed his plate away and tossed his napkin on top of the coffee table.

After a few moments, he broke the silence. "Damn. They're good people. But, you know, I'm not surprised. Now that I think about it, until yesterday, I can't remember the last time I saw Erik at Mass with his family. He's also nonexistent at school and community functions. Hmm…so that's what been going on. And now, you want to talk with Erik about all this, huh?"

"Yeah. But I don't know how much I can help. I mean, after briefly talking with him tonight, I'm convinced he's not interested in the problems at home. It's tricky. He's my best friend. How do I tell him that his goals and ambitions are ruining his marriage and screwing up his kid?"

Nodding his head, Father Anthony said, "I've been through this kind of dicey situation with friends before, and it's tough. What I've learned is that no matter how uncomfortable it is, you can't ignore the situation or shy away from it. Erik probably won't want to hear what you've got to say, and you're gonna run the risk of pissing him off. That's a normal reaction from someone who doesn't want to acknowledge that a problem exists."

"If Erik's ticked off and doesn't want anything to do with me, how can I help?"

"Good question." Father Anthony sat back, tugging at his beard. "In order to fix a problem, a person first has to admit that one exists. Sound familiar?"

Smiling, David said, "That's the first step in A.A."

Father Anthony smiled back and said, "I'm a believer you can't help people until they want to be helped. Hell, if you can't see that something's broken, what's to be fixed? In your situation, about the only thing you can do is get Erik thinking. At the very least, you can fertilize the seed that's already been planted by Lizzy."

David was slowly nodding his head in agreement. "You're right. The alternative of doing nothing is pretty darn bleak. But what should I say? And when's the best time to approach Erik?"

Father Anthony shrugged his shoulders. "There's no magic answer for that one. That's the art of what we do. Each person and every situation is unique. Trust yourself; you'll know when it's the right time, and what to say."

Over the next month and a half, David settled into a routine of leading early morning Masses. Father Anthony appeared to have no intention of splitting or sharing this duty with David anytime soon, or the classroom teaching. There were no requests from parishioners for David to perform other priestly services like baptisms, marriage ceremonies, counseling sessions, or retreats. Regular Church business — confessions, bible study classes, prayer groups — that he led was sparsely attended.

Acceptance wasn't coming as fast as David had hoped and prayed for. The parishioners who disliked him didn't show it as overtly as when he first arrived. Now it was subtler, like the whispers of racism. He tried his best to not let this get him down. In fact, he was chomping at the bit to lead a Mass other than the lightly-attended morning ones. He wanted to reach more people and to challenge himself.

David thought Father Anthony was proceeding too cautiously. After a discussion when David aired his concerns, Father Anthony suggested that David be the lead priest for the upcoming Founders Day Mass – always a popular and well-attended affair. Father Anthony had been allowing David to go at his own pace and was waiting for him to ask for more. The time had come, and Father Anthony was behind David one hundred percent.

There was one stipulation, however, to David leading the Founders Day Mass: Father Anthony would be listed as the lead priest in the Church bulletin.

The elderly priest explained, "I want the people to come out and see you in action. I don't want someone, like Agnes Greene, raising hell and calling for a boycott. When they experience your liturgy, they will begin to believe in you. What you need and deserve is a fair shot, and I think this is the best way we can get you one. Plus, the bulletin is always full of typos…at least that'll be my excuse."

"That's fine," David said. "I just want the chance to prove myself."

Much of David's newly acquired confidence came from his weekly therapy sessions with Larry. As agreed, they met around seven-thirty each Saturday morning at Larry's house and took the sessions to the bike paths and scarcely traveled country highways. Larry was, most of all, a great listener. But he also had the ability to ask probing questions and make insightful observations at just the right time, nudging David toward discussing and working through his personal battles.

After six weeks, they both had agreed that there was no need to continue with the sessions. For David, the toughest part had been letting Larry in on his lifetime secret. From that point on, David was primed to be able to move toward recovery, though he guessed it would be a lifetime of struggle and healing.

During the third week of therapy, David began to join Larry on his morning bicycle workouts. At first, it was just a couple of days a week but soon David was working out with Larry everyday. David enjoyed the rigorous exercise, but mostly welcomed his growing friendship with Larry. They were no longer therapist and patient, now they were friends and confidants. During this time with Larry, David was as peaceful, carefree, and happy as any time in his life.

One early November morning, the two were unable to go biking because of the year's first snowfall. It was a light, wet snow that immediately melted as it touched the unfrozen ground. When colder temperatures moved in and dominated the region, this same kind of snowfall would accumulate and become a nuisance. Today, it was simply a beautiful snow shower with huge snowflakes floating downward like feathers.

Before Mass, David checked the messages on the answering machine. One was from Larry. He said:

"Morning all. David, since snow is finally hitting the pavement, why don't we skip today's bike ride. It's time to move inside to workout, swimming laps. It's a great change of pace. I'm in tight with the principal and athletic director over at the public high school and have an open invitation, key included, to use their pool. If you're game for the change to water, join me tomorrow morning. Talk to you all later."

With a shrug, David said, "I guess I'd better get a suit."

Following Mass, David walked over to the school, reveling in the snowshower. He spent a few moments catching some flakes on his tongue. The first snowfall of the year was always fun and exciting; it was the unofficial kickoff to another winter season. David's enthusiasm, however, tended to dampen as he moved deeper into winter, especially during the months of January and

February. That's when the once novel tasks of shoveling the driveway and scraping the car windows became a downright pain in the ass. But, for now, the change of season was exhilarating.

Entering the school, David was in a festive mood, and it grew as he prepared for his first class. The morning group of students was always the most enjoyable. Everyone's gas tank was full, so it was easier for David to teach and the students to learn. As the day progressed, teaching became more challenging. Many days, it was a struggle just to get to the finish line. It didn't help that he had the younger kids in the afternoon who, by that time, were spent. He would have preferred the high school students at that time.

In the middle of his second class, David heard a child's angry shouts reverberate through the hallways.

"Get the fuck out of my face, bitch!" An enraged voice screamed.

He immediately recognized who it was – Corey. Over the last few weeks, David had begun to worry about the boy. He had heard from Penny that Corey was arguing and yelling at teachers and classmates with greater frequency. Each time, so far, he had regained self-control. That was the good news. The bad news was he was stretching everyone's patience to the limits.

Each day following school and on the weekends, Corey would stop by the rectory for a fill of video games with David. Lately, they had spent less time competing on the machine and more time talking about Corey's life, his problems and how he could deal with people and situations better. Even though Corey had disclosed quite a bit, David felt that there was an even stronger wall built behind the one that was beginning to crumble. The layers of hurt ran deep in this troubled little boy.

David wanted to seek advice from Larry. But, because Corey had specifically made David promise not to tell Larry the things they talked about, David kept his pledge and remained silent. He had always thought that this was an odd request, so one day he asked Corey about it.

"This is between me and you!" The boy had replied sharply. Then, he had said, "Since you're a priest, you can't say nothin' to anyone about what we talk about, right?"

Carefully, David said, "Well, technically that's only when I hear confessions."

Corey shot back, "Okay, when I tell you things, I'm giving you a confession." There was a hint of desperation in his voice. David knew it was best to appease the boy on this issue; otherwise, he would shut down for good.

"Don't worry. I promise not to tell anyone about the stuff we talk about, unless you're in some kind of danger. Okay?"

Corey took some time to think about this. "That's cool."

Currently, Corey was stomping down the hallway toward David's classroom, which was located by an exit with stairs leading to the back of the school. Corey's teacher was in tow and said, "Listen to me, young man. You know if you leave the building, it's an automatic in-school suspension. That would be your third this semester, and the rules say three strikes and you're suspended. Why don't you go to the office and take care of this."

David knew the teacher's threat would only make Corey angrier. David also knew Corey wasn't fond of this particular teacher. She was demanding, headstrong and inflexible; rules were not made to be broken in her classroom.

Right on cue, Corey spat out, "I don't give a rat's ass about your goddamn rules. I'm gettin' the fuck out of this place. Now get your fat ugly face away from me."

Corey was already on thin ice with Penny, and David didn't want to see the boy expelled. Being new to the job, Penny was willing to give Corey a fresh start, but only after David did some fast-talking about forgiveness and second chances. To be on the safe side, he even sprinkled in some good old-fashioned Catholic guilt. Lately, however, she was growing weary of Corey's increased incidents of verbal outbursts.

Up until the last few weeks, Corey had been making progress: He had gone the longest stretch of time staying in school without running away or getting expelled in the last two years. Also, there were no physical altercations with teachers or classmates that had typified his loss of self-control in the past. But, Larry and David were the only ones who were willing and able to see this as progress. Corey's teachers simply saw a student who continued to disrupt their classrooms and cause them unnecessary headaches.

David said to his class of high school seniors, "Why don't you all go ahead and work on any homework you have. I'll be back in a few moments." He knew full well nothing would get done once he left the room.

Entering the hallway, he saw Corey in a frenzied state, trying in vain to open the exit door that led down the stairs. When he realized the heavy metal door wouldn't open, he began lunging at it, violently slamming his right shoulder and upper arm against the thick, immovable barrier. Over and over, he recklessly threw his body against the door, each time more determined and with a little more force than the last.

The self-inflicted beating began to wear on the boy, and he slowed down. Corey was spent. He slumped to the floor, curled up in a ball by the door, and began heaving silent sobs.

David looked at Corey's teacher. After witnessing the boy's eruption, she had a look of sheer terror mixed with disgusted disbelief. "I can take it from here, if you'd like," David said, more a demand than a request.

She snapped out of her daze at David's offer for escape. "Are you sure? I…well…I've got a class full of grade school students and no one to monitor them. I didn't think it would lead to this. All I did was tell him he couldn't use the computer during his free time because he kept talking out, and he just exploded. I thought he was actually going to hit me. I can't work with him anymore."

She turned to go back to her class and stumbled a bit as she hurried away, like someone who came across a gruesome car accident and didn't want to get involved. Yet, out of morbid curiosity, she couldn't resist one more peek. As she looked back, Corey was still curled up in the corner; she picked up her pace and fled to the safety of her classroom.

Taking a deep breath, David walked over to Corey, who still hadn't moved. His first instinct was to bend down, pat Corey on the back and tell him everything was going to be fine. But David's training told him otherwise. Doing that would only reinforce the way Corey went about dealing with others when he was angry, frustrated or disappointed. No, the emphasis here was on teaching, with compassion liberally sprinkled in. Corey had to learn better ways to solve his problems with others – and quickly. The sand was running out of the hourglass for him at school.

David said in a calm voice, "Corey, I know you're really upset right now, and it's tough to work through these things when you're feeling bad. Why don't you try taking some deep breaths like you and Larry have practiced for times like these."

"Fuck that shit! And fuck Larry!" Corey rose and sat against the door, his arms wrapped tightly around his knees. Large trails of tears streamed down his cheeks, which were flushed red with anger and upset. His eyes were fixed on the floor.

David had never seen this side of Corey before. It was something he had only heard about. But David had dealt with worse, so he wasn't shocked or intimidated – not yet.

"Corey, you're yelling. Why don't you just remain quiet for a bit until you're feeling better." David walked over and sat against the wall about ten feet from Corey.

The boy continued to stare at the floor. David saw the opening and said, "Nice job of remaining quiet, Corey. You're starting to get yourself together." David paused to let this sink in, and continued, "I know this isn't easy, but the sooner you calm down, the quicker we can get this over with."

Corey remained quiet, but turned his back to David and started to kick the door.

"Kicking the door won't help anything, Corey. Just sit still and take a couple of deep breaths. That'll help you feel better."

The boy stopped kicking the door and wrapped himself up in a ball again.

"You're listening and following directions." David paused. "Just try taking some deep breaths."

After a couple minutes of silence, he saw Corey's back quickly rise and fall, still shaking from the tears. He was trying. After a couple more shaky breaths, Corey loosened the stranglehold he had on his knees, and the tenseness and rigidity that controlled his posture slackened a bit.

David said quietly, "Great job, Corey. You look like you're starting to feel better. Just let me know when you want to talk. Okay?"

Corey didn't look at David or say anything, but he did quickly nod his head in acknowledgment.

A few more moments later, the door to Corey's homeroom squeaked open and his teacher peaked around the corner. Corey looked up. "What the fuck are you lookin' at?" The teacher's head snapped back behind the door. With an evil grin, Corey chuckled to himself and mumbled, "Stupid bitch."

At that moment, David realized Corey knew exactly what he was doing. He had been using anger and aggression to get what he wanted. Corey had most of his classmates and teachers scared to death that he would snap at any time. But, in reality, he was in complete control, and David could tell Corey liked it that way.

All the things that Father Anthony and Larry had said about Corey began to ring true. Still, David couldn't help but feel pain and sadness over how this little boy got so messed up. Anger was the only way Corey had learned to express himself. The bottom line, though, was that people in this town were sick and tired of Corey's act; they no longer felt sorry for him.

David gave Corey a few more minutes to gather himself. "You look like you've got yourself together. That's tough for anybody to do when they're upset. You should be proud of yourself; I know I'm proud of you. Why don't you make a good decision and walk with me to the office so we can work through this."

"That bitch has been on my ass since they sent me to her class. You gotta get me out of there. I ain't goin' back."

David wasn't going to take the bait and get off the subject of Corey's behavior. This wasn't the first time a kid had tried to suck David in – only this time he knew what to do.

"You know, it sounds like you've got some concerns about your teacher. As soon as you work through this problem, I'm sure she, or Ms. Heins, would be happy to listen to what you've got to say."

"Man, you're just like everyone else around here. You don't give a shit about me."

This one got to David. Now it was his turn to take a deep breath and relax. He remembered Mr. Jordan's maxim: "It's a kid's job to mess up, and it's our job to keep our cool. Never, ever take what they say or do personally. Once you do that, they've got you."

Patiently, David said to Corey, "I do care what happens to you. Now, why don't we go to the office."

Corey upped the ante. He sprang to his feet and began to furiously pace back and forth, then said, "Are you fuckin' deaf? I said I'm not goin' to the goddamn office with you or anyone!"

"I understand you're frustrated. Why don't you relax, stop pacing and stand still. We can work this out."

The bell rang.

Oh shit, David thought. An audience is the last thing a child in Corey's state needs.

As the students poured out of their classrooms and flooded the hallway, the young boy screamed at David loud enough for everyone to hear above the jumbled, upbeat banter typical of classroom changeovers, "What'd you hit me for? A priest ain't supposed to hit people!" Corey grabbed his cheek and winced in mock pain.

Everyone came to a screeching halt. The silence was eerie as all eyes focused on David and Corey, trying to figure out what was going on.

David's first instinct was to vigorously proclaim his innocence and call Corey a liar. Confused, David thought, Why would Corey make up such a serious accusation? The eyes of the teachers and students were now concentrated on David and filled with doubt and suspicion. He became furious as he came to realize that there was nothing he could do to defend himself. He would only appear guilty if he tried to explain what had happened. The damage had already been done.

Like a cornered animal spotting an opening, Corey sprinted down the hall, darting between students, crying and shouting over and over, "He hit me! He hit me!" His voice trailed off as he left the building. Many of the faces in the crowd looked at David, not with uncertainty anymore, but with contempt. Corey had sold them with his act and they had bought it hook-line-and-sinker. David already had been tried and convicted.

Oddly, his one thought was how quiet the usually rambunctious hallway was. Penny appeared and broke the silence. "Okay, everyone, lets get to your next class." No one moved. They were still staring at David. Louder, Penny said while clapping her hands, "Let's go people! Back to class!"

Slowly, the students and teachers began to move and, within seconds, the hallway was abuzz again. Not with laughter or loud barbs between students, rather it was low-level whispering. This would be the hot topic of conversation for days.

David was fuming. Weeks ago, he had decided to concentrate on his strength, and something that brought him tremendous joy and satisfaction: working with young people. He felt that, over time, the parishioners would come around after seeing his commitment and ability to work well with their children. Now his plan was ruined. Over the last couple of weeks, he felt he was making progress. Many of the students were beginning to rib him good-naturedly, and the teachers were less guarded when he entered the teacher's lounge. He thought it was coming together – and now this.

As he stood disoriented and light-headed, a concerned voice said, "Father? What happened? I saw Corey running out of the building. Someone said you hit him?" It was Penny. She took one look at David's ashen face and said, "Why don't we go to my office?"

"We can use my room. I don't have class next period," David said, shaking his head in disbelief.

Penny and David each squeezed into one of the small student chair-desks; it was a snug fit for Penny. "Do you think Corey's safe? Should I call his mother...or the police?" Penny said.

"I'm not sure; I've never seen him like that. You probably should call his mother. As far as the police...I don't know."

Penny uncorked herself from the desk and went over to the intercom. "Mrs. Loeber, would you please call Corey Hansen's mother and tell her Corey has left the school grounds. If she's not around, call the police and tell them we have a student who is upset and may be at risk. Ask them to contact me when they find him. I'll be in Father David's room if you need anything."

She squeezed back into the chair-desk next to David. Penny was on full alert and, for a rookie principal, was remarkably calm. "Now, tell me what happened."

He carefully relayed the incident blow by blow, including his interpretation of the teachers' and students' reactions to Corey's false accusation.

Penny sighed and pursed her lips. "Well, this isn't the first time he's run away because he was mad. It sounds like you did a nice job, and I appreciate you stepping in to help out. Unfortunately, the school board has this archaic policy that requires me to do an investigation into any allegation by a student regarding any kind of teacher misconduct. So, I'll have to interview Corey. Were there any other witnesses besides his homeroom teacher that I should talk to?"

"No. It was just Corey and me. Everyone else was in class."

Penny sighed. "Until I talk to all parties, I better not make any further comments. I'm going to talk with his homeroom teacher, track down Corey, and get this straightened out ASAP."

She got up to leave the room, and David said, "Would you let me know when you find him, and that he's safe?"

"Sure."

For the remainder of the day, David was sleepwalking through his classes; he was distracted and confused. His name and reputation were now pond scum. But he also was concerned for Corey's well-being. Luckily, it was a test day for the younger students. So during the afternoon classes, David had plenty of time to replay the incident and ponder what he could have done differently. At the end of the school day, he concluded that there was nothing he could have done to prevent Corey's reaction.

David felt as if the teachers and kids were eying him with skepticism. Very few kids, and not one teacher, spoke with him. Everyone was business-like and serious. David was devastated. How could anyone think that he would, in any way, harm a child?

The incident was going to be like a festering wound that would take a long time to heal, if it ever did. There would be plenty of rumor and innuendo. And, like all rumors, everyone would hear some bastardized version of the incident, but when it was all said and done virtually no one would hear the real story.

"How you doing?"

Startled, David said, "Oh, hi Penny."

"I had a feeling you might still be here." It was about 4:30 p.m. and the building was empty except for the two of them.

"I wanted to get these tests graded and back to the kids by tomorrow."

Softly, Penny said, "Father, it's Saturday tomorrow."

For the first time since the incident, David smiled and laughed. "Oh well, I wasn't getting much done anyway." He tossed the paper he was grading onto his desk.

"I wanted to wrap everything up before the end of the day," Penny said. "You don't need this thing hanging over your head all weekend. I talked to Corey's homeroom teacher and she didn't really have much to say, other than you 'graciously offered to help out with Corey' – those were her exact words."

"Did you find Corey? Is he okay? Did you talk to him?" David leaned closer to Penny.

"He's fine." A perplexed look came over her face. "His mother wasn't at home and we were about to notify the police when Dr. Peck called the school – about an hour and a half ago. Apparently, Corey picked up his bike at home and rode all the way out to Dr. Peck's house. I know that he's working with Corey, but why would he go all the way out there?"

At first, David didn't think this was odd. But, after hearing the question from Penny, he didn't have a good answer. "I know they've developed a close relationship. Maybe since his mother wasn't home, Corey went to the safest place he could think of, Larry's house."

"Well, he's the first student I've ever come across who ran away from school to see his psychiatrist. I just found the whole thing strange. I mean, Dr. Peck was very guarded during our conversation. He wouldn't let me talk directly to Corey. Instead, he asked me what happened and said he would get Corey's side of the story. So I told him what I knew. About thirty minutes later, he called back and said Corey admitted to making the whole thing up. Dr. Peck also said Corey was trying to save face in front of his classmates. Apparently, the boy's very distraught over what he did.

"I said to the doctor that it would help to hear this personally from Corey; that it would look good in the records. Dr. Peck became very terse with me and said that, as Corey's therapist, he didn't want anyone asking Corey any more questions, that it was over and bringing it up again would only cause more problems for the boy. Since he's Corey's psychiatrist, I guess I've got to respect his request, if that's acceptable to you."

"That's fine. I'm sure Larry had good reasons for handling it that way. I'm just relieved Corey was able to tell the truth, and that he's safe."

Penny squirmed in her chair. "Father, school policy says I can't tell anyone but you, the student, and Corey's legal guardian about the outcome of the investigation.

Supposedly, it's in place to protect the student. Personally, I think it's a policy that's got to be overhauled. I mean, what about protecting the teachers? I've brought it up to the school board, but those dinosaurs are unwilling to admit any error and amend the damn policy. Oops. Sorry, Father."

"I've heard much worse, Penny," he said with a comforting smile.

"This was such a public incident that I don't care what the policy says. I want people to know the real story. So, I intend to—"

"Penny," David said. "I appreciate that you want to help, but I think it's best to let this thing fade away. It won't be good for Corey, and it probably won't change anything. Plus, I don't want to put you in an awkward position. I wouldn't imagine the school board would take too kindly to a policy violation, especially in your first year."

"I don't care what they think. In this case, it's wrong that people don't know the truth."

"Penny, save your first battle with them for another day. Let's just let it drop."

"Are you sure?"

"I'm sure."

Penny tried to rise from the desk; after struggling a few moments, she finally popped out of the tight fitting seat and desktop. She sighed and said, "I simply don't know what to do with that boy. Since he left the building, and due to the seriousness of his actions, he will be expelled for all of next week. Unfortunately, that won't do much to help him; probably won't even faze him. In fact, I wouldn't be surprised if that's exactly what he wants. Maybe it should be longer than a week. He's running out of lives, and I've got to do something to get his attention."

"Penny, give him another shot. He was doing so well. I really think he'll learn from this."

There was a short silence, the kind of tense silence that comes before a jury foreman announces the verdict of guilt or innocence. "Okay, one more chance. And that's it." Then, with a motherly-warmth she added, "Now get out of here. Go have a good weekend, you deserve it."

David remained behind for a while, struggling with how to deal with Corey. He would seek Father Anthony's and Larry's counsel, but David knew it would be a long time, if ever, before he could trust Corey again.

CHAPTER 6

Following a long walk that evening through the rolling hills of the neighborhoods surrounding St. Cecilia's campus, David prepared and ate dinner alone. Father Anthony was presiding over a marriage ceremony that involved a prominent parishioner's daughter and her high school sweetheart, a well-liked kid but from the other side of the tracks. Her parents were irate and objected to her choice in mates, while his were ecstatic and supportive.

Unbeknownst to those at the wedding, including the parents, the couple - currently college juniors – were marrying sooner than initially planned. Father Anthony was the only one besides the groom who knew the bride was pregnant. The two lovers came to him desperate, begging for help. Father Anthony agreed to discreetly accelerate the marriage preparations required by the Church, and to move up the wedding date so a honeymoon baby would be more palatable.

The previous evening, Father Anthony had shared the couple's predicament with David. Intrigued and confused by Father Anthony's actions, David said, "Why are you marrying a couple who you know had sex before marriage? Church doesn't look too kindly on that."

"You know, it would be a disaster if her parents found out. They would finally have the ammunition they've been looking for to call off the wedding, and an ugly finger-pointing feud would ensue between the two families. They – and I know her parents well enough to say this with complete confidence – would send their daughter on a long vacation. You know why?"

"An abortion?"

"You betcha. These two kids are happy and full of love for each other. What possible good could come from telling her parents? All it'd do is create a train wreck. I've spent a lot of time with this young couple and they know they messed up. Both wish like hell they could take it back, but they can't. There's no question in my mind they're committed to each other, and to the baby. Getting married was part of their future. They had set a date for next summer and were going to announce the news to their families over Christmas break. I may not agree with what they did, but should one mistake destroy their lives, and the life of an innocent baby?

"Sometimes, David, we have to play the role of King Solomon and weigh what the Church says against the circumstances. It's not a matter of right or wrong — there are always shades of gray in situations like these. But the way I've learned to handle something like this is to ask myself, 'Would Jesus have loved these two people less, labeled them sinners or made them outcasts?' The answer is clearly, 'No.'"

David thought about this conversation as he picked up a plate of tuna noodle casserole, peas and two homemade cinnamon sticky buns. He wasn't very hungry. Thoughts of the day's debacle with Corey rattled around in his head, driving out any desire to eat.

He was about to give up on dinner when a familiar screech of tires sounded from the rectory driveway. Father Anthony was back from the wedding reception, and David guessed the old priest was feeling no pain.

Stumbling through the back door, Father Anthony said with a slight slur, "Hi ya David! Whatcha eatin' there? I'm hungry as a bear. Great wedding. Went off without a hitch. Best wedding buffet I've ever set my eyes on. It was enormous. Everything from caviar to chips. But, as usual, I didn't get to eat anything. Someone always needs to talk for just a minute; next thing you know, all the food's gone and it's time to go."

Father Anthony's presence lifted David's spirits. He pushed the plate of food toward the other side of the kitchen table. "Here. I'm not really hungry. I just heated it up."

"Ahh," Father Anthony said, rubbing his hands together. "Mrs. Watson's tuna casserole, always a masterpiece. Are you sure you want to part with this marvelous creation?" He sat down, landing heavily on the kitchen chair, ready to pounce on the food.

"Bon appetite."

"Could you be so kind as to fetch me a Guinness? It goes wonderfully with this dish."

"I could use one myself," David muttered, as he rose and headed to the refrigerator.

He set the beer bottle down on the table next to Father Anthony who was studying David's face. "Just an old expression. I was kidding."

"I heard about what happened today. Penny said you handled things very well."

"I don't think anyone else thought so. People see what they want to see and, from the looks I saw on the teachers' and students' faces, they saw a priest who hit a child. Corey was very convincing. I'm sure it's all over town by now."

Father Anthony had already inhaled the small serving of food and was putting a heftier helping on the plate. "You're upset and reading way too much into this. Don't worry, I've been around here long enough to know that it'll all blow over before school starts on Monday."

"I hope you right. I'm just so damn disappointed. I've given Corey as much of myself as possible, and for him to do and say something like that just blows me away. I don't know what to think anymore."

"You're disappointed – and you're pissed. Right?" Father Anthony said, while setting the microwave timer.

"Yeah, I guess I am. You know, I was making headway. I felt like people were finally starting to warm up to me, and now this."

"What're you going to do about it?"

David stroked the now thick whiskers on his upper lip and chin. "Part of me wants to punish Corey by cutting off our relationship, but that's going overboard and wouldn't help anything. He suffers and I'd feel like crap for giving up on him. Hell, I don't know what to do."

Father Anthony carried his plate over to the table, sat down, took a long draw off his beer and set the bottle down hard. "Listen to me: You're human, not a damn saint. It's normal and perfectly okay for you to feel angry and frustrated, along with all the other ugly emotions that everyone else feels. Just because you're a priest doesn't exempt you from that. Hell, I'm angry with the kid for what he did to you. I also believe the boy deserves to be disciplined. Otherwise, we both know it'll just happen again and again. It's up to you determine what his consequence should be."

David continued to brush his goatee, while Father Anthony shoveled in a few heaping forkfuls of casserole.

With his mouth half-full of food, he continued, "I know this sounds cliché, but I truly believe that people learn more about you, and you learn more about yourself, when adversity hits. Believe it or not, you can turn this whole mess into a positive experience."

David squinted and said, "How do you figure?"

"You can show Corey and all the teachers and students and everyone else in the community that even though people screw up, they can be forgiven, if they ask for it and really mean it, and that life goes on. It's like the wedding tonight. This couple made a mistake but learned about forgiveness. They'll go on to live happy, full lives together. And I guarantee you that both will be more tolerant and willing to forgive had this not happened. You know, it's true: Actions speak louder than words, and this is a golden opportunity for you to show folks what you're really made of."

Laughing, as one does when a burden has finally been lifted, David said, "How'd you get to be so wise?"

Father Anthony held up the beer bottle and gazed into the dark brown glass. As he brought it to his lips, he said, "Practice, my boy, years of practice."

———

David's schedule was light on Saturday. Father Anthony had graciously volunteered to take the two morning Masses. He and Larry had planned on attending the Crusaders football game against the Southridge Skyhawks, St. Cecilia's longtime rival, and, because David was being left behind once again, he was sure that this gesture was Father Anthony's way of easing the guilt. The game was at night and both teams were undefeated and highly ranked. Whatever team won would continue its run toward the playoffs and a state championship. The town and parish were lathered into a frenzy.

Since the Crusaders were playing at Southridge, a three hour drive from Willa, the game was being televised on a local cable channel. The 5:30 p.m. kickoff meant that David's 5 p.m. Mass would be, at best, sparsely attended. That was fine. He planned on making the service short so everyone, including himself, could make it back home in time for the coin toss. With his popularity waning, a short Mass on game day was a sure-fire way to gain some brownie points.

At 5:10 p.m., David peered out the sacristy door for the third time, only to see empty pews again. Saturday evening Mass was usually well attended, but in Willa even God took a back seat to a Crusaders football game. David figured another five minutes and he would pack it in. It looked like he might make it over to the Pattens in time for kickoff.

Before leaving, David didn't even bother to take one last peek out into the church. No one could have possibly come in; it had been so quiet that he could hear the blood pulsating through his veins.

To David's delight, Erik and Christopher were going to Southridge for the game. Lizzy had invited David over to watch it with her, and he was looking forward to spending time alone with her. He was curious how things were going with Erik and Lizzy, but mostly David wanted to check up on Christopher.

Just before kickoff, he arrived at the Patten's house. David had stopped to grab a six-pack of O'Douls – the caffeine in Diet Coke practically gave him an anxiety attack during games like these. He had avoided Harmon Liquor and happily paid more for the non-alcoholic beer at the local Kum & Go.

The front door was open, and David could hear the TV announcer through the screen glass door. He was droning on and on about some far-out statistic about how the Crusaders were undefeated over the last ten years when the game was played at night under the lights, in front of a sellout crowd, on a Saturday, when Jupiter was aligned with Mars and all sorts of other goofy crap that, when all put together, made perfect sense to crazed Crusaders fans.

"Hello?" David shouted as he opened the door and walked into the house.

"In here."

David walked toward the living room and saw a shard of glass lying on the hallway floor. It was opaque and thick. As he got closer to the entrance, there were more fragments of glass strewn about.

When he walked into the room, David saw Lizzy on her knees, picking up broken glass by hand. She looked up at David; her eyes were puffy and streaked bloodshot.

"Lizzy, are you okay?" David kneeled down.

"I'm fine," she said, voice cracking. "Go watch the start of the game. I'll finish here and be right in." She hastily scooped up the remaining glass with both hands. A sharp point broke through the skin on her palm; blood began seeping from the wound. She flinched, but rose to her feet and walked toward the kitchen. Every two or three steps drops of blood fell and spattered on the floor.

"Lizzy," David said, following the trail of blood into the kitchen. "You cut your hand; it's bleeding."

She said nothing and tossed the glass into a trash can under the sink. Zombie-like, she picked up the broom and dustpan. Blood was streaming down her fingers and onto the broom handle.

"Lizzy," David commanded, "Stop. You're bleeding."

Dumbly, she lifted her hand and stared at the puncture. "Shit."

David gathered she wasn't talking about the wound. "Come over here," he said. Turning on the faucet, he gently took her hand and placed it under the cool stream; the pooled water quickly clouded red. Lizzy recoiled her hand at the sudden pain. Within seconds, she adjusted to the water's frigid temperature and relaxed her hand. The bleeding receded but didn't completely stop. He looked closer.

"It's not bad. There's a sliver of glass still in your hand. Do you have any tweezers?"

"Umm, yes...upstairs. I'll go and get them."

"No. Just keep your hand under the water and I'll get 'em. Where are they?"

"In the guest bathroom, top right hand drawer."

"How about some Band-Aids?"

Lizzy, starting to show signs of life, said, "Same drawer. David, I'll go get—"

He smiled. "I know where to go. I'll be right back."

David located the items and returned to Lizzy examining her hand. "Thanks," she said. "I can take it from here."

She used the tweezers to pluck out the small piece of glass, ran cold water over her hand, wiped it off with a clean dishtowel and covered the puncture wound with a Band-Aid. When done, she looked up at David and smiled.

He shrugged his shoulders. "It was all I could find."

"Well, Dino was always my favorite Flinstone's character."

"Lizzy, I don't want to pry, but what happened here?"

Sighing, she said, "It's a long story. Let's go to the living room and I'll fill you in. First, let me run up and check on Christopher."

"I thought he was with Erik at the game."

"Nope."

While Lizzy was upstairs, David grabbed a broom and dustpan and cleaned up the tiny pieces of glass that remained hidden on the floor. He saw that there was a broken lamp tipped over on top of a coffee table. The cord was severed toward the base of the lamp; only a small tail with splayed copper wire sticking out remained. He went back to the kitchen, emptied the dustpan, put it and the broom away and returned to the living room.

He lowered the volume on the TV and heard the score was tied seven to seven in the first quarter. Within minutes, David was engrossed in the game; it never took long. At the end of the first quarter, Lizzy still hadn't returned. Southridge was now ahead ten to seven and driving for another touchdown. Out of concern for Lizzy and Christopher, and also because he couldn't bear to watch Southridge score again, David tore himself from the tube and went to go check on them.

"Fumble!" the announcer bellowed. "The Crusaders recover on their two-yard line!"

David felt like yelping in delight, but caught himself – this wasn't the time or place. Instead, he walked upstairs in time to see Lizzy quietly closing Christopher's bedroom door.

"Is he okay?"

Lizzy nodded her head, and said in a whisper, "He's asleep."

Walking down the hallway, he said in a low, concerned voice, "Sleeping? Christopher never misses a game. And why isn't he there with Erik?"

When the two arrived back to the living room, Lizzy plopped down on the couch and stared at the TV screen. She seemed to be looking right through it. "He went with one of his fucking partners."

"What?"

She sat up and leaned toward David. "During breakfast this morning, Erik walks in and casually announces, like he's about to take out the garbage, that he's going to the game with one of his senior partners. Erik had promised Christopher they would go together; Christopher's been excited for days. After Erik saw the look on my face, he started going on and on about how this all happened unexpectedly and that his hands were tied. It was such bullshit."

"You should have seen Christopher. He was decked out from head to toe in Crusader red. He even finger-painted a red "C" on his cheek. And when Erik told Christopher they weren't going...oh, I could have strangled Erik right there. You know what Christopher did?"

"What?" David said softly.

A tear trickled down Lizzy's cheek and fell harmlessly onto her sweater. "He said, 'That's okay dad, maybe another time." As the last word left her mouth, the dam burst and she began weeping.

Instinctively, David moved closer and put an arm around her. She fell into his arms. He gently patted her on the back.

After a few minutes, her tears were spent. She leaned back and vacantly looked up at the ceiling. David grabbed a Kleenex box that set on the table next to the broken lamp.

Without a word, she took a couple of tissues and dabbed her eyes and nose. The two sat in silence. He knew that words would be no comfort. She needed to get her bearings. At the moment, the presence of a friend was all that was required.

"What's the score?" she said in a drained voice.
"It's half-time. I think it's ten to ten."
"David, I want to ask you a favor."
"Name it."
"It's Christopher. Right after he saw the first shot of the football stadium on TV, he knocked over the lamp and walked off to his room. It was eerie. He was so quiet and reserved during the whole thing. He didn't seem enraged; there was no yelling or screaming or crying. When I went to his room, he said that he didn't want to talk and that nothing was wrong.

"I don't know what to do. A mother's love is just not enough anymore. I think he needs counseling...or some kind of professional help. For the last couple of months he hasn't been the same outgoing kid he usually is. He spends most of his time in his room. It's been weeks since he's had a friend over to play. You know how much he loves basketball, and now he wants to quit the team. His school grades are dropping. Even his teachers have noticed a change. At conferences last week, his homeroom teacher said that he's having difficulty paying attention, that he doesn't participate in class and that he's seems to be isolating himself from the other students. He just picks at his favorite dinners. When I try to talk to him about what he's thinking or feeling he says he's too tired, and then sits in front of the TV or goes off to his room. I'm really worried...and frightened for him. David, Christopher loves you like a big brother, and I think a male influence might open him up. Would you consider counseling him?"

David said, "Erik still doesn't see the problem?"

"Fuck him, he's no damn help. I've done everything I can to open his eyes to what's happening with Christopher and to our marriage. He's blind, completely blind to it all. Remember I said we were going to visit with Father Anthony about all this stuff?" David nodded. "Right on cue, Erik backed out at the last minute. He called from work and said he couldn't get away and to reschedule. I told him if he really wanted to work things out he could be the one to schedule another appointment. Guess what? It's been weeks and I haven't heard a word about it. No, he can screw up his own life, but I will not stand for him wrecking Christopher's life anymore."

David heard the conviction in her voice. These were the words of a mother and wife who had experienced the last straw and was now out to save her child. At best, Erik and Lizzy's marriage was on tenuous ground and headed for a defining confrontation.

As David prepared to respond to Lizzy's request, doubt and insecurity raced into his consciousness. Can I really help Christopher? How do I approach Erik? Do I have the ability and experience to deal with this kind of crisis? What if I mess things up and Christopher gets worse? Consumed with apprehension and panic, David looked for a way out.

"Lizzy, you know I'd do anything for Christopher. I also love him like a brother, and you guys are family to me. I hate to see anyone suffer, especially those I love. But, I...I think I might be too close; too emotionally involved with Christopher, and with you and Erik, to be effective. More often than not, this is a recipe for disaster when counseling someone."

The TV announcer blared to life, "Blazek flips the ball to Nolting. He breaks a tackle at the forty, cuts to the left sideline. Oh, what a block by Pickett! Flattened two Southridge defenders! It's a foot race now! No one's going to catch him! Touchdown, Crusaders! Man, woman, and child, they're dancin' in the aisles now!"

David and Lizzy watched and heard the play, but there was no joy, no celebration. He saw that his comments devastated Lizzy. Her once hopeful eyes now stared toward the floor, sad and defeated. He felt like hell for copping out. As the TV camera panned out with a wide shot of the wild Crusaders' crowd raising the roof, David thought of Father Anthony and Larry.

That's it! David thought.

"Lizzy," he said, trying hard to contain his excitement. "I've got a better idea about how to best help Christopher."

"What? How?"

"Larry Peck." David grinned, as if he had just discovered the cure for cancer.

She took a deep breath; an unsettled look crossed her face. Right away, he knew the idea may have been genius, but it wasn't going to be easy. There would be strings attached.

"Lizzy," David said calmly. He didn't want to sound desperate. "Larry's the best there is. He's renowned for his ability to treat kids with all sorts of issues. And he's right in our backyard. I've spent lots of time with him since I've been back. I think he's a great guy, and he's one of the wisest, most compassionate persons I've ever met.

"Lizzy, you're one of my dearest friends, so I know I can trust you with something very personal. I've had therapy sessions with Larry. He helped me work through a problem that I've struggled with since I was a kid. It surfaced once I came back home and has caused me lots of grief. It was painful stuff, but Larry somehow made it easier to confront and overcome. I've experienced how good he is, and I have the utmost faith in his skills. He and Christopher would work great together."

David saw he was having a positive affect on whatever was holding Lizzy back, so he continued to pour it on. "Larry believes in setting goals and timelines for treatment. That way, a person isn't in therapy forever. It also means he's able to achieve results quickly. I'd bet it wouldn't take long for him to help turn Christopher around. Just think, you could have the old Christopher back in no time." David stopped. He was taking this too far, getting too carried away. After all, he had no idea if Larry had the time or was willing to take on Christopher as a patient, let alone help fix the boy in short order. But David was convinced that Larry was the man for the job, and he desperately wanted to sell Lizzy on this too.

"I don't know…Erik would throw a fit. You know, the stigma of his son being in therapy. I just thought it would be easier if you could talk to him."

"Easier for who?" David said kindly. This was a harsh question, but a fair and important one.

Disgusted, Lizzy said, "Easier for me, and Erik. You're right. If Larry's the best, then that's what my little boy deserves. I don't give a damn what anyone else might think. And Erik, well, I'll take care of him. This is one battle he'd better not fight. Do you really think Larry can help Christopher?"

She was sold, and before David could catch himself, he said, "I'd bet my life on it."

"How soon do you think he could see Christopher? Next week? Since you know Larry so well, would you talk to him for me?"

"I'll talk to him tonight or tomorrow after Mass."

"Thank you. Thank you. This has been like a bad dream the last couple of months. It's time to do something before things get worse, and to stop feeling sorry for Christopher – and for myself. David, you've given me some hope again."

"You won't regret this, I promise. I really think it's the best option for Christopher." David felt like a coward. He had found a way out, but had pushed way too hard. He took comfort in the belief that Larry was far more capable than he was at helping Christopher out of his tailspin.

Lizzy and David sat in silence, each alone with their thoughts, watching as the St. Cecilia's place kicker split the uprights with a twenty-four yard field goal. Their team was comfortably leading the Skyhawks as the game's final seconds ticked off the clock.

It was a tough victory and hard fought, but it was worth it, David thought. The game wasn't bad either.

David stayed a few more hours. He wanted to make sure Lizzy was doing okay. Also, he hoped Christopher would wake up and come downstairs. Talking to his godson would allow David to assess the damage, and to help him feel more confident about his decision to convince Lizzy that Larry was the answer.

David was confused about Christopher and the depth of his problems. Why didn't I see how bad things were? David thought. Looking back, there was nothing unusual about the boy's behavior during religion class. Although he was uncharacteristically quiet at times, he did get involved when prodded.

Unfortunately, there wasn't a peep from Christopher. Lizzy checked on him several times only to find him asleep. Erik hadn't come home from the game yet. Lizzy said, "I'm sure he's drunk at some bar with his partner. He won't dare come home; he'll sleep it off on the couch in his office. Tomorrow morning, he'll show up saying he had some important work that had to get done after the game. Work. It's his patent excuse for everything."

David left around midnight. Lizzy gave him a long hug and thanked him for his suggestion about help for Christopher. David promised to talk to Larry, and reassured her that everything was going to work out.

David took a longer route back to the rectory. He needed time to think. The Patten's situation looked grim, though he felt better knowing that the cavalry might be on its way. The one thing that worried him was Larry's busy schedule. David prayed that he hadn't jumped the gun and made promises he couldn't keep.

His thoughts shifted to Erik. What had happened to him over the years? David fondly recalled the many long, late night talks the two had while growing up. These conversations weren't dominated by superficial guy talk, like sports or getting laid, rather they centered on friendship, family, and how they were going to change the world. It was during these late nights that David had his first inkling he was destined for more than just a nine-to-five job. These were defining moments in his life, and he refused to accept that they had no effect on Erik.

David didn't recognize the man Lizzy spoke of. Erik had always been a fun-loving, caring person. David recalled how excited and happy Erik was when Lizzy accepted his marriage proposal, and the thrill in his voice when he phoned David at 4 a.m. to announce Christopher's birth, asking David to be the godfather. That person's still there somewhere, David thought. He's got to be.

David recalled an impactful lecture he attended while at the seminary. The instructor had said that the seduction of power, greed, and status was much like a lost soul who was brainwashed by a cult into becoming a member. After this evening, David felt safe that his earlier assumptions were correct: Erik had indeed fallen prey to the belief that money, prestige, and possessions were the measuring sticks of success and the keys to happiness.

This wasn't new to David. He'd seen the intoxicating effect and unyielding hold this belief had on people. Many floundered like drug addicts, eventually losing what really mattered in life: family and friends. But the pursuit of this drug was accepted, even encouraged by society, making the battle difficult.

He pulled into the driveway. Father Anthony was back from the game, and his Jeep was parked as usual: angled so that it took up two parking stalls. The rectory was lit up, which took David by surprise. Father Anthony was a zealot about conserving energy and money, so he was constantly roaming around turning off lights.

Entering the front door, David heard two voices coming from the den. He stood in the entryway trying to figure out who was with Father Anthony. It didn't take long to recognize who it was.

"Corey? What the hell is he doing here so late?" David said under his breath.

The unpleasant memories of the previous day's events came rushing back. Not ready to see or talk with Corey just yet, David thought about slinking off to his room unnoticed and letting Father Anthony send Corey home when he tired of the boy. But escaping wasn't the answer; he had already done that once tonight. Besides, David thought, I have to deal with him sooner or later.

Collecting his thoughts, David attempted to form a plan. He looked up at the picture of the Crucifixion and, just like the first day he had arrived, he looked into the mesmerizing eyes of Jesus. "Any ideas?" David sighed. "Lord, I'm angry and upset. I know it's not right to be vindictive, and I want to forgive this boy, but it's hard. Please give me the strength to forgive."

He made a quick sign of the cross and walked into the den.

"There you are," Father Anthony said. "And just in time. I can't seem to get the hang of this." Father Anthony held a video controller in his hand and was sitting on the floor next to Corey. David couldn't help but be amused by the scene and it took some of the edge off. Corey was so absorbed in a video game that he didn't hear Father Anthony greet David.

"Hello," David said, watching Corey play. It was then that David's plan was born.

With a yawn, Father Anthony said, "Well, I've about had it. Long day. I'm going to hit the sack."

Corey didn't react to what Father Anthony had said. The child was completely lost in the game. David couldn't tell if it was real or by design.

"Corey," Father Anthony said. Still, no acknowledgement "Corey!"

Without looking at the old priest, he said, "Yeah?"

"Father David is here, and I'm off to bed. Remember what we talked about, okay?"

Corey paused the game. "I'll remember."

Laboring up from the floor, Father Anthony winked at David and said on the way out, "I'll take the Masses tomorrow. Assist me at noon Mass and you're done for the day. Get some rest."

David looked over at Corey. The boy glanced down to the floor and back up to David several times; Corey was unable to sustain eye contact. David remained silent and let the tension and uneasiness build.

"Father David, I want to say that I'm sorry for what I did and said at school yesterday. It was stupid. I...I just didn't want all the other kids to see me like that."

His voice quivered with emotion. David recognized how hard this was for Corey and trusted the sincerity of his apology. All of this took David by surprise. The frosty layer of hostility he had developed toward Corey weakened a bit; however, David was still determined to use a firm hand in dealing with the boy.

"I appreciate and accept your apology, Corey. I do want you to know that I was hurt by what you did. You embarrassed me in front of a lot of people who now think I did something very wrong. I understand you were trying to save face, but you can't treat people like that. If you do, you're going to be a very lonely boy. No one wants to hang around someone they can't trust. Do you understand that?"

Hanging his head, Corey said, "Yes."

"Listen, I'm not really worried about what others think of me. There's not much I can do about that. I am concerned about what's happening with you. Do you know you're suspended from school?"

"No."

"Well, you are. Ms. Heins decided to suspend you for one week. She thought about kicking you out for good. I asked her to give you another chance and she agreed – reluctantly. Listen bud, you've used up all your chances at school."

Corey looked toward the television screen; the picture showed a video game character paused in mid-jump. Switching the game to life, Corey grumbled, "I don't need fuckin' school anyway."

"Excuse me?" David said with authority.

Corey whipped his head around and glowered at David. "I said I don't need school. It's bullshit! I haven't learned a fucking thing from those teachers. They don't like me, and I don't like them. I'll just learn for myself."

David was neither shocked nor upset by Corey's little tirade. He was getting used to just about anything coming out of the boy's mouth. "Turn the game off." David said quietly.

Corey continued to play.

David walked over to the TV and turned it off. "No more video games."

"What?" Corey said with a mixture of annoyance and disbelief.

"I've spent a lot of time with you since I've come back to Willa, and I've really enjoyed it – until recently. Yesterday, you showed me an awful lot of disrespect. And I will not accept or tolerate behavior like that. If you don't want my friendship and help, that's fine. If you do, that's also fine. But you gotta decide what you want. I hope you choose to continue our friendship because I like you and enjoy hanging out with you." There was a hint of fear in Corey's eyes.

"I've been thinking about what happened yesterday, Corey. You've apologized and I've accepted it. That's a good start. But, as you've probably heard before, it's your actions that count. It's important you prove to others, yourself, and to me that you mean what you say. And here's how you can do that: Every day next week, you come over to the rectory after I'm finished with school – four o'clock sharp. I'll pick up your homework from the classes you're going to miss, and you will sit here and do that work until it's finished. No Nintendo, no games until you're back in school."

Corey looked dumbfounded. "You're jokin', right?"

"No, I'm not. And there's one more thing: When you're done with the schoolwork, we will continue your First Confession preparations. The sacrament is set for Sunday. The work you'd be doing in class next week is important, and you need to finish it in order to participate. This is a big event in your life and I don't want you to miss it."

David paused to let it all sink in. "That's the deal. The ball is in your court now. If you agree and follow through with what I've laid out, then you're welcome to come over to play video games with me, or Father Anthony, anytime after next week. If you don't agree or follow through with this, then I don't want you to come over to the rectory anymore. It's your decision."

Corey's shoulders slumped. He knew David wasn't bluffing. After a short silence, Corey mumbled, "This isn't fair."

"Life isn't always fair. And you haven't been fair with me or others." David continued with more conviction. "Corey, it's time for you to stop blaming everyone else. Everything that happened yesterday was the result of your actions, not mine or anyone else's. You may think this is all bullshit, but if you look again you'll see I'm extending my hand in friendship. I'm not going to tell you what to do or try to talk you into anything. It's all up to you. But I do want to say that this is a chance for you to shine. How? By taking responsibility for your actions and accepting the consequences. That's all anyone can ask of someone who messes up. This is a great opportunity for you to show everyone that you want to repair the damage you've done."

Corey looked at the blank TV screen. He began to fidget as he wrestled with what to do. David guessed that very few people had called Corey to the carpet when he misbehaved, and the choice was uncharted waters.

Corey stayed still. The rhythmic "tick-tock, tick-tock" emanating from the old grandfather clock grew louder and amplified the silence with each passing second. David knew the boy had to make a tough choice: retreat to the world that was familiar and comfortable or choose a new path filled with uncertainty. Corey had to make this decision himself; otherwise, what David had proposed would never work. The silence continued.

"How about if—"

"There will be no ifs, ands or buts. It's all spelled out for you."

This didn't seem to bother the boy. David had expected Corey to try and change the rules, but he seemed to understand David wasn't going to budge.

"How long do I have to sit here and do homework?"

"Until it's finished."

"Man, that could be hours!"

"Yes, it could."

"Will you be here to help me?"

There it was. The choice had been made. David was pleased. "I'll be around as much as I can. I have meetings and other responsibilities almost everyday after school, and at night. You will have to do most of the work on your own. Each night, we'll check over your homework and I'll bring it to your teachers the next day."

After a short pause, Corey said, "Whatever, I'll be here." He got up, snatched his windbreaker off the floor, and left.

David was about to offer Corey a ride home; after all, it was after midnight and the temperature was close to freezing. But David let the boy go. He wanted Corey to leave knowing that he meant business. Besides, the cold walk home might do him some good.

Sitting back on the thinly cushioned couch, David wondered if his plan would work. His head told him he had done the right thing, but his heart was heavy. Corey needed a person who not only had kind words to help heal the hurt, but someone who also had the guts and stamina to discipline and teach, to define boundaries.

"Shit," David said, looking at the alarm clock. It read 6:21 a.m. He shot up out of bed to a sitting position, panicked that he would be late. The hazy fog of slumber began to lift, and he remembered that Father Anthony was covering Masses today. This was one of the few mornings David had the opportunity to sleep late. His body was programmed for rising early and he found it impossible to get back to sleep. So, he did his Liturgy of the Hours and decided a workout was in order. After a quick bowl of instant apple and cinnamon oatmeal, he hopped into his car for the short drive to the high school pool.

It was a crisp mid-November morning. The sky was clear and the sun was shining brightly. A light layer of freshly fallen snow covered the landscape. The ground was now frozen, so the snow no longer melted on contact. As the Honda slipped over the snow-covered streets, he figured it was time to replace the worn tires.

David slid to a stop in the school's back parking lot, which was where the entrance to the pool was located. He barely missed smashing into the side of the only car parked in the tiny lot. It was Larry's Landrover.

David got out the duplicate key that Larry had made, with the principal's blessing, and opened the door. He checked the pool. Larry was already swimming laps. David changed at his usual locker into baggy, multi-colored Nike swim trunks, faded from the chlorine. Larry preferred a skimpy Speedo suit. David couldn't bring himself to wear one. It wasn't about vanity or self-consciousness; he simply figured he wasn't about to break any world records so why dress like an Olympic swimmer. Plus, he had a certain image to uphold and a butt-thonged swimsuit wasn't exactly priest-like. Larry frequently gave David grief about his "Grateful Dead" look, but it was all fun banter between workout partners.

Larry stopped swimming when he saw David stretching. "What? Leaving the flock behind to fend for themselves?"

Smiling, David said, "Father Anthony's taking care of business. He gave me the day off."

"Rough one on Friday, huh?"

"Yeah, that's probably why Father Anthony took all the Masses today. After all, who's gonna support a Church that houses a child-beating priest? And, lest we forget: small turnouts at Mass lead to small tithing."

"Come on, David, don't even joke about that. Once people have the weekend to think about it, they'll dismiss the whole thing as just another one of Corey's performances. I guarantee you things will die down quickly."

"Really think so?"

"You bet. Once they hear Corey is suspended, they'll know what's going on. Don't give it a second thought.

Around here, this kind of stuff sparks interest for a day or two, then dies as soon as the next rumor starts up."

"Then let's get another one going," David quipped, trying to hide his surprise that Larry knew about Corey's suspension. The boy didn't even know about it until late last night. David dismissed the thought, realizing the doctor could have learned it from a number of different sources. The man was plugged into the community, and he probably could find out just about anything he wanted with one phone call – most likely, to his good friend, Father Anthony.

"Things will be fine," Larry consoled. "Have you talked with Corey yet?"

"Yeah, last night."

"He was extremely upset over what happened; as distraught as I've ever seen him. You've really had an impact on him. What did you two talk about?" Larry's odd tone made his words sound almost like an accusation, like David had done something behind Larry's back. Maybe it's got something to do with Corey's therapy, David thought. After all, the two have been working together for a long time, and it's only natural Larry would be curious.

To avoid breaking the privacy pact he had made with Corey, David said, "I think we came to an understanding and straightened things out. Hey, I've got a big favor to ask you."

Larry scowled. David was unable to tell if Larry was irritated because the conversation about Corey was cut off, or because David was about to request a favor. The look on Larry's face caught David off guard; he had never been on the other end of a harsh look from the man. This small, almost insignificant act would have gone unnoticed if it were from Father Anthony or anyone else. But it was magnified with Larry because it was novel. David thought, Hell, the guy's actually human.

"What's the favor?" Larry said. He spat into his swimming goggles and wiped away the condensation that had built up during his workout in the humid indoor pool.

"It's involves Christopher Patten. I'm really worried about him, and so is his mother."

Larry seemed to snap out his funk almost instantly. "What's up?"

"In a nut shell, Christopher's a very unhappy child. I'm worried he might be experiencing depression. He's lost all interest in the things he usually likes doing, his school grades are dropping fast, he doesn't talk much to anyone – friends or family – and he's isolating himself in his room or plopping down in front of the TV for hours. Lizzy is at her wits end and has finally come to the realization that Christopher needs help beyond what she can provide. She's never seen Christopher like this, and I've never seen her so troubled."

Larry's game face was on now. The dark side he had briefly flashed vanished like a shadow. "Do you or Lizzy have an idea of what might be causing this?"

"Her marriage is in on shaky ground. Basically, Erik has been nonexistent at home for a long time now. He's extremely wrapped up in his work. Erik's always been driven, and he's currently one of the rising stars at the law firm."

Larry shook his head. "Let me guess: Christopher's been regulated to a second-class citizen, along with Lizzy."

"That's her take on the situation and I think she's right. Lizzy's not a complainer or one to burden others with her problems. The fact that she's reaching out to me for help tells me that she's desperate.

"Also, I'm seeing the same things from Erik. I've been back home, for what, about three months now and I've spoken to him a grand total of one time. And he cut that conversation short because of a business call. I've only seen him in the flesh once: briefly at my first Mass. Even that

Sunday, he went to work; didn't even attempt to make a short appearance at the reception.

"Larry, I know I should have talked to you about this first, but if you could have seen how distraught and worried Lizzy was last night…well…I didn't know what else to do, until I thought of you. I'll get right to the point. I know you're a very busy man with a full schedule, but I promised Lizzy I would ask if you would be willing to take on Christopher as a patient. I'm not trying to blow smoke up your ass, but you're the best I've ever met at what you do, and it just kills me to see Christopher suffering like this and—"

"Of course, I'd be happy to see Christopher. Tell Lizzy to call me at home. We can set up an appointment for early next week if she likes."

A wave of relief swept over David. "Thanks. This means the world to me."

Larry didn't appear to hear this. His lips were pursed as he looked out over the calm water. He turned and said, "I'll tell you right now that there is only so much I'll be able to do for Christopher without Erik and Lizzy's support and cooperation. The real key here, from what you've told me, is Erik. If Christopher's going to get better, it'll take a team effort. That means I will need to work with Christopher one-on-one and with his parents – together. It sounds like there won't be any problem with Lizzy, but what about Erik?"

David hesitated for a moment. He thought about telling Larry about the depth of Erik's denial regarding Christopher's problems. However, David feared that if Larry knew the whole story he would back out, and the whole thing would blow up. So, David said, "I will personally make sure Erik's on board."

Larry eyed David skeptically. "Okay, but be careful." Larry put on his goggles and pushed off the side of the pool to finish his workout.

David returned from the pool invigorated, physically and mentally. He immediately phoned Lizzy and told her the good news, along with Larry's conditions about parental involvement. Her voice was overflowing with excitement and relief. She told David the more she thought about his suggestion the better she felt about it. Lizzy also assured him not to worry; Erik would be available and involved. She was going to discuss the matter with him right away, even if she had to go drag him out of the office.

Apparently, she was right. Erik had spent the night at his office, calling early to say he had worked late into the night. After hearing the certainty in her voice, David was confident Erik, like it or not, would be committed.

With that taken care of, David planned to relax the rest of the day. He assisted Father Anthony with noon Mass. Following the service, the elder priest left to make the two-hour drive to Falls City. He was going to spend the day with his sister and also attend his niece's volleyball game. According to Father Anthony, his sister was a surprise; she was born almost twenty years after him. She also was a single mother of a sixteen-year-old all-state volleyball player. Father Anthony had told David that his sister had planned to be a single parent; to her, men were a nuisance. At first, he didn't approve of her decision, but over the years he had accepted it and supported the two any way he could.

Since David had the rectory to himself and nothing to do, he decided to lounge in front of the TV. He was an avid Kansas City Chief's fan. He had attended many of their home games when he was at the seminary. This year, he hadn't seen them play one game on TV, and he was anxious to watch the Chiefs play their archrival, the Oakland Raiders. It was always a war.

Around 4 p.m. the back door bell rang. Annoyed by the disruption, David let the bell ring again and hoped whoever it was would go away. At the third ring, he snapped out of his football stupor and realized he'd better get the door. It could be someone in need or, better yet, someone with food. David was getting hungry.

"Corey? We're supposed to start Monday after school."

"But you said we were gonna do First Confession stuff. So I thought I better come over today."

David's irritation receded as he realized that the boy was trying to make amends and do the right thing. "Come on in. Let's get you started."

For a moment, he thought about blowing off the lessons and letting Corey watch the game. But the rest of the week would be a disaster if David sent this kind of message from the get-go. So he hustled over to the school and got Corey's religion book, along with some worksheets. David decided to have Corey work silently at the kitchen table. Today, he didn't intend on working with Corey individually; that kind of attention would be extremely reinforcing to the boy. He needed to work alone for a while. Plus, David wanted to catch the end of the game.

Once Corey was all set with his work, David spent his time walking back and forth between watching the game in the den and monitoring Corey in the kitchen. As usual, the game was a barnburner with the lead flip-flopping between teams. Corey studied silently and had very few questions. It was eerie having him so cooperative.

Toward the end the game, the front doorbell rang several times in quick succession. Exasperated, David tore himself away from the television. "Now what?"

It was Erik.

David said, "Hey! How ya doin' stranger?" Even though he was confused and bothered by Erik's actions with his family, he was still David's best friend and he was glad to finally see Erik face to face.

Erik looked hard at David. "I need to talk to you."

"Sure. Come on in. I was just watching the Chiefs - Raiders game. Let's go into the den and watch the end. We can talk in there."

"No," Erik responded firmly. "I don't have time. This won't take long."

It was the first time in nearly two years David had seen Erik up close for more than a few seconds. The man's once lean frame was carrying extra weight. His shirted belly hung over the belt of his dark-gray suit pants, and his face was round and puffy. David could see Erik's scalp through his receding hairline and thinning blond locks. This was the most startling change to the man, because Erik's defining physical characteristic had always been a thick mane of blond hair. Now it was withering away, like colorful leaves when nasty winter weather creeps in. Erik's brown eyes caught David off-guard. He remembered them as lively and upbeat, now they were replaced by the bitter and dull eyes of a man that David didn't recognize.

Erik stepped inside. David closed the door behind him. "Can I get you something to—"

"I don't need a goddamn thing from you. You've already done enough. What gives you the fucking right to get so involved with my family?" Erik's voice trembled.

This was it: The confrontation David hoped would never happen had materialized. It was inevitable, and he had already decided what course to take.

Erik's voice grew louder. "Lizzy just told me what you two decided to do with my son. Why the hell are you planting those kinds of stupid ideas in her head? Christopher doesn't need a goddamn shrink. He's a little kid…and he's fine."

"Erik, I think you're wrong," David didn't back down from Erik's aggressive posturing. "Christopher's not well right now and he needs some help, professional help. Listen, I didn't try to butt in here. Lizzy came to me with some concerns and in search of advice. She asked me to talk with Christopher, but based on what she told me and from what I've seen, I really felt like he needed a different kind of help than what I could offer. That's why I suggested Dr. Peck. Erik, Larry's the best there is, and he's excellent with kids."

"Not with my kid! He doesn't need any help. You and Lizzy are making a big deal about nothing. After this next year, things will settle down at work and I'll be able to spend more time with Christopher. Until then, I want you to call off all this shit and tell Lizzy that you shouldn't have gotten involved."

"I can't do that, " David responded evenly. "It's obvious that Christopher's hurting. I've seen it when I've been over at your house, and his teachers are saying the same thing. I simply want to help him."

"And I don't?" Erik roared.

"Of course you do. That's not what I'm saying. I'm sure you want only the best for your child, but I don't think you realize the magnitude of what's going on." David decided to throw caution to the wind and continued more forcefully, "Your job is important to you, I understand that, but it's hurting your family. Both Lizzy and Christopher feel like they're not important to you, and that work is your first and only priority. And that hurts them deeply. I think a lot of what Christopher is going through is tied to that. He just wants his dad around."

Erik took a step closer to David, pointed a finger toward his chest and said, "How the hell do you know how anyone feels? You're just a goddamn drunk who couldn't make it in the real world. Now your hiding behind a God you flipped the finger at all your life. And suddenly you think you're the expert on people and what they feel and what they need. Well, I think you're full of shit.

"I want you to listen to me, Father," Erik said, his shouts echoing off the stone walls. "Stay away from my family. I don't want you to contact Lizzy again – and keep clear of Christopher. If you want to play Clara Barton, stick with that crazy little fuck, Corey Hansen. You can't do any more harm to him. I refuse to let my kid be your or Dr. Peck's fucking experiment."

Just then, Corey stepped around the corner into the dim light of the hallway. Stoically, he stared at Erik. Corey's penetrating gaze made Erik look away toward David and back again to Corey, like a rodent unable to decide what hole to hide in.

Erik was way out of line, and David was livid. He could deal with the disparaging remarks that were thrown his way, but attacking an innocent child who had no connection to what was taking place at the moment was another matter. Through gritted teeth he said, "Erik, I think you'd better go."

Erik turned to leave, then wheeled back to face David. "I mean it. Stay away. I can handle my own family. We do not need your help." He opened the front door and slammed it behind him.

Immediately, David turned his attention to Corey who was staring at the closed door. "He was upset. It was wrong of him to say those things...he didn't mean them."

Corey paused, looked at David thoughtfully and said, "Fuck him. At least I know I've got problems. I came to tell you that I'm done with my work. I'll be leaving now."

David didn't know what to say as he watched Corey shuffle to the front door and walk out. At that moment, David was reminded of a former world champion boxer he saw fight in St. Louis years ago. The boxer was well past his prime. A younger, more skilled opponent savagely beat him in the fight. The old boxer tried to proudly leave the ring as if he were unhurt. But the damage done on the inside was as obvious as the cuts and bruises on the outside. And it had made David sad, just like now.

CHAPTER 7

At least one thing was back to normal on Monday morning: 6:30 Mass. David took comfort in arriving at the Church early, spending some time each day in prayer and reflection. As such, the early time slot had grown on him. He felt like it was his Mass, and that he was responsible for making each service more than just an early morning duty of the devout. That meant putting in time, energy, and enthusiasm. It appeared to be paying off, as the attendance had risen from a mere smattering of people to more than two-dozen regulars.

Over the months, David had grown more comfortable and confident as a celebrant. He had moved past the self-consciousness stage, and his natural abilities as an inspiring preacher were beginning to shine through. He liked to think that the growth of early morning churchgoers was directly tied to this.

Following every Mass, David patiently waited at the church door, thanking those who came. He was always gracious and friendly, even to those who didn't look at him or hurried by. Over time, however, more parishioners were approaching David to offer their appreciation for a job well done. Their kind words were encouraging and rewarding; it made the effort he put into each morning worth it.

David began to understand that there was actually a method to Father Anthony's madness. The man wasn't too lazy or hungover in the morning to lead services. Hell, he could do it in his sleep. Father Anthony's intention was to have David take baby steps, to experience many small successes that would help build his confidence. And it was working. He wouldn't give up early morning Mass for anything.

This morning, however, David wouldn't have been surprised if the church was empty, given the rumors he was certain were already circulating. But it wasn't; the regulars were there, sitting in their usual seats, seeking solace on their own private islands. Following Mass, there was no noticeable indication from the early morning crowd that word had spread about Friday's incident. But David knew better. This was a small town where gossip spread like cancer, slowly killing some while sparing others.

These folks believed in David because they had witnessed his effort, devotion, and passion almost everyday. They were allies now and would give him the benefit of the doubt. It was the people on the bubble, those who didn't know him well, that were more likely to shoot first and ask questions later.

As the final few people were leaving, David sat down in the last row of pews. He wanted to put off going to school for just a bit and take a few minutes to soak up the kind of solitude found only in an empty church. He watched as the sun's rays began to peek through the stained glass windows. This atmosphere helped to charge his battery. He needed a boost before facing the firing squad of doubting teachers and students.

"Father David," a frail, old voice said from behind.

"Yes?" Startled, he turned around and was surprised to see Mrs. Loeber. He didn't recognize the school secretary's voice because it was usually amplified to a rock concert's decibel level as it blared over the school's speaker system. The busted intercom made her presence seem larger. David smiled as he thought of the scene in the *Wizard of Oz* when the curtain was pulled back revealing that the great and powerful Oz was just a mere mortal.

Mrs. Loeber was an early morning regular who left right away. David assumed it was so she could get over to school on time.

"I just wanted you to know that I enjoy your Masses, especially your homilies. They're real; not just a bunch of flowery Bible talk." She shuffled over to where David sat, as if the floor was full of land mines, and sat down in the pew right in front of him.

"It's nice to hear that."

"Father, I don't want to be nosy, but I have to tell you that I don't trust that boy, and I don't think you should either."

"Corey?"

"He's trouble, rotten to the core. I've seen many kids come through St. Cecilia's, both good and bad. Most of them good, I'm happy to say. But, that boy…he'll smile at you one minute and steal the clothes right off your back the next. Just like he did Friday. I know what went on in the hallway; I didn't have to see it. You know, it's not the first time something like that has happened with him. That boy has burned a lot of bridges, and the teachers and kids want nothing to do with him. You're going to do what you think is right, and I respect that. Just be careful."

"Thanks for your concern," David said. "I'm learning more and more about Corey every day, but I'm gonna stick with him for a while longer. There's some goodness there, it's just harder to find than it is with most kids. Maybe I'm being naive, but I couldn't live with myself if I didn't try."

She gave David a warm smile. "I thought you'd say something like that. You're a good boy; I can tell that by your homilies." She got up, patted his arm and said, "I better get to school."

"Bye."

He watched as she left, her aged body slightly bent over, valiantly fighting the laws of gravity. She was a wise woman with decades of experience, and he knew her warning held merit. He liked her and was uplifted by the short conversation.

Walking up to school, he chuckled at his runaway imagination that included, among others scenes, a mob of angry parents picketing and chanting his demise as he struggled to enter the front door. The extra time thinking and praying in church had calmed his anxieties. Like anyone else, he would have supporters and detractors.

As David was preparing for his first class, Penny poked her head into the classroom, and said, "How are you?" She sounded like she was visiting a terminally ill patient in the hospital.

"Fantastic," David said. A curious look came over Penny's face as she walked into the room. "Friday's in the past, Penny. I spoke with Corey this weekend and we worked things out. He was honest about his actions, gave a sincere apology and accepted the consequences I laid out. He handled it all extremely well, though I think he had some coaching from Father Anthony."

Penny crossed her arms and said, "I don't mean to be cynical, but when it comes to Corey Hansen I can't help it. His history of broken promises is too long. Over the weekend, I spent a lot of time thinking about the injustice that was done to you on Friday. Frankly, I'm second-guessing my decision of suspending him for only a week. I mean, when is enough enough?"

"Penny, I understand Corey's a thorn in your side, and I can only imagine the kind of pressure you're getting from teachers and parents to get rid of the kid, but let's not give up on him just yet. Not after what I saw this weekend." David spent the next few minutes detailing to Penny the arrangement he had made with Corey, his response, and how things played out the previous evening.

When he finished, Penny was silent for a few moments. "Okay. I'm going to trust your instincts here. On one condition."

"And that is?"

"That you keep me informed of how the week goes with Corey – the good and bad. If he can make it without screwing up, I'll stick with the week's suspension. If he doesn't, he's expelled."

"Deal."

"I admire what you're trying to do, but with some kids, there comes a time when you have to throw in the towel. Up to this point, nothing has gotten Corey's attention. Don't get me wrong, I'm not into punishing kids, but Corey doesn't seem fazed by anything. There have been some changes since you've been working with him. But is it enough? Is it too late?

"I'm sorry, I'm babbling...just thinking out loud. What I want to say is don't hang on too long. Unfortunately, the reality is we can't save every child, especially the ones who don't want our help."

The intercom clicked on. Penny stopped talking and jerked her head up, like a laboratory rat that's learned an electric shock is about to be delivered. "Ms. Heins to the office! Ms. Heins to the office!"

"Oh, I hate that thing," Penny said. "Before I go, one more item: Let me round up Corey's homework from the other teachers. That way, it'll give them a chance to infer the outcome of my investigation without any rules being broken, and they'll see you have my full support."

"Penny, that's not necessary."

"I know, but I think it's needed. I won't take 'No' for an answer. I'll drop it by after lunch." She sped away before he could thank her.

The school week was uneventful. There were no rallies or demonstrations calling for his head, bomb threats or investigative reporters lurking in the shadows to get the dirty scoop on "priest strikes student" for the local news.

There were, however, subtle looks of distrust from a few of the teachers and a handful of students. But these were far outweighed by words of encouragement and statements of support.

Corey came to the rectory on time every day and completed his homework and First Reconciliation lessons without objection. It was almost too easy, too good to be real. David noticed a faint change in Corey, but was unsure if it was a positive one. In a somber way, he was compliant, like a wild horse whose spirit finally had been broken and now was ready to serve a master. Conversation between the two was sparse, other than what was required from Corey's studies. He didn't respond to David's good-natured ribbing or attempts at chitchat. Corey came, did his work, then left.

David relayed all this to Father Anthony at breakfast on the Saturday before Corey's First Reconciliation.

"I don't know; it's a fine line," David said, as he took another bite of the blueberry pancakes Father Anthony had whipped up. "Corey's got to learn, but you hate to strip a kid down and suck out all of his spirit and fight."

Muffled by a mouthful of food, Father Anthony said, "Can't have it both ways. His spirit may be bruised right now, but it can always be built back up. A dose of humility never hurt anyone. He's just got a case of the guilts, which is good; means he's got a conscience. This will pass soon enough. He may be on his best behavior only until he's back in good standing. Corey's smart enough to know when to lay low; you can't rule out that this is an act, or another game."

David pushed his plate away, then poured another cup of coffee. Since he had taken over the coffee making duty, the brew was no longer at toxic levels and he could handle more than one cup. "I think there's more to this. Maybe there's something going on at home. I get the feeling something's occupying his thoughts."

After working his way through a mountain of pancakes, Father Anthony finally settled back into his chair. David often wondered why Father Anthony wasn't larger than he was; the man had an endless appetite. It has to be his schedule, David thought. The man is constantly on the move.

Father Anthony rose for more coffee and said, "You're going above and beyond the call of duty on this one. I hope it pays off – that the boy actually starts to get it. You just never know with some kids."

Father Anthony poured a large helping of coffee and sat back down at the kitchen table. "I want to talk with you about Mass tomorrow. It's all yours. I'm assisting."

David was in mid-sip, and the directness and unexpectedness of this statement caused him to swallow too much coffee. He quickly put the mug up to his mouth and spit back the hot liquid before it could do any serious damage. He grabbed a paper napkin and dabbed at the drops that spilled on his blacks. "You can't be serious! I thought we were going to wait for a couple more weeks...for the Founders Day Mass."

It was obvious from Father Anthony's amused grin that he got a kick out of David's reaction. "Damn right I'm serious. You're ready. Plus you've been the one who has prepared these boys and girls for their First Confession. It's only right that this Mass be yours."

"But everyone will be there. They'll want you, not me. I mean, come on, there will be some angry people if I do it." Inside, David was nervous, but thrilled at the prospect of finally leading a public Mass that had more than the usual importance. He felt obligated, however, to point out the downside, even though he was sure Father Anthony hadn't made this decision on a whim. He was smarter than that.

"I don't give a damn. You've earned this, and I will not be strong-armed by the possible negative reactions of a few pin-headed parishioners."

"It'll be more than a few."

"That's fine. My mind is made up. If people can't deal with the fact that you deserve to do this, then shame on them." A smile came across the elder priest's face. "It's time to take you out of the oven, you've been cooking long enough."

David didn't put up any more resistance. "Well, it's got to happen some time. I guess tomorrow's as good as any."

"Now you're talkin'. If you need any help preparing your homily, let me know. I'll be around most of the day today. Tonight I'm heading over to Larry's house to watch the state semifinals. What a run we've made. Can you believe we're undefeated and only two games away from our first state championship! This might be the best Crusaders football team ever – best I've seen in all my years. Oh, Larry said to tell you to come on over if you'd like."

David's head was already swirling with ideas for his homily, "Huh? Oh…umm…maybe. Let's see how far I get in my preparations."

"Don't worry, David. We can go over the logistics this afternoon and do a quick run-through tomorrow morning. All you need to bring is your enthusiasm – and a homily."

The idea of a dry run calmed the queasiness in David's gut. "Can we do it right now?"

Laughing, Father Anthony said, "Sure, sure."

The two priests cleaned up the breakfast mess, all the while discussing the football game. It was almost impossible to talk to someone or turn on the TV or open the newspaper without hearing or seeing something about the Crusaders' run at a championship. With the football team being the pride and identity of many in Willa, winning and losing were a part of life. Now, David had another reason besides loyalty to his team to be rooting for victory: A win meant tomorrow's Mass would be upbeat and happy; a loss meant the atmosphere would be like a funeral. He decided right then to watch the game alone. There was more than pride or a bet riding on the outcome, and the thought of being around others was not appealing.

The walk-through should have taken about twenty minutes, but with all of David's questions and concerns it took a little over an hour. Throughout the neurotic dry run, Father Anthony remained patient and helpful. To soothe David's nerves, Father Anthony answered and re-answered all of David's procedural questions, and rehearsed all the various aspects of the Mass.

After a request for a third practice, Father Anthony threw up his hands in mock surrender and said with an amused chuckle, "Relax. You've got it. Everything will run like clockwork. You've got the upper hand here."

"Now how do you figure that?"

"All the folks in church tomorrow will have no idea how this works. It only happens once a year and they leave the nuts and bolts up to us. If a mistake's made – and I emphasize 'if' – no one will know. Simply keep on going, act like everything that happens is supposed to happen. Trust me, as long as you appear confident and in command, no one will doubt you. Now, let's enjoy the rest of the day."

David couldn't help but laugh at himself. "Okay, okay, you're right. I promise I'll mellow out – right after Mass tomorrow."

Father Anthony slapped David on the back. "Never lose that sense of humor, it's a necessity in our line of work. You know, all this practice has made me hungry. How about some lunch at Mama's? I'm in the mood for a double-crusted potato and broccoli pizza."

David panned the massive church and took in a deep, self-assured breath. "You're on. As long as you're buying."

"Me? After all I've done for you? I've got a better idea: I think the people of St. Cecilia's owe us a pizza for all the great work we did this morning. What do you think?"

"Absolutely. It's the least they can do."

———

Only a few hours had passed since breakfast and David wasn't all that hungry. But he knew food was Father Anthony's favorite pastime and Mama's, a small family-run restaurant, was his favorite pizza joint. David didn't want to disappoint his mentor, so he proceeded to stuff himself full of pizza, salad, spaghetti, lasagna, bread and homemade Neapolitan ice cream, specially made for Father Anthony.

When he asked for the bill, the gnarled, old owner said, "On the house." The man was paper-thin, with white hair shooting in every direction, like a balloon had been rubbed on his head. He reminded David of an old elf – a tragic elf, not a happy, carefree one. During lunch, David had learned that the man was eternally grateful to Father Anthony for his support during his wife's long battle with breast cancer, another battle that cancer won. This was a ritual between the two: Father Anthony always asked for the bill but was always denied.

"They were an odd couple," Father Anthony had said at lunch. "Always bickering. I guess it was their way of communicating, and it worked for them. They were inseparable; soulmates you might say. Poor guy, he'll never be the same. That's one of the risks of falling in love that you're not warned about. I try to check up on him once or twice a week."

When they got back to the rectory, all David could think about was a nap. Father Anthony checked the answering machine and was right with his prediction: zero calls. Normally, there would be five or six messages waiting for the elder priest when he returned.

Father Anthony said, while chewing on a toothpick from Mama's, "It always amazes me how emergencies suddenly become non-emergencies on game day."

"I'm gonna head to my room and get started on my homily," David said, his eyes as heavy as the lunch that sat in his stomach.

Yawning, Father Anthony said, "I'll be in the den watching TV; come and get me if you need any help."

David sat down at the antique roll top desk he had purchased at a local garage sale a few weeks ago. It was the style of desk he had always wanted but could never afford, and it was in mint condition. When admiring it, he met the young lady who was running the sale for her father; he had been stricken with Alzheimers. She sold the desk to David for what he had in his pocket, thirty dollars. The desk easily could have sold for twenty times that amount. David had tried to get her to agree on a more reasonable price but she would have none of it.

"Sometimes, the money doesn't matter," she said wistfully. "Papa loved the Church. He would be happy knowing a man of the cloth was using it." The next day, before David had a chance to locate a truck to fetch his purchase, two men showed up at the rectory and hauled the heavy desk into his room. The woman had made arrangements and paid for the delivery; it was a kind act that David would always remember whenever he sat down to work. Since then, he had researched Internet sites on antiques to learn how to care for the desk and dutifully followed each instruction.

Recalling what the young lady had said and done that day caused him to think about Erik, Lizzy and Christopher – and their troubles. Since the confrontation with Erik, David had not talked with Lizzy, although he did see Christopher in class and learned that he was meeting with Larry. Christopher said he really liked Larry. This encouraged David. Also, it helped him justify the brutal honesty he had used with Erik that day and the gaping wound it left on their friendship.

David shook off the thoughts of his friends and started searching the Bible for scripture that might provide inspiration for his homily. After some time, he grew frustrated; the right passage had yet to leap off the page and grab his imagination. So, he went to the den. Father Anthony was snoring loudly, asleep in his Lazyboy recliner. Instead of waking him, David retreated to his room and laid down for a short rest.

"Wake up, my boy." Father Anthony gently shook David's shoulder. "It's almost game time." He turned on the lamp by David's bedside and the pitch-dark room was suddenly flooded with light.

Shielding his eyes, David said, "What time is it?"

"About six o'clock," Father Anthony said. "You want a ride over to Larry's house? I'm taking off pretty quick; got to get in some tailgating before kickoff."

David's eyes were beginning to adjust; he propped himself up on an elbow. "Thanks," he said with a big yawn. "But I think I'll stay here and listen to it on the radio. I've got to work on my homily. I haven't done a damn thing yet. I intended to rest for a few minutes, not take a two hour nap."

"Suit yourself. If you want, come on over when you're finished."

"I will." David was now fully alert. He started to panic, realizing what was ahead of him.

Father Anthony rubbed his hands together. "We're gonna kick Cedarburg's butts up and down the field tonight!" Then, he bolted from the room, like a child who had been told it was finally time to go to a birthday party he had been waiting for all day.

David laid back on his pillow, hands behind his head, and thought about how he could pull off a miracle for tomorrow's homily. After ten minutes of serious reflection – and no divine intervention – he got up, took a quick shower, got dressed, found the game on the radio and sat down at his desk. With pen in hand, he was armed but he didn't feel very dangerous.

The motto drummed into his head at the seminary, "Most inspiration comes from perspiration," now resonated in his brain. He opened the Bible and began skimming the scripture from the beginning, Genesis. He was determined to hunt down the perfect piece of scripture to draw from, even if it took all night.

The longer and more intensely he searched, the more discouraged and desperate he grew. Soon, David was keeping both ears on the radio and one eye on his task. Around 10:00 p.m., he switched off the radio. It was a distraction and an excuse to delay the inevitable. Plus, St. Cecilia's was so far ahead that he didn't recognize the names of the substitutes; the rout was on. David was invigorated. Knowing that the congregation would be happy and filled with conquest, he was better able to concentrate. Now on full alert, it didn't take David long to find exactly what he was looking for.

He had read from the Gospel of Mark many times. He knew it well; some of his favorite pieces of scripture were contained there. Reading chapter 10 verses 13-16 out loud, David grew more enraptured with each word:

> "People were bringing little children to him in order that he might touch them; and the disciples spoke sternly to them. But when Jesus saw this, he was indignant and said to them, 'Let the little children come to me; do not stop them; for it is to such as these that the kingdom of God belongs. Truly I tell you, whoever does not receive the kingdom of God as a little child will never enter it.' And he took them in his arms, laid his hands on them, and blessed them."

David was moved and immediately began writing. Basing his homily on the theme of this passage was effortless. His pen seemed to move on the paper on its own, as if someone was gently guiding it. This had happened to David on two or three other occasions. However, this time he didn't question what was happening, but instead went with the flow.

Thirty minutes later, after putting a period on the last sentence, David snapped out of the zone. He had been in a trance, totally oblivious to the world around him. Now, the occasional hiss from the steam heater, the slow drip from the faucet and the dank smell that permeated his room all came flooding back like they were brand new. Putting the pen down, David knew he wouldn't have to use the words as a guide during Mass; they were etched into his memory forever.

David woke before the alarm clock sounded. He was refreshed and hungry. After a shower and shave, he went to the kitchen and ate two toasted onion bagels – one smothered with grape jelly, the other with peanut butter. He polished off a large glass of apple juice then poured himself a cup of coffee. On the way to get dressed, he passed Father Anthony, who was only wearing his lucky Crusaders boxer shorts. He was headed for the bathroom.

"Mornin', Padre," David said.

Father Anthony put his hands over his ears and whispered, "Not so loud."

"Sorry," David said, suppressing a laugh. "A little too much celebration last night?"

Eyes bloodshot, Father Anthony looked at David, shook his head and said, "You're smart, my boy. Unfortunately, I strayed from the friendly confines of Guinness and wandered into the unfamiliar and dangerous world of scotch. I was lucky to get out alive. Whenever you have an urge to drink, remember this encounter."

Father Anthony continued walking toward the bathroom door, his gait unsteady. At one point, he veered sharply to the right while reaching back to scratch his rump.

He disappeared through the bathroom door, and David figured it wouldn't be prudent to venture in there for some time.

David got dressed in his newest blacks and went to the kitchen for more coffee. Father Anthony was sitting at the table dressed in a tattered, yellowed robe. He was sipping from a large mug of steaming coffee; an opened bottle of Advil sat off to the side.

"All ready for the big day?" Father Anthony said, rubbing his hands together. David marveled at the man's recovery power. He was violently hungover but didn't let it get in the way.

"I am," David said. And he meant it.

Father Anthony looked slightly bewildered. "Want to do one more quick walk through?"

David stroked his freshly clipped goatee. "Nah, I think I got it."

Father Anthony sat up straighter and said, "Okay, what gives? Last night you were more nervous than a long-tailed cat in a room full of rocking chairs, and this morning you're acting like a grizzled veteran."

Laughing, David said, "I'm not sure. Last night, I found some scripture that really inspired me. I wrote my homily in about half an hour. It seemed so easy, and this morning I feel calm. I'm as surprised as you are. I don't know how to explain it. The Holy Spirit was with me last night, still is. Knowing this gives me tremendous comfort and peace."

"The Holy Spirit always comes through if you don't get in the way." Father Anthony looked up and toasted the heavens with his coffee cup. "Give me a few minutes to get ready, then let's go over and set up."

"Why?" David said. "We've got plenty of time."

"I want to try and keep the Holy Spirit around as long as we can."

The Mass was going to be packed. People were streaming into the church forty-five minutes early. In small towns, nearly everyone was related to someone somehow, and events like this were a big deal. Old and young were decked out in their best suits and prettiest dresses. And they all wanted a good seat.

When David brought out the hosts and the wine to be used during Mass, he peered out at the early arrivers. Lizzy was seated in the third row, which was as close as one could get – the first two rows on both sides of the aisle were reserved for the children. Erik was nowhere to be seen. After placing the items on the server's table, David walked to where Lizzy was sitting and, in a hushed voice, said, "How are you? I'm so excited for Christopher. How's he doing?"

Lizzy grasped David's hands. Her grip was tight and her fingers were lightly trembling, but she was smiling. "Better. He's really excited about today. You were right about Larry. I can't believe the impact he's already had on Christopher. He is spending less time alone in his room, and he's actually starting to open up with me. Oh, he even decided to stay on the basketball team! Thank you for leading us to Larry. He's a godsend."

"You don't know how happy that makes me." He crouched down and was eye to eye with Lizzy. "What's Erik's reaction?"

She looked down and sighed. "Not good. We had a blow out over the whole thing. In the end, he gave in and agreed to give it a chance. He's upset. But the odd thing is I can't tell if it's with me or himself or Christopher…or what. Since then, Erik's had to work late or has been out of town, so we haven't talked much. Something's rattled him; I sense a real sadness. I don't know…I'm just giving him some space. We'll see what happens."

David held her hand. "Erik will come around; he's a good man. He's just confused about his priorities right now. Giving him some time and space to sort things out is a great idea."

"Maybe," Lizzy said.

David rose up. "I'd better get going. I'm running the show today. Wish me luck."

Lizzy's eyes opened wide. "Really? You'll do great. Break a leg!"

"I hope that's all I break."

As he turned to go back to the sacristy, he saw Larry enter the church with Corey. Larry had a hand on Corey's shoulder. David assumed that Corey's mother was in no condition to attend, so Larry was Corey's escort. When David made eye contact with Larry, he quickly took his hand off Corey's shoulder, waved hello and smiled at David. Corey left to join his classmates' who were gathering downstairs in the reception room, while Larry found a seat in the middle of the church.

No one, at least overtly, appeared bothered that David was the head celebrant. There was no uprising of parents gathering their child and walking out in protest. This sacrament was an important milestone in the Catholic faith, so even the adults were on their best behavior.

Father Anthony's advice was sound: The people in the pews had no idea how this particular Mass was to proceed. At the beginning, when David was supposed to be quietly praying and reflecting, he thought, I'll bet they're all waiting for Father Anthony to take over. But it wasn't going to happen. Instead, the stately priest sat at rapt attention in a small pew to David's right.

Father Anthony did the first two readings and the responsorial Psalm. David followed with the scripture from the Gospel. Once finished, he lifted the Bible over his head like it was a fragile infant and said, "The Gospel of the Lord."

"Praise to You Lord Jesus Christ," the crowd responded in unison.

Then, the jam-packed church fell quiet. There were no coughs or throats cleared, not a baby cried or even fussed and not a soul squirmed in his or her seat. The only sound was the low, steady hum from the halogen lights in the overhead chandeliers, which were spread throughout the church. All eyes were on David. To his amazement, he wasn't freaked-out. Rather, he felt serene, as if he was speaking to a couple of people, not a full congregation on a special day.

Instead of hiding behind the lectern during his homily, he made his way down the sanctuary steps. He stopped in the center aisle, just in front of the first row of pews. As he was doing this, Father Anthony stealthily slipped into the sacristy. Seconds after David arrived to face the kids in the front of the church, the lights went dark.

At David's request, Father Anthony had killed the lights. For this to work, David needed his mentor's assistance. While setting up for Mass, David informed Father Anthony what was going to be said and done. At first, he was skeptical, but agreed to be an accomplice when David reasoned, "This isn't a traditional homily, I know that. But it's not intended for the big people, it's for the little ones. This is the best way for me to help them understand, enjoy, and remember the uniqueness of this day. Anyway, I've got nothing to lose."

When the church went dark, a worried murmur spread through the crowd of adults. They were confused and peered around at each other and at the lights, as if they searched hard enough they could figure out the reason for the power outage. The children, on the other hand, muffled their giggles and laughs as well as nervous kids who were to be on their best behavior could.

Even during the day, the church was dark. The deep colors of the stained glass windows absorbed much of the sunlight and blocked the rays from penetrating the holy building. Today, this was exacerbated by an overcast sky.

David let the suspense build. Then, just before he felt someone might rise and try to solve the problem, he slid a flashlight that he had hidden in his pant pocket under his alb and shined it on his face. He held it under his chin; his face was illuminated, but not in a spooky, Halloween way. There was a short gasp from the parishioners and snickers and squeals from the children. Then, silence.

"Darkness," David began quietly, a wireless microphone amplifying his voice. "It's strange and scary, isn't it?" He panned light on the little faces fidgeting in the pews. "When it suddenly goes dark, we want the light back on, don't we? When darkness hits, we reach for something – like a flashlight – that will help make it light again. Darkness is cold and unfamiliar. It makes us feel uncomfortable and frightened. Light, on the other hand, is warm and familiar. It makes us feel good and gives us comfort and hope.

"Who's ever been afraid of the dark?" The next couple of seconds were tense for David. If he didn't get a response here, his homily was shot. David's eyes had adjusted to the darkness and, to his delight, he spotted a couple of brave little hands slowly rise up. The children looked at their neighbors and more and more hands shot into the air. Within seconds, all hands were raised high, except one – Corey. This didn't surprise or bother David.

Relieved, he continued, "We all get scared in the dark. Even moms and dads and teachers and priests are afraid of the dark sometimes." As he spoke, David continued to pan the light from one child's face to another; it was a spotlight shining on each child for a brief moment. The kids were on the edge of their seats, staring right at David, hanging on his every word.

"Most of the time, we're unsure what to do when darkness suddenly strikes our lives. We can't see what we want to see, so we become mixed-up and frightened. But we don't have to be afraid. There's a light that shines bright in each of us, even during the toughest moments. Today is a special day for all of you. It's a day when each one of you can tap into that light and begin to discover the beauty, peace, and love it offers."

David switched the flashlight off and turned around to face the front of the church. A spotlight turned on and lit up the large crucifix over the tabernacle. The timing was perfect, and he imagined that Father Anthony was having a ball in his role as lighting director.

David turned back to face the kids. "Who is the light in our lives? Who can help us when we are afraid of the dark?"

Together, the kids said, "Jesus!" David thought he heard a few adult voices sprinkled in but wasn't sure.

"That's right. Jesus is our light. Today is your First Reconciliation; it's the day that you can let Jesus, the light, into your life. We all sin. We're not perfect, and God knows this. We all have troubles that we want to let go. Holding onto our sins and secrets makes us feel bad. Today, you can give your sins to God, simply by asking Him for forgiveness. When you give your deepest, darkest secrets to God, the darkness turns to light. You have a chance to start fresh – to try to be good and honest again." David panned the light from face to little face. "Who wants to come out of the dark? Who wants to come with me to discover the light?"

The little voices shouted, "I do!" All the traditional rules of expected Church behavior were now suspended, and the kids loved it. David asked the question one more time, and all the kids, even Corey, shouted louder, "I do!"

David shined the flashlight on the little girl in the first row seated closest to the middle aisle. He hadn't planned this part, but it seemed right. Spiritedly, David said, "Then follow me. Let's go find the light." The girl jumped out of her seat and followed David as he illuminated the first Station of the Cross. Walking over to the large statue that seemed to be magically attached to the wall, David looked back and saw that all thirty-two kids were quickly and orderly filing out of the pews.

When they all arrived at the first Station, David gathered the kids around him. "As you look at each one, think about what Jesus did for us so that we could have light in our lives." Silently, he led them through all twelve Stations of the Cross. Each one dazzled as the beam lit it to life. Briefly, he stopped at each Station, allowing the kids to take in the depicted scene.

Out of the corner of his eye, he noticed that the crowd of adults was following every move. They were hushed, but he sensed they weren't outraged; rather, intrigued and fascinated, like fans at auto race anxiously waiting for a violent wreck to happen.

On a whim, after the last Station, he said to the remarkably well-behaved children, "Where's the light?"

Like an expert choreographer, Father Anthony caught David's improvisation and turned on another light that further illuminated the large Crucifix. David repeated the question and the kids said, "There! It's up there!" They all pointed to the front of the church.

"Who wants to go to the light?"

"I do! I do!" The children clamored.

"Then let's go!" David turned on his heels and began walking toward the back of the church.

Laughing, the kids said, "No, not that way! Up there!"

David turned around. "Where?"

"Over here! Up this way!"

"Show me the way," he said.

The children ran up to the Crucifix and David followed, as if he was lost and confused. Beseechingly, the kids said, "It's right here. Come up here!"

On the way, he clicked off the microphone. Then, he huddled the kids in a circle and said words to them that only they could hear. David could feel the necks of the adults stretching out to hear his words. When he finished, the kids shouted, "I will!"

A moment later, David blessed them all. They were more subdued as they responded, "Amen." Quickly, but silently, the children scattered to their seats. David sat down in the celebrant's chair as the church lights flicked on. Father Anthony came out of the sacristy; he was beaming ear to ear.

When the last child was seated, Larry began a slow, solo clap. Without hesitation, the kids joined in, and it spread through the rest of the crowd. Before David knew it, the whole church was applauding. Father Anthony was furiously clapping and grinning like a proud parent on graduation day.

David did his best to remain composed. He sat, giving thanks to God in silent prayer. Exhilarated, all he could think of was, "It worked! And they loved it!" As the applause began to subside, David realized that the fat lady hadn't sung yet; he still had to finish Mass and the ceremony for First Reconciliation. The thought quickly sobered him, and he concentrated on the task at hand.

During communion, David was pleasantly surprised to find as many people in his line as Father Anthony's. While serving communion, David noticed that the adults and kids looked at him differently; they made eye contact and most smiled. This Mass was a turning point for David as a priest at St. Cecilia's. First impressions, he knew, were so important and, many times, all one got. For a majority of these people, this was their first look and, so far, he was passing with flying colors.

As David moved to the First Reconciliation ceremony, he felt like an athlete in a zone; he didn't have to think about what he was doing, he just let it happen. Everything was going smoothly. He was on cruise control.

He took up station for confessions by the sacristy door. It was the only place in the sanctuary that provided a hint of privacy. A lectern blocked the view straight on, while the altar obstructed any gawkers from the other side of the church. David would hear the kids' confessions face-to-face and Father Anthony was available for the adults in the traditional manner: Behind the closed door of a confessional, where a flimsy screen separated and concealed one from the priest.

One by one, the children came to David to reveal their little sins and to ask for forgiveness. Most were nervous, and either unsure that what they were about to say even qualified as a sin, or that it was such a major transgression that they were going to get into serious trouble.

"Bless me Father for I have sinned. This is my first confession," Harry Strenstrom said. After a few moments of contemplation, the young boy said, "I called my little sister a bad name after she messed with my Gameboy. I saved the game I was playing 'cause I almost had it beat, and she erased it. And…I got a "D" on a math test 'cause I didn't study real hard. I threw it away on the way home from school so my dad couldn't see it." Harry looked to David like a student who wasn't listening during a classroom lecture and provided the teacher with a guessed answer to a posed question.

He couldn't disappoint the boy. So, as he pondered young Harry's fate, David put on a grave face and stroked his whiskers. Doing his best not to smile, David said, "God forgives you for these things. For your penance, say one Our Father and one Hail Mary." Harry broke out into a huge, pleased grin. David added, "Also, say one nice thing to your sister every day for one week, and come clean with your dad about the test – he's going to find out about it sooner or later. It'll be better if it comes from you than from your teacher." Harry's smile disappeared.

David thoroughly enjoyed sharing this sacrament with the children. Their little voices rang with innocence, awe, and fascination. Some of this was due to the pomp of the ceremony, but David hoped that most of this was because he gave them his full and undivided attention. Kids weren't used to this. Rarely did big people listen, really listen to what the little voices had to say.

When Christopher arrived, David smiled warmly, listened patiently to his godson's sins, and gave him his penance. Christopher's eyes were more alive than when David saw him last, but there was still a void. David figured that Larry was helping the boy. But it had to be an uphill battle; nothing could replace a father's presence and love. Christopher politely thanked David, and his heart ached for the boy and his dad. As Christopher walked back to his seat, David saw Erik sneak in through one of the side doors at the back of the church. He stood there pressing out the wrinkles in his suit. David thought, Another night at the office. Well, at least he showed up; that's a good sign.

After a couple more kids, Corey made his way to David. The reflective look on the boy's face surprised David. He had fully expected Corey to remain seated in the pew with his arms crossed, holding his breath in defiance. Not only was David happy that Corey had decided to participate, but David also was relieved that now he wouldn't have to go drag the boy by his collar to confession.

Corey sat down on the padded chair across from David. "Bless me Father for I have sinned. This is my first confession." He looked right at David and opened his mouth as if to speak, but nothing came out. He dropped his head and wiped his eyes with a shirtsleeve. Corey was crying. A chill ran up David's spine.

Carefully, David said, "Corey, it's okay. Tell me what's bothering you."

"I...I can't." More tears. David moved his chair slightly to the side to block Corey from the wandering eyes of the crowd.

David had seen Corey angry, but never so anguished and uncertain like this.

"Why don't you take a couple of deep breaths; it'll make you feel better. Then, we can talk about what's troubling you."

Between silent sobs, Corey said, "I know it's wrong, but he made me do it. He said it would make me feel better, but it doesn't. It only makes me feel worse. If I stop, he said he wouldn't help me anymore. I don't want to be alone."

Corey's words were too familiar; a troubled, sick feeling invaded David's gut, and his heart began to thump and race inside his chest. "Who? What are you talking about?"

"Larry," Corey said quickly and angrily.

David felt dizzy; he shuddered. The boy was speaking in riddles, giving pieces to a puzzle. There could be no mistakes or misunderstandings or misinterpretations here. His thoughts flicked back to Corey's accusation in the school hallway. Taking hold of the boy's arm, David said, "What about Larry? What are you saying?"

"You're hurting me," Corey said.

David didn't hear this; he wanted answers and he wanted them now. He wasn't about to mess around with any of Corey's bullshit. The sting of his lies still lingered fresh in David's mind, and he grew more and more intolerant as he recalled what happened in school ten days ago.

David's balloon had burst. He felt like this day was ruined, and he blamed Corey. All the joy David had experienced so far, and the breakthrough he had made at Mass, was now tainted. For the moment, David was blinded. He tightened his grip on Corey's arm, moved closer and said in a low, stern voice, "Corey, tell me about Larry…and make sure what you say is the truth."

David's eyes were filled with the doubt and contempt that he felt. Corey became confused and quickly retreated, yanking himself free from David's grip. In a whispered voice, Corey hissed, "Fuck this. I thought you'd listen."

Corey rose to leave, and David snapped out of the dark cloud that had engulfed him. "Corey, I'm sorry. Don't go. Stay and tell me what's wrong. I shouldn't have reacted that way. I'm not mad at you. Please, sit and let's talk."

It was too late. Corey had shut down. There were no more tears. With icy calmness, he said, "Why? You won't believe me, nobody will. I'll show you – and him." Corey quietly moved into the sacristy, and David heard the door that led outside squeak open and close shut with a muffled thud.

David sat stunned. Unanswered questions raced through his head. Was Corey playing games again? What was he going to say about Larry? Why the hell did I react like that?

"Father David," a little voice said. "Am I next?"

David turned around, forced a smile and said to Margaret Coles, "Yes…yes. Sit down." As he slid his chair back into place, he looked out into the congregation. He expected angry stares and accusing looks, but no one seemed to have noticed what had just taken place.

David's gaze wandered over to where Larry had sat. He was returning from confession with Father Anthony. Larry slid past a rather large lady to get to his seat, kneeled down, made the sign of the cross and began his penance. David watched for a few seconds as Larry dutifully and silently mouthed prayers of forgiveness. He suddenly looked up and right at David. While continuing his prayers, he shot David a wink and smile. David smiled back at his friend and thought about all the help and support Larry had given him.

For some reason, Corey was lashing out at Larry. But still, David reacted wrongly, and he couldn't ignore what the boy had to say. He would apologize to Corey and follow up with him, find out what was so upsetting. But that had to wait. David's festive spirit was dampened; however he was determined not to let Corey make this wonderful day a complete disaster.

"Bless me father for I have sinned…" David turned, smiled, and gave his full attention to Margaret.

CHAPTER 8

On Monday morning, several students stopped David in the hallway and came by his classroom to applaud yesterday's Mass. In the teachers lounge during lunch, David was enjoying strokes to his ego, when he noticed Father Anthony at the door. He motioned for David to come out into the hallway.

Smiling, David strolled out and said, "Hi. Man, everyone sure liked—" Father Anthony's face was ashen, his expression grave. David clammed up and swallowed hard.

"I've got some awful news. I just received a phone call from the police and…well, Corey was found at Neihardt Park. He's dead. Chief Gardner said it looks like suicide."

"What? Not Corey. No…he wouldn't do anything like that."

Father Anthony put his giant hands on David's shoulders and said, "I'm sorry."

David felt ill. He rushed over to a trash can and threw up his lunch. His stomach heaved twice more. David didn't fight it.

"Here." Father Anthony handed David a handkerchief. "Why don't we go over to the rectory for a bit. You've got the next two periods free, don't you?"

Dabbing his mouth with the handkerchief, David looked at Father Anthony as if he was speaking a foreign language. The elder priest repeated his suggestion.

"Okay…sure," David stammered.

He was reeling. His mind was overloaded, like a computer that freezes up from too many commands.

Blindly, he followed Father Anthony out of the building. Once at their home, David plopped down hard on the couch in the den.

Father Anthony said, "I'll get us a couple of sodas."

David stared straight ahead at nothing in particular.

When Father Anthony returned and handed David the soda, he took a short swig and said, "What the hell's going on? What happened?"

Father Anthony was pacing back and forth. "I don't know all the details. What I've been told is that an officer who was doing a routine sweep of the park discovered Corey this morning. Chief Gardner said that Corey...well...he hung himself – from the jungle gym on the playground."

David's thoughts immediately shifted to the memory of Bobby Harmon. The fact that another hideous death of a child had taken place at Neihardt Park's playground was too much to bear, and David broke down. He was crying for Corey and for Bobby and for every child who dies too young.

Through the tears, David said, "He killed himself? He's too little to be thinking of that."

"I know, I know." Father Anthony gently massaged David's shoulders. "Good Lord, kids are just too damn young to realize suicide's a permanent solution to a temporary problem."

David knew this was true, but it was no consolation. He also knew that most who hurt themselves made a cry for help, gave some kind of sign. The incident at Corey's First Confession came storming back. David gasped.

"What?" Father Anthony said. "What's wrong?"

David buried his head in his hands and was about to tell Father Anthony everything Corey had said yesterday. But he stopped, remembering both his vow of silence and the fact that Larry was the focus of Corey's confession. Frantically, David thought, I can't tell Father Anthony of my suspicions! There's no way he'd believe his best friend of fifteen years might have sexually abused Corey, a patient – a child! It's just conjecture on my part; I don't know anything for sure. Shit, I don't even believe it.

David had intended on following up on Corey's outburst, but over the last twenty-four hours he'd been so busy basking in his own glory that the boy's troubles weren't even an afterthought.

Instead of the full story, David said, "During confession yesterday, I think Corey might have been trying to tell me something."

Father Anthony scooted to the edge of his chair. "What?"

David had to tread lightly; stay on the fringes of the complete truth. "He never told me. He was trying. But he became upset and left the church through the sacristy door."

"Do you have any idea of what he was trying to tell you?"

David hesitated. He hated to do this to his mentor, but before he said anything more he had to be absolutely sure. "No, not really. My god, I should have…I never thought he'd—"

"No," Father Anthony said sternly. "I know where you're headed and I won't allow it. This is not your fault; you're the good guy here. From the word go, you did everything possible to reach the boy, putting up with a lot of his shenanigans at your own expense. We are priests, not God. We are not omniscient, we can't read minds. I know this won't ease your pain, but tragedies like this happen and will continue to happen. On a daily basis, we encounter death and suffering because of the work we've chosen to do. Our calling involves both life and death. David, I know – and you know – that if you had any suspicions of this, you would have done everything in your power to prevent it."

"Listen to Father Anthony, David. He's right." It was Larry.

Father Anthony smiled at his old friend. "I'm glad you got my message. Thanks for coming over."

Larry appeared unruffled, like it was just another day. There were no outward signs of upset: no red, puffy eyes or distraught expressions. This bothered David.

The phone rang and Father Anthony picked up the receiver. After a few seconds of hushed conversation, he pressed the hold button and put the receiver back on the phone. "I have to take this in my office. I'll be back shortly."

Larry sat in Father Anthony's recliner, across from David. The silence was uneasy; neither man looked at the other. Finally, David said, "Did you see this coming?"

"No. Looking back, I can honestly say Corey didn't give off any classic signs of being suicidal. When we first started working together, he had threatened to harm himself, but it was always a way of seeking attention. It was never about suicide or self-harm. At no time did I ever consider him lethal. Lately, he was working through his issues without any unusual distress. I'm convinced this was a spontaneous act and not something he thought about for a long time or carefully planned out."

David thought, Why is Larry so matter-of-fact and analytical? Is this how he copes with tragedy? Are his feelings hardened from the years of working with mentally ill kids? Or am I misreading him? At the moment, David didn't know what to think, so he remained silent, consciously taking deep breaths in an effort to stay composed.

Larry squirmed in his chair. "Did Corey say anything to you yesterday that indicated he was upset about something?" The psychiatrist squinted sideways at David, and he couldn't help but feel Larry's suspicion.

David decided to take the same approach that he had with Father Anthony: tell the truth, but not the whole truth. "Yeah, there was something, but he never told me what it was. He became upset and left the church. Damn it, I should have followed him, stopped him."

Larry leaned forward, his fists clenching and unclenching. "What exactly did he say?" Larry demanded.

This commanding display caused David to become defensive. "Nothing in particular, I just sensed he was upset. I probably pushed him to talk sooner than he wanted to. He started to cry and then shut down."

Nodding his head, Larry said, "Okay, so he didn't tell you anything specific." He relaxed his fists and sat back in the recliner.

David said. "Larry, you know that I can't tell you or anyone what Corey told me during confession. I take that vow very seriously, and I don't feel comfortable talking about what we may or may not have discussed." David almost added, "I'm sorry," but didn't because he wasn't. Larry's behavior – angry looks, demanding questions, aggressive body language and complete lack of mourning over Corey's death – was beginning to anger David and legitimize his suspicion of what Corey wanted to reveal.

David locked onto Larry's eyes; neither man backed down. David's mind was now brimming with doubt and innuendo about Larry's true relationship with Corey. The man appeared desperate to find out if David knew more than he was letting on. At that moment, the trust that had built up between the two over the last few months began to wilt.

"I'm sorry," Father Anthony said, stepping back into the room. Larry and David quickly broke eye contact. "That was Chief Gardner. Of all the damn things." Father Anthony's voice cracked, and he took a moment to regroup. "Apparently, Corey's mother is pretty messed up. She's probably been drinking since this morning when the police told her about Corey. Larry, I hate to ask, but would you mind coming down with me to the coroner's office? They need me to identify the body. I could use the company."

Like a light switched from off to on, Larry smiled compassionately and said, "Of course, Anthony."

As Father Anthony was putting on his parka, Larry got up to leave. He walked over and patted David on the shoulder; David flinched at his touch.

"Are you going to be all right?" Larry said.

"I'll be fine."

Larry was putting on an act for Father Anthony's benefit, and this pissed David off. He ignored Larry and addressed Father Anthony, saying, "I'm gonna go fill Penny in on what happened and then go over to see how Corey's mom is doing. Drunk or not, she's hurting and shouldn't be alone right now."

Larry shot David a callous look and appeared poised to refute his idea, when Father Anthony said, "That would be great. Call me on my mobile phone if you need me."

Father Anthony walked over and gave David a long, hard hug. He whispered, "He's with God now. You did all you could. Bless you, my boy."

David's body stiffened. Then, he closed his eyes tight and did something he thought he could never do again: He hugged back. It felt good, and David didn't want to let go. When opening his watery eyes, he looked over Father Anthony's shoulder and saw Larry snatch his coat from the chair and wheel around to leave.

Penny was horrified when told of Corey's demise. It took David quite awhile to help Penny pull herself together. Like David, she felt guilty and somehow responsible for the boy's actions. For the time being, her painful thoughts and feelings were quelled. However, he knew they would rekindle, like flames on a smoldering fire, for both of them for many years to come.

Penny volunteered to oversee David's remaining classes, and asked him to relay her condolences to Corey's mother, Rhonda. Also, Penny gave David the rundown on Rhonda and insight into what to expect from her. He thanked Penny for the information, gave her an awkward but sincere hug and headed out into the frigid afternoon air.

On the drive to Corey's home, David took a detour. He was drawn to visit the playground at Neihardt Park. It wasn't out of curiosity, rather a yearning to pay homage to Corey and maybe, just maybe, to find an answer or a clue as to why a little boy would choose to take his life in such a gruesome way. As he made his way to the park, David mercilessly beat himself up over how he mishandled Corey's confession. There was no excuse for David's reaction and conduct. *What I did probably threw Corey over the edge!* David couldn't shake this thought; it clattered round and round in his brain.

When he arrived, David expected to see a swarm of police cars and rolls of yellow tape cordoning off the area where the suicide took place. But there was nothing. The cops were finished, and one couldn't tell that a child had hung himself there that morning. There were no gawkers yet; no one driving by, wondering if they could still get a glimpse of Corey's limp body hanging from a noose. Word must not have spread yet. Soon, this spot would be teeming with cars loaded with onlookers who didn't give a damn about Corey, but thrived on the catastrophe and misfortune of others.

As David sat in the car staring at the jungle gym, he replayed Corey's attempted confession. "Why did I get so cross with him? Why didn't I just shut up and listen?" David cried out.

Drained, he slumped in the bucket seat. He was too tired to think and too sad to cry. He scanned the park and, through the forest of leafless trees, he saw the snow and ice that covered Cather Lake, the place where Father Emery had kidnapped and quashed his youth and innocence. Now, David was able to look at that lake instead of wanting to flee from it. And he had Larry to thank for that.

David studied Cather Lake, and the answers began to come. Yesterday, he had no desire or time to figure out Corey's riddle. To complicate matters, David was forever indebted to Larry for helping him accept and come to peace with the past. Discovering that Larry might be like Father Emery, a monster preying on children for his own pleasure, would be a crushing blow.

"Judas! Coward!" David yelled at his distorted reflection in the windshield. He had failed Corey, and he had failed his vow as a priest to seek the truth. For both, he could never forgive himself.

He understood what he must do: search for the truth, no matter where it led him, no matter the cost to himself. David pledged to Corey's memory to do everything in his power to find out if his suspicions about Larry were true. To do this, David would have to wrestle the demons of his past once more. This time, however, there would be no one to help him, not even Father Anthony. David was on his own again. The failure he felt toward Corey would be enough to fuel and push him through the fear and danger.

Right there and then, David began to focus on the task. First, he brought his concerns about Corey and Larry's relationship out into the open. David clearly recalled the possessiveness that Larry had over Corey. Also, David detected that he and Corey shared a vulnerability that Father Emery had preyed on and one that Larry could have easily taken advantage of: no father, and for all intents and purposes, no mother. As a child, David had coveted Father Emery's attention, and Corey would find Larry's attention just as intoxicating.

Tires screeched; a vehicle was rounding the sharp curves that led to the park's entrance. The freak show had begun. David put the Honda in gear. As he exited the gravel parking lot in front of the playground, he looked in the rearview mirror and saw a van from one of the local TV stations pull up and skid to a stop. Immediately, two people jumped out; one a woman with a microphone and note pad, the other a young man who was balancing a camera on his shoulder. The two ran out to the playground, like a couple of hyenas ready to scavenge a fresh kill.

Finding Rhonda Hansen's house was a difficult chore. David had never been there, not even to pick up or drop off Corey. It could have been pitch dark at night, pouring rain, or so cold that the only place to escape the sub-zero wind chill was in a hot bath, and the boy would insist on walking to the rectory or back home.

Rhonda Hansen lived on the other side of the tracks – literally. To get to her neighborhood, David drove across the railroad tracks that bordered the downtown area, clanking across the four sets of tracks, lucky that the Honda's muffler stayed intact. He continued on a gravel road past deserted grain elevators, a couple of junkyards and the town dump. After a few miles, he came to a cluster of houses right off the road. Miles and miles of snow-covered fields surrounded the homes. In the spring, summer and fall, these fields were alive with corn and soybeans and men and mice, but in the dead of winter the fields were like graveyards: quiet, deserted, spooky; a place you didn't journey into unless you had to.

David turned onto a frozen and rutted dirt road that served as the main artery for the two-dozen or so homes that made up the neighborhood. Each home had the same layout: A small square plot of land, a single story ranch house with a peaked roof and a detached one-car garage.

The front yards were tiny, and there were no backyards because the fields butted right up to the rear of all the homes. David noted how close the houses were crammed together. He figured every neighbor knew all about the skeletons in each other's closet.

The yards were littered with old, deserted tricycles and bikes, along with other traveling toys and playthings. Rusting metal trash cans, many overflowing with garbage, set on the sides of the homes or right out front. Jalopies, dead and decomposing, were scattered in more than just a few of the dirt driveways, many with the hoods open, vainly waiting for someone to bring them back to life. Most of the garage doors were open and filled to the brim with old junk, like empty paint cans, tattered couches and chairs, broken washers and dryers and other useless large items the garbage trucks refused to haul away. Without a backyard, there was no place to store or hide anything, so the homes were overrun with physical remnants of the occupant's past.

Some of the houses had addresses attached to the peeling paint on the wood by the front door; this allowed David to estimate the address sequence. He pulled up to what he calculated was Rhonda Hansen's home and saw an address on the mailbox that confirmed his guess. David was surprised to see the yard was void of anything indicating a child had grown up there. Next to three full trash cans by the front door was a pile of black garbage bags. Many were broke open – David figured by raccoons or dogs – spewing spent beer cans, empty bottles of hard liquor, cigarette butts, soup cans and, what he determined to be, syringes all over the front walk. The hungry scavengers had gobbled up all of the perishable items.

The driveway was vacant. David pulled in and lingered in the idling car, gathering his thoughts. Anxiety began slithering all over his body, increasing in intensity with each passing second. He peered out the car window. Through the transparent drapes, which covered a large plate-glass window on the front of the house, he discerned no movement inside. Maybe no one's home, David thought hopefully. He had a powerful urge to leave; his gut was tied in a knot. But he couldn't run away. He was there in the capacity of a priest to comfort a suffering parishioner, not to confess his failings to Corey's mother – that would be selfish and cruel at this time. This sense of duty was enough to propel David through the fear and panic, exit the car and make his way to the front door.

The plastic doorbell cover was broken and torn away, leaving the guts exposed. Expecting a shock, David hesitantly pushed the cold bare metal. Nothing. No shock and no sound from inside the house. He tried once more. It was busted. So, he knocked on the wooden door and waited. After thirty seconds or so, he knocked again; this time a little harder and longer. And he waited. David began to relax, relieved that no one appeared to be home. He turned to leave and was about to get into the car when he remembered that Father Anthony had said Corey's mother was in bad shape; that's why Father Anthony was doing her dirty work at the coroner's office. Now, David became concerned for her safety.

He thought, Maybe she's passed out, or high on something and out of it. She might even need medical attention. The last possibility was very real. He took his hand off the car's door handle, turned around and hustled back to the front door. He pounded on the door several times and said loudly, "Hello! Is anyone home? It's Father David, Father David Cooper. I'd like to talk with you for just a moment."

David heard a door hinge creak from inside, then footsteps. They were slow and heavy, a shuffling sound, like sandpaper on wood.

"Go away. Leave me alone." The woman's voice sounded weary and beaten.

"Rhonda," David said, "I just want to see how you're doing. I promise not to stay long. Please, open the door."

David heard muffled babbling, then the sound of metallic locks coming undone. The door opened slightly and the reek of rotten eggs and sour milk, beer and cigarettes and other odors that he couldn't identify immediately jarred him.

David heard the shuffling sound fade away. "What're you waiting for? Come in!"

Pushing the door open wider, he cautiously entered the home. No one was in the living room. "Hello?"

"Just a second." It came from the kitchen.

When Rhonda Hansen appeared, the first thing that caught his eye was how emaciated she looked: tight skin clung to her skull; sunken, dulled eyes bulged out like a bug; and long, stringy hair that was thin and greasy hung down past her shoulders. She was wearing baggy black jeans riddled with holes and rips in the knees and back pockets. Her tie-dyed Grateful Dead T-shirt read, "Once Your a 'Head' You're Never Behind." Her long bony fingers with chipped, black-painted nails held a blue plastic cup. It wasn't full of water or V8 juice.

Rhonda bumped into the arm of the couch and took a step to the side; she swayed and almost fell over. Father Anthony was right. She was blasted. She didn't try to hide it or fake anything or apologize; this was her way of life. She plopped onto the couch, took a sip from her cup, cringed as she swallowed and said, "Whadda you want? You come to minister to my sorry ass?" A quick, bitter laugh, a look of misery and another gulp from her cup.

"Rhonda, I'm very sorry to hear about Corey. I had the chance to be around him the last few months. He was a good boy with a good heart."

She reached to the end table next to the couch, put her cup down and hunted for something under a stack of magazines and papers. As she pulled out a pack of

Marlboros, a magazine fell to the floor and opened to a two-page color picture of a nude man and women humping doggy style. Rhonda didn't notice that the magazine fell; she was concentrating on pulling a smoke from the nearly empty pack.

"Fuck!" She ripped off the cover, grabbed the last cigarette, crumpled up the spent pack and threw it to the floor. When she lit the cigarette, her hands were trembling so violently that she had to use two hands to hit the mark.

After a long drag on the butt, she said as smoke seeped from her mouth and nose, "I couldn't handle him. I was too fuckin' young to be havin' kids. Sixteen. Shit, I shoulda been at the fuckin' prom instead of home with a baby." Another swig from her glass.

"I know it's hard to raise a child by yourself," David said.

"What the fuck do you know! You ain't never had a kid to take care of!" Rhonda's eyes welled with tears, but she didn't cry. Another shot from the glass and drag on her cigarette.

David remained silent for a moment. Rhonda was doped up and upset, and David knew her anger wasn't directed at him. "You're right," he said quietly. "Is there anything I can do? Anything you need? I'd like to help."

"Help?" Rhonda said in a shrill voice. "Help? Haven't you and that fuckin' shrink done enough already!"

"I'm sorry...what do you mean?"

"Don't give me that shit. I may be a fucking drunk, but I ain't blind." She stopped and stared at her cigarette. Quietly, she continued, "I didn't have no choice. They would have taken my boy away."

The front door flew open and slammed against the wall. David was startled to see a huge man dressed in black from head to toe: bandanna, leather jacket, shirt, pants and boots. His hair was pulled back into a long ponytail; two gold-colored earrings dangled from his left ear lobe. David could see the legs and feet of a woman on a colored tattoo that ran under the man's jacket and down his right hand almost to his knuckles. He shot David a menacing look. "Who the fuck is this?"

"One of Corey's goddamn guardian angels," Rhonda said.

"You that motherfuckin' head doctor?" The man moved closer and reached inside his jacket. David thought he was dead. But the man produced a small brown paper bag and threw it at Rhonda. "Here," he said.

Rhonda greedily snatched the bag from the floor and said to David, "I don't need your help, mine just got here." She weaved her way out of the room.

David's winter coat covered his white collar, so he said to the man, "I'm Father David Cooper. I knew Corey and…and I just came by to see if there was anything I could do."

The man forced a laughed. "You know how you can help? Get the hell out of here and leave her the fuck alone." He moved closer and towered over David. The man was breathing heavy, and David could see the glassy, far-off look in his eyes. He was even more juiced up than Rhonda. David became worried about what the man might do in this state, so he got up to leave. "I'm sorry to bother you. I'll—" David was shoved back into the chair.

The giant took one look at David's reaction, laughed and said, "Don't wet your fuckin' panties, I ain't gonna hurt you. I want you to pass on a message: Tell that fuckin' shrink, Dr. Peckerhead, that he'd better be watching his motherfuckin' back. You tell him Reggie wants his sweet, tight ass; that Reggie's gonna string him up, give it to him just like he did to Corey. Understand?"

"I'm not sure that I do." David squirmed in the chair.

"Don't fuck around with me. Perkerhead's been puttin' his prick where it don't belong. That ain't right. Now get the fuck out of here!"

Reggie backed off and opened the front door. As David passed by Reggie and through the open door, he prepared himself for a boot in the ass, but nothing happened. When the door slammed behind him, David didn't look back. He headed straight for the car. Once inside, it took him a few seconds to steady his trembling hand enough so he was able to put the key in the ignition. In a hurry to leave, David almost backed into Reggie's pickup truck. It was an old style Chevy from the 1950s or 1960s and appeared in perfect condition: shiny black paint, silver rims, high wood sideboards. David pulled on to the grass to sneak around the truck – he wasn't about to go back and ask Reggie to move it – and sped off.

Exactly what had happened between Larry and Corey wasn't clear to David, but he firmly believed it played a major role in Corey's death. The problem was there was no solid evidence, no irrefutable facts to indicate Larry was guilty of anything. At this point, it was all conjecture.

Father Anthony wasn't back from his gruesome visit to the coroner. David was relieved. He was still shaken by his encounter with Rhonda and Reggie and needed time to sort things out; to put the fragmented pieces together and figure out what the hell, if anything, to do next.

Even though they would never acknowledge it, Rhonda and Reggie had Corey's blood on their hands. It was easier, David knew, for the tormented mind and soul to cast blame onto another, and that person was Larry. As fucked up as Rhonda and Reggie were, David couldn't deny the loathing and utter contempt they had displayed for Larry. Their character and credibility was, at best, questionable, yet all of David's instincts told him that what they had intimated was not concocted or some kind of act to cover their own asses.

David felt the need to be clean, to scrub his body raw with water so hot that he could barely stand it. Once in the shower, David backed away from the spray, then leaned into it several times until his skin adjusted and he no longer felt the burn. The pain felt good. It gave him a brief reprieve from thinking about the whole tragic mess before him.

Exhausted from a long day of powerful emotions, the scorching shower was the last straw. David melted, sitting in a heap in the bathtub, while water continued to pour over him. With agony, he returned to his dilemma and realized one thing: He knew what he could not do. He couldn't go to Father Anthony for advice, he couldn't confront Larry with innuendo, and he couldn't tell the authorities, especially Chief Gardner, about his suspicions. No one would believe him! After all, Larry was the pillar of the community, the pride of the city. And Corey was just a menace that no one cared about. He wouldn't even be missed. To top it off, David certainly wasn't anyone's darling. He didn't have enough clout to allege anything about anyone.

"Shit," David said. "What the hell should I do?"

The hot water began to fade, and he let it get colder and colder until it felt like ice was being sprayed on him. This woke him up; forced him out of the haze he'd been in since the dreadful news that morning. With a clear focus, David recognized his next move: He had to uncover something, any kind of solid fact that would exonerate or implicate Larry.

But how and what? David thought, as he rose and turned off the shower.

He reached for a towel, but there were no clean ones left. Dripping wet, he threw on his boxers and scurried down the hall to the closet where the fresh towels were stored. He grabbed the door handle and pulled; the door didn't budge.

Is it locked? David thought. Why the hell would it be locked—? Then, it hit him. Larry's house: The room in the basement that was locked when David was looking around the morning after he had slept over. At the time, he thought it strange it was the only locked door in the house. And the noises I heard! David thought. An ominous feeling crept over him. All his instincts hollered to him that this was the place to start.

David yanked on the handle once more and the closet door popped open. He grabbed a towel and started drying his hair and body. "Now, how can I get in there?"

Preparing for Corey's funeral was the most depressing experience of David's short life as a priest – as a person, it was crushing. The day after Corey's death, Father Anthony collaborated with David in planning the funeral, believing Corey deserved the same treatment that one would get who was greatly loved and admired. Father Anthony had pulled rank and would be the celebrant. When informed of this, David was peeved, but shortly came to realize this was Father Anthony's way of showing David, and all the parishioners, that everyone was worthy of the best St. Cecilia's had to offer.

The rosary would be held Wednesday evening, the Mass and burial the following morning. This seemed speedy to many outside the Church, but David had been involved with enough funerals to believe this was the best way to lay a loved one to rest. The hours and days leading up to a funeral were like a time warp for the family; the world stood still and nothing else mattered.

Beginning Tuesday morning, both priests had repeatedly tried to contact Corey's mother and invite her to help plan the details of the service, like picking out scripture and choosing hymns. When David finally got a hold of Rhonda on the phone it was late in the evening. "You take care of all that funeral shit." She slurred. "Ain't that your job?"

David wanted to rip into her for what she had allowed her son to endure. Instead, he said, "We'd be honored to take care of the details for you. The wake is tomorrow at seven in the evening at Crosby Funeral Home, and the Mass will be held at St. Cecilia's Thursday at ten in the morning. Following the burial at the cemetery, we'll have a lunch in the church basement."

David heard voices in the background and music blasting. Just another drunken, drug-filled evening for Rhonda Hansen. David tried not to judge her; he had to believe she was hurting and knew of no other way to cope.

"Fine," she said quietly. The line went dead.

Earlier in the day, Father Anthony, David and Penny had addressed Corey's death at an all-school gathering in the gymnasium. The bleachers were packed, full of loud, rowdy kids. The local news had already reported on the suicide, so the kids were aware of what had happened. Per Larry's counsel, Father Anthony told the students Corey had passed away and skipped any details. Then, the pastor led the student body in prayer, followed by a moment of silence, though no tears were shed. When finished, the students were dismissed back to class. For these kids, life immediately returned to normal, and they dispersed with the joking and bantering typical of any other assembly.

Father Anthony had wanted all the students to attend the funeral Mass but, after meeting with Larry and Penny, decided to allow only those kids to come who felt a strong need to be there – with their parents' approval. Father Anthony agreed that Larry and Penny were justified in their concern about the possibility of copycat behavior that often accompanies the suicide of a young person. According to Larry, kids who are already vulnerable see the outpouring of attention the deceased receives and it can be enough to push them over the edge.

Larry volunteered to clear his schedule during school hours for the rest of the week so he could be available at school for any kids who might need help dealing with Corey's death. Father Anthony and Penny were grateful to Larry for this selfless act, but David was guarded in his enthusiasm. What's his motive here? David thought. He began to carefully study Larry from a distance, thinking he appeared almost too accommodating, too willing to lend a helping hand.

Larry was the professional here and all of his advice would be followed to the letter, not only because he was an expert, but also to keep the school free from any accusations or lawsuits that it didn't do enough for the students, as if suicide was some kind of contagious disease that could be caught through germs in the school's restrooms. David had found this standard drove most of the decisions made by those in charge. Instead of doing what was right and good for kids, it was all about protecting the school's ass.

David knew these kids well. His hand was on the pulse of the student body, and he firmly believed, like Father Anthony, that attending Corey's funeral would be good for all of them. A little remorse and guilt was healthy for the conscience, and these kids, most of whom treated Corey like a leper, needed to reflect on their behavior and see the reality of what happens when someone is treated so cruelly.

The wake and funeral were sparsely attended. David was pleased to see Rhonda show up early to both. At each service, she dressed appropriately in the same plain black dress, and appeared to be sober. Rhonda never showed any emotion. Her face remained blank and she sat stiff. Not once did she peer around or fidget in the pew; it was as if she was expecting a bolt of lightning to come from above and strike her down.

Father Anthony put his heart and soul into Corey's funeral services. Those in attendance who knew Father Anthony well recognized his effort and were deeply moved. Penny was almost inconsolable. Every time David looked at her, she was dabbing her eyes with a Kleenex or shaking with silent sobs. He made a mental note to get together with her later, after all this was over, to remind her and thank her for all she did to try to help Corey.

Larry was perfect: reserved when appropriate, choking up at the right moments, politely smiling and softly laughing at Father Anthony's charming recollections of some of Corey's more subdued escapades. Throughout, Larry graciously offered to lend a hand wherever needed. But, when Reggie arrived at Thursday's Mass to pick up Rhonda right after communion, David noticed that Reggie scanned the crowd and locked in on Larry. Reggie's glowering eyes never left the man.

That's the second interesting thing I've observed at Church today, David thought.

The first came when lighting the sanctuary candles in preparation for the funeral Mass: Lizzy and Erik walked into church together. Initially, for the first time in days, David's heart soared. He thought, Maybe things are getting better between the two. God knows a tragedy like this would make parents rethink their priorities. His thoughts drifted to Christopher and how he was doing. Then, as fast as seeing Lizzy and Erik together made his heart soar, the sight of Larry entering the church right behind the two filled David's mind with dread and alarm.

Larry dipped two fingers into the marble bowl filled with holy water and made the sign of the cross. David's hands began to shake. The taper he was using to light one of the large white candles next to the lectern struck the candle, causing it to fall to the floor. David picked it up and placed the candle back on its perch. All the while, he continued to watch Larry, who was now greeting Lizzy and Erik. As the three stood in the back of the church chatting, David was frozen with panic. He had been so preoccupied with what had taken place over the last couple of days that he had completely forgotten that Christopher remained in therapy with Larry.

The Pattens and Larry ended their conversation and went to sit down. As Lizzy and Erik walked up the aisle, she gave David a short wave and a melancholy smile. When Erik was seated, he quickly looked up at David and acknowledged him with a nod. He wasn't sure how to interpret this gesture. Was Erik embarrassed about his rant at David? Was this an initial attempt to make amends? Or was Erik civilly acknowledging a former friend? David returned the gesture, but it was too late; Erik was looking away.

Seeing the two talking with Larry left David shaken. After all, he was solely responsible for Christopher being in Larry's care. David thought, I begged Lizzy to send Christopher to Larry, all because I was afraid that I might screw things up. Now the mystery surrounding Larry took on an added meaning, and the urgency to find out the truth rushed through David like a raging river plunging over a waterfall. He had to do something, and fast.

Larry was a no-show at the burial and luncheon. According to Father Anthony, Larry had received an emergency phone call from a colleague in Minneapolis who needed a consultation on an unusually difficult case. So, Larry was now on the road to Falls City to catch a plane. Father Anthony mentioned this was odd because it had never happened before. Larry always consulted over the phone or scheduled a visit well in advance.

David suspected something else: Since there were only a handful of people in attendance at the funeral and burial, there would be an even smaller group of mourners at the lunch. That meant Larry would have to come face to face with Rhonda – and, if he showed up, Reggie. These were encounters David had hoped to observe.

Later that evening, while sitting alone in church, David knew that what he was about to do was wrong; a sin any way he sliced it. There was no way to rationalize his way out of this one. But it was the lesser of two evils, he had reasoned. This was one of those King Solomon decisions Father Anthony had warned David he would face many times as a priest. He wasn't in church to pray for guidance; that wouldn't be fair. Plus, he knew what the answer would be, and he didn't want to hear it. No, David was there to ask for forgiveness for what he was about to do.

Father Anthony had left that afternoon for a weekend visit he had scheduled weeks ago with his sister and niece. A snowstorm had been forecasted to blast across the plains later that night, and Father Anthony wanted to get an early start and outrace it to Falls City. His niece, a senior in high school, was playing in the finals of the state volleyball tournament that weekend. Father Anthony was a regular at all her big games, and he desperately wanted to be there for her last high school match.

"I hope you don't mind, but I can't miss Fae's last game" Father Anthony said. "And to be honest with you, I need to get away." David could see that the last few days had taken a tremendous toll on the man, so he encouraged Father Anthony to take off before the storm hit.

Everything was in place. The stage was set. Larry was out of town. Father Anthony was on the road, speeding toward the welcome distraction of his sister and niece. David sat in a pew at the back of the church. He was dressed in his blacks. Slowly, he removed the white collar; he couldn't wear it where he was going. With a heavy heart he stood up, slid into the aisle, genuflected and made the sign of the cross while looking at the crucifix at the front of the church.

"Forgive me."

Around 9:30 p.m., David decided to leave. Six inches of snow were already on the ground and the forecast called for another three to six inches. Fierce northerly winds were gusting up to forty miles per hour, forming huge snowdrifts all over the city. Snowplows were out in full force, clearing the streets and highways, but it was a futile endeavor. Ten minutes after the plows cleaned a path, the cold winds swept the snow back over the roads. Traveling conditions were treacherous: Interstate 16 was closed west of Willa due to jackknifed semis and cars spinning off of the slippery highway. The winter storm that the National Weather Service had predicted was now a full-fledged blizzard.

The police and state patrol were asking people to stay at home, but David had to do this tonight, no matter how bad the weather. He wasn't sure when Larry was due back. Father Anthony never mentioned it and David didn't think to ask. Plus, he thought, with the poor weather, there probably won't be any phone calls to the parish tonight, so no one will know I'm gone.

David's greatest fear was that he would be seen headed towards Larry's house. That fear was now abated by the fact that very few people, if any, would be out in these conditions; the town-folk had too much respect for a snowstorm of this magnitude. This could be the only opportunity to get a look inside Larry's house and find something, anything to prove or disprove Larry's connection to Corey's suicide.

To protect himself from the elements, David dressed in his warmest winter garb: a turtleneck covered by a heavy cotton sweatshirt, thermal long underwear, black jeans, thick wool socks under heavy hiking boots, ski parka, gloves, and a black stocking cap. He trudged through the snow to start the Honda. First, he had to sweep the drifted snow piles off the front and back windshields. He let the car warm up, and soon realized the sub-zero wind chills wouldn't allow the heater and defrost to spit out air much warmer than the outside temperature. "Piece of shit," David said, as he wiped fog off the inside of the front windshield with his glove.

Driving cautiously, he crawled along the streets. As an added precaution, he took back streets to get to the main highway that led to Larry's private road. This was a much longer route, and the going was slower and tougher due to the unplowed streets, but David wanted to avoid being seen by a plow operator, policeman or some other city emergency crew member. The whole scheme knotted up his stomach, but if he was going to do this he was going to do it right – and that meant not getting caught.

The usual twenty-minute drive to Larry's took over an hour, and David had to temper his desire to speed things up. He had to get this done quickly; the conditions were deteriorating fast. In a couple of hours he might not be able to make it back to the rectory.

Once on the highway he kept both hands locked on the steering wheel as he fought with the strong gusts of wind that were pushing the car off the road. With the snow coming down almost sideways he had to lean forward, his head inches away from the front windshield, to see the outline of the road. On a couple of occasions only quick reflexes kept him from crashing into a snow-drifted ditch.

Traveling at the slow pace caused David to become disoriented. The snow-covered terrain blended together so that the once familiar natural landmarks were now unrecognizable. He kept his eyes peeled for the wood mailbox right off the highway that marked the entrance to Larry's property.

The mailbox was easy to spot; it was out in the open and not covered by drifts – yet. He turned off the highway and stopped before heading up the private road. It disappeared into a forest of trees, so it was impossible to see or determine how much snow and drifting had taken place on the twisting uphill path. The towering trees provided some shelter, but that only meant the snowdrifts would be haphazardly spread out along the road. To be prudent, he decided to drive only as far as the snow would allow. If he ran into any problems he'd hoof it the rest of the way.

"Anyway," David said, as he surveyed the situation, "I can't leave the car right out in the open."

Inching forward, he disappeared into the trees. Within one hundred yards, David spotted the first questionable drift. Any other day he would've just plowed through it, but he wasn't willing to gamble getting stuck. He looked for a wide area to turn the car around, but the road was too narrow and elevated. So, he decided to leave the car right where it was and back it out later if he needed to. David blasted the heater fan to high. Since the car was now sheltered from the cold wind, he decided to leave it running so it was warm and ready to go as soon as he returned. Digging out was the last thing he could risk when finished.

The walk on the snow-covered road was long, about a mile or so, but not too strenuous. The overhanging branches and thick brush shielded the road from the foul weather, and David encountered only a couple of large drifts. When he arrived at the driveway, he concluded that a trip up the road in his small car with bald tires would not have been possible.

He walked directly to the front door, took a glove off and reached into his front jeans pocket. "What the hell?" David ripped off his other glove and let both fall onto the snow, as he frantically searched his pockets for the key to Larry's front door. Father Anthony had a spare one for emergencies, and also for a welcomed retreat from the rectory when Larry was out of town. Before Father Anthony left for Falls City, David had snatched the key from the elder priest's key chain.

"Where did I put the damn thing? The ashtray!" David pictured himself setting the key there for safekeeping. "Shit!" He plucked his gloves from the ground and put them back on.

For the hell of it, he tried the front door. Locked. Looking around, he decided to check two other doors and even some windows before going back to retrieve the key. This was taking a lot longer than he had envisioned, and his intuition said to hurry up.

David tried the garage door – nothing. Peering inside a small garage window, he could see that Larry's Landrover was gone. Next, he tromped to one side of the house and checked another door, then two ground-level windows – one on the other side of the house and one by the front door. No luck. They were all shut tight. Defeated, he was about to make the long trek to the car when a thought occurred to him, What about the sliding glass door on the back deck?

"Might as well give it a shot."

A deep snowdrift, all the way up to David's knees, covered the narrow path that led around to the back of the house. He plodded through the drift and up the slick stairs to the deck. Huffing and puffing, David tugged at the sliding glass door. It moved slightly. Encouraged, he thought snow and ice might be keeping the door from opening, so he began brushing snow off the runner. After a couple of swipes with his gloves, he discovered a round wooden pole wedged inside. Quickly, David worked to get the bar out. It was packed in with the snow, so he used his bare fingers to scrape and, eventually, pull it out. He rose and gave the door one hard pull. It moved. Another pull and the door was open wide enough to squeeze through.

David hesitated. Once he went though, there was no turning back. On the other side was sin, and a crime. Everything he preached against was staring him in the face. He thought about why he was there: Corey's memory, Christopher's future. David's inner struggle ended with the thought of these two boys. He grabbed his gloves, held his breath – like one leaping from a plane on an inaugural parachute jump – and entered Larry's home.

Some snow had blown through the opening and was melting on the tiled kitchen floor. Also, David had to brush off the snow that clung to his jeans and boots before going any further. Looking around the kitchen, he spied a roll of paper towels. He took some time to clean up the puddles and dry off his clothes before beginning the search. Satisfied that evidence of his presence wouldn't be tracked through the house, David balled up the paper towels and shoved them into his coat pocket.

Some lights had been left on throughout the house, although he didn't need them. Even in the dark, David knew the layout of the house well enough to negotiate his way to the basement. Once there he went directly to Larry's office; the same room where David had spent time getting his life together, finally finding some freedom and serenity.

He had a hard time rummaging through Larry's desk to find Corey's file. It felt dirty. But David focused away from the act itself and thought only of the purpose of his actions. It didn't make it any easier but, at least, it allowed him to get the job done. He found Corey's files with relative ease. They were massive. All the information was tightly packed into two brown accordion folders, both about three inches thick. After five minutes of scouring the files, David concluded there wasn't anything telling or useful. They contained a mountain of detailed notes of Corey's sessions, all chronicled in psychobabble David didn't understand. He put them back.

David reasoned, If any of this stuff was incriminating, it wouldn't be kept where it would be easily found. It would be hidden, or even destroyed. After probing the rest of the office, he realized this room held no answers. It was squeaky clean. So he double-checked to make sure everything was back exactly where he had found it. Once satisfied, he went out into the main room of the basement. David's curiosity immediately pulled him toward the door that led to the only room he had never entered or seen in all the time he'd spent there. Hand trembling, he reached for the doorknob and tried to turn it.

"I can't get a damn break." David felt like kicking the locked door down, but he knew better. Instead, he dropped into a beanbag chair and thought about his options. Quitting at this point was out of the question, so he focused on how to get in the room.

"Maybe in his desk drawer," David said, after a few minutes of contemplation. He labored to get up from the mushy chair and hurried back to Larry's office.

David walked over to the desk and opened the middle drawer. There was office supply junk spread all over. He began rummaging through the contents in the drawer.

"Bingo." From the back depths of the drawer, he pulled out a metal ring that held two keys. Examining them closely, they had a similar cut and generic appearance – the type of keys that typically come with a new desk or filing cabinet...or doors for the inside of a home.

First, David looked at the desk and couldn't find any keyholes. Next, he examined both filing cabinets; the keys were much too large for their locks. These were keys to a door; David was sure of it. On the way out of the office, he stuck one in the lock built into the doorknob. It fit. David turned it and felt the doorknob latch. Hopeful, he returned to the locked door. When he put the key in, it fit. With one turn, the lock clicked and the doorknob moved. He was in.

Slowly, hesitantly, he opened the door, as if the devil himself was waiting on the other side. The room was pitch dark. With one hand clinging tightly to the doorknob, David fumbled around, feeling the wall next to the entrance for a light switch. "There it is," he said in a whisper. He flicked on the lights and scanned the room. His first impression was that this was some kind of production studio. It was bare and stale. David's nervous, heavy breaths amplified off the white-washed walls and cement floor. There was a door leading outside to the back of the house, but no windows.

This was strange for a number of reasons. To start with, every other room in the house had at least one window; most rooms had several. Also, Larry believed that windows were healthy because they provided one with a sense of openness. Finally, he cherished the views of the surrounding forest that the windows provided.

David spied a video camera perched on top of a tripod that was positioned by the far wall. It was aimed in the direction of a black-leather sofa. Behind the video camera was a bookcase with shelves full of neatly stacked videotapes. An empty video case and two cameras, one with a large lens attached, sat on the floor close to the tripod. To his left was a long table. Sitting on it was a computer monitor with a large screen, a color laser printer, and a scanner; all were connected to a computer tower underneath the table. Other than a phone, an answering machine – the old kind that required a cassette tape – and a folding metal chair for the table, that was it: no paintings or decorations or knickknacks.

After debating where to start searching, David walked over to the table and opened a fat drawer built into the table's lower left side. In it, dozens of computer diskettes were scattered around. He reached in, rummaging through the disks, when he felt a cold metal object. Right away he knew what it was, and carefully brought out the gun. He had seen and used shotguns and rifles many times, mostly during hunting trips for pheasant or duck when he was young – a normal pastime for kids growing up in small Midwestern towns. But he had never seen a handgun up close. It looked like the type of gun used in old western movies. He inspected it and clicked open the chamber that held the ammunition. It was loaded. This made David nervous, like the gun would go off by itself, so he put it back.

David picked up a couple of diskettes. They were labeled with one or two capital letters and numbers, such as EO 10, M 13 and so on.

"What does it mean?" He examined a couple of disks to try and find any other identification marks. There were none. His curiosity was piqued, so he turned on the Macintosh computer. It revved to life. He flicked on the monitor and the computer was already finished with the startup process.

Choosing a disk labeled JP 11, he inserted it into the floppy drive on the tower. Once opened, there were ten separate files to choose from. They were simply labeled 1, 2, 3 and so on, all the way up to 10. David stroked the whiskers on his chin with his left hand and clicked on the first file. It hesitated, then opened, revealing its contents.

"Oh, my lord." His head and shoulders slumped forward, and his left hand and arm dropped to the table, as if the nerves and muscles had gone dead. The image on the screen was repulsive, but he couldn't take his eyes off it.

"God, he can't be more than nine or ten years old." David opened another file only to find a similar image. He viewed all ten files, hoping that these were mistakes, some kind of electronic accident, and that the real content would appear and explain this all away. But the substance of every file on the disk was the same.

He took his glasses off and rested his head in his hands. The images of the naked little boy in provocative poses went around and around in his mind's eye, and he couldn't erase them. David's eyes welled up, but knew he couldn't lose it; not here, not now.

The phone on the table rang out. Alarmed, he fumbled for his glasses and they fell to the floor. Another ring, followed by four sharp, static-filled beeps. The cassette on the answering machine began to rewind. David picked up his glasses, put them on and stared at the recorder in horror. It stopped. Another click and the tape began to play. A voice said, "Hello Dr. Peck, this is Dr. Greenberg returning your call. You can reach me at my office at…" Panic set in, overwhelming David's senses. He didn't hear the rest of the message.

"Is he...?" David said. "No, he can't be."

One short, static-filled beep activated another message.

After a few moments of study, the answer hit him. "Larry's checking his messages from his car phone!"

David ejected the disk, and stuck it in his coat pocket. Seeking to get out of the house quickly, he neglected to properly shut down the computer. Instead, he pressed the power switch on the tower and the computer went dead. He scanned the room to make sure that nothing was disturbed or out of place, then raced for the door. Half way there, he stopped and whirled around.

"I need more," David said, clenching his fists tight.

Backtracking, he ran to the table, opened the drawer and snatched another disk. Then, he hustled to the bookshelf and grabbed a videotape. They weren't titled, and he didn't have time to peruse them, so he randomly picked one. David bent down and lifted up one of the cameras; it was heavy and unfamiliar. "Where is the film?" he said. Turning it over, he saw the name and model. "Digital? For the computer," he reasoned out loud. "I don't know how these damn things work." He set the camera back down in the same spot. Except for the lens, the other camera looked identical, so he left it alone.

He shut off the lights, closed the door and sprinted upstairs to the sliding glass door he had entered earlier. Once outside, David struggled to place the bar back into the runner. Looking over his finished work, he closed his eyes and sighed heavily. In his hurry to bolt from the premises and shove the bar in place, he had cluttered the snow in front of the sliding glass door with footprints. He scooped snow into the imprints and tried to smooth them over. It looked awful.

Not wanting to repeat the same blunder, he aimed each step for a footprint that he had made on his way in. Carefully, David tiptoed and treaded lightly across the deck, retracing his tracks to the stairs. His thoughts drifted to the answering machine. He hoped he was wrong and that Larry wasn't calling from his car phone. David thought, If Larry was, he's headed back this way. But he wouldn't drive in this crap, would he?

His focus elsewhere, David slipped and skidded down the first few stairs. He grabbed the railing to keep from tumbling all the way down. At the bottom, he looked back up at the snow that had splashed off the stairs and railing. Disgusted, he shook his head and hoped the storm would continue raging – or even pick up in intensity. Scanning up and around at the dense cover of the surrounding trees and brush, he knew it would take a while for the mess he had made to be masked.

After the debacle on the deck and stairs, he determined he couldn't afford to leave any more calling cards. So, instead of traveling back down the road to his car, he would trek through the forest. He entered the woods about ten yards from the road. From there, he sped as fast as he could through the dense woodland, swatting snow-covered branches out of his way, falling twice when he tripped over some shrub or stick hidden under the deep snow. A sharp tree branch slapped him in the face during his first fall and, as David emerged from the woods, he touched his cheek and found blood on his glove.

With the car still idling, hot exhaust had sputtered from the tail pipe melting a large space in the surrounding snow. David hopped into the car. He was huffing and puffing from the frantic run and sweating profusely due to the heavy layers of clothes he had on. Warmth radiated from the car's heater. David felt as if he had stepped into a sauna. Instantly, his glasses fogged over. Several times, he wiped the condensation off, only for it to return. The glasses were useless; they needed time to thaw out. He tossed them onto the passenger seat.

As he squinted out the back windshield, David put the car in reverse and started moving. Without his glasses, there was no hope of finding a place to safely turn around. Slowly, he backed out, using the blurry outline of the trees as a guide. Without incident, he arrived at the clearing in front of the highway. Once past the tree line, the strong wind and blowing snow smacked the car and forced him to adjust to keep a straight path. Snow was beginning to drift and cover the entrance, so he was very careful as he turned the car around. Before getting on the highway, he tried on his glasses. Again, no luck.

"Fuck'em," David said, as he threw them back on the passenger seat. The front and side windows also were fogging up, and he had to wipe a peephole on the front windshield with the sleeve of his coat in order to see the road.

David eased out onto the recently plowed highway and headed for the rectory. As he gained confidence that the road was passable, he shifted into second gear and began to speed up. He checked the rearview mirror and noticed two small points of light approaching. Headlights, David thought. And they were getting closer. Abruptly, they appeared to go backwards, and he stared in alarm as the vehicle stopped and turned into the entrance of Larry's property. It hesitated at the tree line. David grabbed his glasses. "It better not be him!" He frantically wiped off the condensation. This time they didn't fog over. He put the glasses on, but it was too late. The headlights had already disappeared into the trees.

CHAPTER 9

On the way home, the snowfall began to taper. However, the winds picked up and howled across the land, haphazardly shaping snowdrifts, some the size of boulders, that David was forced to maneuver around. It was nearly 1 a.m. before he made it back to the rectory. Once inside, David peeled off his soggy clothes and set them in the laundry room to dry. His jeans were soaked from the clinging snow that had melted on the ride home. As he emptied the pants' contents, he pulled out the two keys he had snatched from Larry's desk drawer. David blankly stared at the keys dangling from the ring. Rubbing his matted-down hair, he took off his glasses and massaged his weary eyes. The adrenaline was spent; he was drained from a long night of struggle and startling discoveries.

Replaying each step, the scads of clues he had left behind came tumbling back: the footprints littering the snow; the keys to the room also meant the door was unlocked; the computer shut down improperly would lead to an error message when turned on; and, of course, the disks and tape – the booty of the ordeal. All this was the obvious evidence that would provide Larry with proof someone had invaded his home.

Disgusted, David threw the jeans against the dryer. "Well, at least I know I'm in the right profession."

In need of dry clothes, David went off to his room. He slid into sweats and thick wool socks. Fingering the three keys to Larry's house, two keys to the inside doors and the key to the front door that was swiped from Father

Anthony's key ring, he scanned the room. At this point, it was impossible to put the keys back where they belonged, so they had to be hidden. David hoped the two men wouldn't miss the keys before he had a chance to plant them back in their rightful places. He settled on a spot: the top dresser drawer, his junk drawer. He stuffed the three keys into a leather pouch that also contained a treasured possession, a rosary blessed by the Pope.

After a hot bath, David went to the kitchen for some leftovers. Even though he hadn't eaten since breakfast, he had no appetite and grew nauseated at the sight of the warmed-up pizza. David threw the slices in the trash and went to the den to check for phone messages. To his surprise, there were five.

Beep. "Father Anthony, are you there?" David recognized Janet Manelli's voice. "I've got to talk with you right away...it's my father. I'll try you on your mobile phone." David wrote a message to Father Anthony on a yellow-sticky note and tacked it to the corkboard the two priests used for messages and other correspondence.

Beep. "David, it's Father Anthony. Just wanted to let you know that I arrived safely, only a few inches on the ground here. It wasn't a bad drive at all, the farther south I went the better it got. Sounds like the bulk of the storm stayed up that way. Anyway, I'll see you Sunday. Have a great weekend. Oh, I heard on the car radio that Tasker won't be playing. Hurt his knee. Of all the stupid things...I mean, couldn't the kid wait until after the game to go sledding? With our best linebacker out, I don't know if we have enough fire power to—" *Beep.* Typical.

David had completely forgotten about the state championship game Friday night between the Crusaders and the Taylorville Tornadoes. In comparison to what was currently happening in his life, the game was just that: a silly, inconsequential game, one that didn't pique his interest anymore.

Beep. "Hello, this is Lizzy calling for Father David. Give me a call when you're free." She sounded good. Upbeat.

Beep. "David, this is Erik...Erik Patten." David sat down at the desk and leaned toward the answering machine. He sounds tired, David thought. "Hey, I've been sitting in my hotel room thinking...and...well, I'd really like to get together and talk whenever you're available. I'm scheduled to land in Falls City late tomorrow afternoon. By the time I drive up, and with all the snow it sounds like we're getting there, it'll probably be...umm... Why don't I just call you when I get in and see if you're around. Thanks. Oh, if you happen to run into Lizzy or Christopher please don't mention when I'm coming home. Goodbye." David stared at the machine, as if another message would immediately follow Erik's and explain what that all meant.

Beep. "Anthony, hello, it's Larry." David's back stiffened. "I just walked in the door and wanted to give you a run down on the roads before you left in the morning. After the first twenty miles or so out of Willa, it's pretty smooth sailing all the way to Falls City. Just take it easy on the way out of town. Hey, I know this sounds weird with the storm and all, but did you stop by the house tonight? It's no big deal. I was just curious because—" Larry stopped; the hair on David's neck and arms began to tingle. "Ah, if I don't talk with you, have a great visit." This was said quickly, as if something very important just came up that had to be attended to right away.

"He knows I was there."

David took a deep breath. "Maybe I'm wrong and just being paranoid." His gut told him not to be a fool. The man knew. It was time to prepare for the worst-case scenario. This meant viewing the videotape and the other disk. Knowledge of what these contained was David's only protection – and ammunition.

He brought the items to the den. First, he went to the computer. The rectory had inherited an older model

Macintosh from the school last year after some new ones were purchased for the students and the school office. Flipping the power switch on, the machine came to life.

The disk he put in the floppy drive was labeled TR 9. Several files required more memory than the old computer could handle and couldn't be opened. After a few clicks on other files, David found one that the computer was capable of launching. The content was the same as the other disk: A boy, this time younger and smaller, laying naked on the studio's black-leather couch. David's heart fell to his stomach. Of the thirteen files on the disk, the computer was able to open four others; all were similar photos of the same little boy.

David snatched the videotape off the desk. He was getting past the initial shock and disgust. Slapping the tape in the VCR, he pressed the play button. It was seeing the movement and actually hearing the voices and other sounds that caught David completely off-guard. He stood in stunned silence, watching as another young boy buried his head in the crotch of a much older boy. The young boy's head awkwardly jerked up and down, like a slinky with bent metal rings. David wanted to take his eyes off the screen, but couldn't; he was spellbound.

After a few minutes, the tape cut to a different scene. In it was Corey. He looked younger – a year, maybe two – than David remembered. The boy was standing next to the same black-leather couch. He began to take his clothes off. His face was stern. Once undressed, Corey looked at the camera – not right at the lens, more off to the side. Unlike the last scene, there was no sound. David speculated that Larry was choreographing. Corey laid down on the couch and began fondling his penis until it was stiff. David fell heavily into the recliner and watched the rest of the scene play out. Once done, the tape ended and the VCR clicked to a stop.

The TV screen was now black and white fuzz, and the sound snapped back on, filling the room with loud static. But it didn't annoy him; it was simply white noise. His mind was elsewhere.

How could he do this kind of perverted shit? David howled in his head. I mean, this is Larry! A man who's committed his life to helping kids. An expert on the subject of sexual abuse. Then, David added out loud, "And, the man that helped save me. How in God's name could he be involved with stuff like this?"

David hurled the VCR controller against the wall. The top exploded off and the innards flew around the room.

"That son of a bitch!" Tears stung his eyes. He wiped them away with a swipe from his sweatshirt. David thought frantically, That bastard needs to be stopped before another boy winds up hurt...or dead.

David took a deep breath and reasoned, If Larry's harboring this kind of filth, he's got to be involved in more than just downloading pictures off the Internet or shooting videos.

Now, David's chief concern and greatest fear was for Christopher. He could be Larry's next target. David's godson was the perfect victim: in crisis and desperate for the attention of a male figure. Knowing what it felt like to live and recover from a monster's rape, David cried out, "I will not allow that to happen!"

David awoke to brilliant rays of sunlight – illuminated even more brightly from their reflection off the fresh snow – penetrating the den's windows and piercing his dry, tired eyes. Hesitantly, they fluttered opened. He had fallen asleep in the recliner. The TV was still on, blaring out static. Pushing himself out of the chair, he turned off the irritating noise. His head was pounding from lack of sleep, and his body was stiff and sore from the old chair. He looked at the

VCR and knew that the memories and visions from the night before were no dream. No, this was all very real.

The clock read 6:16 a.m. David had less that fifteen minutes to get ready for Mass. And, because confessions were heard on Wednesdays and Fridays during the weekday, he also would have that duty.

"Well, at least school's got to be canceled." Groggy, he stretched his arms wide in an attempt to get started. He went to pop the tape from the VCR – it was gone. "What the hell?" He walked over to the computer and found that the disks also were missing. David looked at the clock again and saw time ticking away. "I'll look after Mass."

With all of the snow, attendance would be very light, only a few of the devout. David made a pot of Father Anthony strength coffee and shuffled down the hallway for a quick shower and change of clothes. Grabbing a fresh towel, he decided a short Mass would serve him, and those who showed up, well. After his priestly responsibilities, he would wrestle with when and how to confront Larry. Right now, David needed a hot shower, a heavy dose of caffeine and some help from God.

The snow that covered the church's parking lot and walkways had already been cleared by Tom Meyer – a well-meaning parishioner who for years had put the church at the top of his list for snow removal and grass cutting. David was grateful, but he also knew old Tom wouldn't be at Mass this morning or the next day; after all, there was money to be made, and that always seemed to change plans.

When David peered out of the sacristy door toward the pews, he chuckled to himself. The exact people that he had guessed would be there were kneeling, patiently waiting for Mass to begin. He sleepwalked through the first portion of the service. When he got to the homily, he realized he wasn't prepared. But he was too tired and distracted to fret, so he calmly did what Father Anthony was so good at: Letting the Holy Spirit take over. David did his best, in the fewest words possible, to spontaneously attach some significance to the readings and Gospel. From the looks, or lack thereof, on the faces of those in attendance – all four of them – he felt like he did a pretty good job of working without a net for the first time.

When Mass ended, David went to the confessional, opened the door, and turned on the light that signaled it was showtime. These folks were traditionalists and preferred the artificial privacy and anonymity of the small booth and screen. Younger kids seemed to be the only ones who were open to face-to-face confession.

"The innocence of youth," he sighed, as he sat down on the padded bench seat.

Confession was a sacrament David dearly loved and held in the highest regard. During this time, he truly felt like God's instrument. He allowed others to cast off burdens, and provided those who were suffering and racked with guilt an opportunity to wipe their conscience clean. The transformation many people made after confessing their sins and carrying out their penance was awesome and remarkable.

David slid open the wooden panel that covered the screen.

"Bless me Father for I have sinned, my last confession was two days ago." It was Mrs. Horst. She was always the first one. The other parishioners would sit in the pews until Mrs. Horst was kneeling and saying penance before they made a move to the confessional. As a matter of fact, David knew the sequence of who would come first, second, third, and fourth this morning. There was an unspoken hierarchy among the regulars, with the pecking order usually determined by age or the amount of service given to the Church and school.

As usual, Mrs. Horst was done in a matter of minutes. There's not a lot of sinning an 86-year-old woman can do in a couple of days.

"For your penance," David said, "Say two Our Fathers and one Hail Mary."

"Don't you mean two Hail Marys and one Our Father?" Mrs. Horst retorted.

The penance David had given was the reverse of her usual one. But he was ornery and tired and in no mood to be pushed around.

"Well," he said, "I think it's best if we stick with the two Our Fathers and one Hail Mary."

"But…I— Oh, fine!" There was some rustling as Mrs. Horst struggled to get up from the kneeler, her cane banging against the walls of the tiny room. He heard the door burst open, then shut with a force that caused his ears to pop.

There wasn't any ruckus during the next two confessions; both parishioners were in and out in a hurry. But he had to wait on the fourth person. After three or four minutes, David rose from the bench. He wanted to see if Mr. Obera – the only other person who was at Mass, and a sporadic participant during confession – was still around. David sat back down upon hearing the confessor door open. While uncovering the screen, he put a hand over his mouth to stifle a yawn. *Man, I need some more coffee*, he thought.

Once settled in, there was no sound from the other side. So, he said, "Go ahead, whenever you're comfortable." More silence. This wasn't unusual; some people needed to get up the gumption.

"Bless me Father for I have sinned." The man's voice was barely audible, just a hair above a whisper. David thought, *That's not Mr. Obera.* Uncrossing his legs, David scooted to the edge of the bench and bent forward so his face was inches from the screen.

"My last confession was a week ago," the man said.

David sat straight up, his body rigid and tense, as if the dentist was about to drill without using Novocain. His mouth dropped open when he finally placed the voice.

Larry! David scooted back from the screen as if it was on fire and spitting flames.

"Father," the voice said a little louder. Now he was sure it was Larry. "I have sinned." His voice cracked and he hesitated to continue.

"Go on," David said gently, as he always did with those who were having trouble spitting something out.

"I'm...I'm afraid."

David was unsure what to do or say next. So, he continued to encourage Larry to open up, like he would for anyone else. "I know it can be difficult but don't be afraid. What you say here is between you and the Lord."

"But my sins are unforgivable." Larry stopped. David let the silence hang in the air. There were sniffles from the other side, a cough, a clearing of the throat.

Finally, David said, "All your sins will be forgiven when you ask and repent."

He couldn't believe what was happening. He thought, What the hell am I supposed to say and do here? This man's the devil himself. David took a deep breath, gathered himself and reasoned, Okay, Larry's still one of God's children and I have to honor that. While in the confessional, I must treat him like anyone one who is suffering and asking for God's forgiveness. I may not like it, but it's not up to me to pass judgment.

"These times can be very difficult," David said. "Take comfort in knowing that God loves all of His children, and that He is a forgiving God. Put your faith in His hands. Give Him your sins so that He may take away your burdens."

The exhalations from Larry's nostrils whistled at a higher and higher pitch. David moved closer to the screen again. He could feel his heart pounding; the vessels in his temples pulsated with the burden of added blood. His fingertips were icy cold, and he had to rub his hands together to rid the numbness.

"I have a sickness," Larry said. There was no emotion in his voice now. It was detached and cold, as if he was repeating his social security number to someone for the millionth time. "I know it's wrong, but I can't control it. I want to stop. I've tried...God knows I have. I'm like an alcoholic who can't stop drinking."

"Go on," David prodded, doing his best to ignore the last remark.

"I've touched kids...and taken advantage of the vulnerable ones. It's easy for me to get them to do what I want. I've used them. I don't know what to do. Help me."

As Larry talked around the edges, David squirmed in his seat.

Larry continued, "I know these kids have been hurt by what I've done. But, the last boy...I never thought he'd go that far. He was a lot sicker than I ever imagined. And now he's gone. He was just so...so messed up." Larry was seeking David's support, but he would give nothing. As a priest, he would do what was required, but no more. Larry was responsible for Corey's death, and David wasn't about to personally give the man any relief. So he remained quiet.

After a few seconds of silence, Larry said, "And now there's another one. A boy who I'm afraid I might not be able to stay away from." David detected a change in Larry's voice; an edginess, like a child who wasn't getting his way and needed to switch to a new tactic. Christopher! David screamed in his head. *That bastard is talking about Christopher!*

"He's a good boy, and I want to leave him alone. I know I could if I try real hard. I just hope my activities with the other boy don't somehow get in the way."

Larry knows that I was in his house and that I know his secret! He's threatening me, telling me to back off and keep my mouth shut or else Christopher's next!

David could tell by the steeliness in Larry's voice that he meant business. On the defensive now, David wasn't about to do or say anything to piss off this man.

I've got to protect Christopher at all costs, David thought.

"I'm asking for...I need God's forgiveness," Larry demanded.

David's hands began to tremble and his breathing accelerated as his fury grew. He wanted to blast through the screen, pull the bastard out of the confessional, and drag his ass kicking and screaming down to the police station.

Christopher, David thought, as he tried to calm himself down. Remember Christopher. David realized he had no alternative except to play Larry's game.

"Are these your sins?"

"Yes, Father," Larry said smugly.

"Then God absolves you of these sins. For your penance, stop at each station of the cross and say one Our Father. Go in peace and sin no more." Larry's door shut before David finished.

His back hit the wall as he slumped on the confessional bench. "Larry wasn't here to ask for forgiveness," David said in a whisper. "He was here to deliver a message. And he did it during confession because he knows I'm vowed to silence and can't reveal anything to anyone now." David sighed, as if the damage was beyond repair.

Maybe if I just leave things alone Christopher will be okay, David thought desperately.

He shot out of the confessional, then stopped in his tracks and slowed down. He scanned the church. Everyone was gone. Hurriedly, he straightened up the altar, put his alb away and hustled back to the rectory. He had to develop a plan; a way to stop Larry from ever harming another child, especially Christopher.

David waited about an hour before he called Lizzy; the first step in the strategy he was developing on the run. "I'm glad you called," she said. "Survive the storm last night? I was a little worried. I tried to get a hold of you but all I got was the answering machine. You weren't out in that stuff were you?"

"Oh, just for a bit. It really wasn't too bad," David said. "Hey, I got your message."

"Good. You know, it's been ages since we've seen you. I'll bet you're busy now that you've settled in. But if it works with your schedule, and the roads are drivable, I wanted to invite you over for dinner tonight – chili's on the menu – and to watch the football game. Erik's on a business trip, so it'll be Christopher and me. I know it's kind of late, but—"

"That's the best offer I've had in a long time," David said. "I'd love to come over." Lizzy's chili was temptation enough, but he saw the opening he needed. Obviously, she was unaware of her husband's demand that David stay away and of their confrontation. At this point, however, David didn't care. Plus, with the storm, Erik probably wouldn't be back until very late. "What time?"

"Game's at seven." Lizzy was obviously delighted. "Come on over around six, or earlier if you can. We'll be around all day."

"Sounds great. Can I bring anything?"

"Nope, just yourself. With your car, I'll just be happy if you make it here."

David laughed. "Hey, it's like an old pair of shoes, plus it gets the job done – most of the time anyway."

"I'll believe it when I see you. Maybe we should make it five o'clock, give you a big cushion."

Clearly, Lizzy was in a good mood, and that meant trouble for David and his mission of eradicating Larry from the Patten's lives. "Well, I've got five o'clock Mass tonight. But if attendance is anything like what happened on the last game day, I'll be there before five-thirty."

"Just come on over whenever it's good for you," Lizzy chirped.

David laid on the couch in the den and put his hands behind his head to cup it. The flimsy pillows and cushions that covered the wood couch provided a little more comfort this way. Without thinking, he turned on the TV – the same one Corey had spent so much time playing video games on – and quickly turned it off at the memory of this. The last thing he wanted to do was watch anything on that television set.

David looked up at the yellowed ceiling with paint peeling around the light fixture and weighed his two options: To tell Lizzy what he had heard in confession and break his vow of silence, meaning life as a priest was over. Or try and talk her out of continuing to use Larry as a therapist, while revealing nothing about his lurid behavior. Once Christopher was out of harm's way, David could figure out some kind of a plan to bait Larry into showing his true colors – without breaking the vow. There was no surefire answer. David would have to play this one by ear. The thought of no longer being a priest, of giving up what he was called to do, banged around in his mind until his head throbbed.

"Stop!" David barked. "I don't have to make any decisions right now, and maybe I won't have to make any at all."

Tiredly, he sighed. From Lizzy's upbeat tone, it didn't take a genius to gather that all was going well with Christopher and Larry. After all, the man was exceptionally good at what he did as a therapist – David knew this firsthand. For the second time in one day he would have to wing it, to trust himself and his instincts.

He closed his eyes and began praying, " Our Father who art in heaven…"

It was closing in on 3:30 p.m. when David woke up with a start, bolting upright to a sitting position. Even though there was a chilly draft in the room, his shirt was soaked with perspiration stains on his chest and back. Vaguely recalling a troubling dream, David let the memory fade. He had no desire, and made no attempt, to try to recall it. He got up and walked around to try to rid the dream's ugly shadows from the fringes of his mind.

After a long, hot shower, a shave and a couple of Diet Cokes, he felt revived. Due to Father Anthony's absence, David had all the weekend Masses. So, before going over to Lizzy's, he decided to work on his homilies. Sitting at the desk in his room, he read the Gospel three times before its familiarity even registered. He tapped a pen on the antique desk and stared at the blank sheet of white paper lying before him. After scribbling down a few words and reading them over, David ripped the paper from the legal pad, crushed the paper in a tight ball and threw it in the trash can.

He looked at his watch and saw it was time for Mass. "Good." He dropped the pen and almost sprinted to the laundry room to grab his coat, gloves and hat out of the dryer.

"Just what I thought," David said as he looked out at the empty church a little before 5 p.m. said a quick Mass to himself before leaving.

All the main roads had been plowed but it remained extremely windy, causing the snow to continue drifting. Peering out the Honda's frosted windows, David could see that very few people had bothered to begin digging out.

With the wind still howling and the game tonight, there's no reason to be out in this mess, David thought.

It was nearly thirty minutes of slipping and sliding before he arrived at Lizzy's. By that time, the car's defrost finally began throwing out enough heat so he could cease with the manual defrosting. He had no problem traveling down the long road that led to the Patten's home and into the driveway. There were some things money could buy, and quick snow removal was one of them.

Lizzy was at the door almost before the sound of the doorbell subsided. "David, get on in here. It's freezing."

David stomped his boots on the front landing before stepping into the entryway. Once inside, Lizzy hugged him; it lasted a little longer than normal. He wasn't sure if it was a reward for something he had done or her desire for a bit of human touch from a good friend. Either way, David didn't care. After tonight, this might be the last hug he ever got from her.

"Let me take your coat."

David handed her his jacket and gloves.

A wonderfully familiar scent wafted in the air. David inhaled a couple of deep breaths and, in an attempt to recognize the aroma, closed his eyes. "What is that?"

He hadn't eaten in over twenty-four hours. His stomach ached and began growling, while his salivary glands began to work double time. Lizzy closed the closet door and laughed. "It's ready and waiting. Taco pie, remember?"

"That's it!" David said, as if he was just given the last word to the New York Times crossword puzzle. "I haven't had taco pie since college."

"Well, back then it was made out of desperation – and imagination. I thought you'd get a kick out of it. And, if it's not as good as you remember, we've always got chili. I've made a few improvements in the pie I think you'll approve of. Come on, let's eat."

He wolfed down the first piece without saying a word. Lizzy didn't seem to mind. She rattled on about the storm and the game, all while attending to David and preparing other foods. As his empty stomach began to fill, he forced himself to slow down. He passed on a fourth piece of pie; he didn't want to appear too much of a glutton. Plus, he could see all the other treats Lizzy had prepared. If he wanted to run the full gamut of the buffet, which he fully intended on doing, he'd have to pace himself.

"Well, you think we can do it without Tasker?" Lizzy said while rinsing off his plate and loading it into the dishwasher.

Now full, David wanted to move right into the substance of why he was there, but knew it would be wiser to tread lightly and move toward it slowly. Bringing up the subject right away might backfire. He had only one shot and couldn't afford to blow it. He thought, Be patient, the opportunity will present itself.

"It'll hurt us, no doubt. But we're still pretty deep at linebacker," David said.

"I don't know. Remmers is going to have to take Tasker's place." Lizzy put liquid soap into the dishwasher. "For a sophomore he's pretty good, but in a game this big I wish he had more experience." She closed the dishwasher door and turned it on. "Oh well, it probably won't make that big of a difference. Come on, let's go watch the Crusaders kick some tail!"

They both sat on the couch in the living room. The pre-game hype of the television announcers murmured in the background. There was plenty of time before kickoff and Lizzy was intent on talking about innocent community gossip, no personal stuff yet. David didn't want to let this chitchat go too far because once it got rolling it was hard to stop. So, in an effort to short-circuit the dialogue, he was reserved with his responses.

Once the game got underway, he doubted there would be many opportunities to talk about anything other than bad officiating, great or poor play calling, and all the other blabber that came with watching a sporting event. So he decided to test the waters.

"How's Erik?" David wanted to ease into the subject of Larry and Christopher, and going through the side door was the best plan he had come up with.

When she turned to face David, Lizzy had a stern look of concentration. A pit developed in his stomach. Wrong question, he moaned in his mind.

"Good…pretty good."

Surprised he had read her wrong, David took the subject a step further. "How about you two? Are things getting better?"

She took a slow, deep breath. "I think so. It's funny, even though Erik's been out of town most of this month, we've been talking more, you know, about our relationship and how things got to be so messed up. We're not to the fixin' part yet, but we're talking. It's a start, I suppose."

David stayed quiet and looked Lizzy in the eye, nodding his head every now and then. He wanted to keep her talking.

"The last few weeks when Erik's been out of town, he's called home every night to check in, ask about my day and see how Christopher's doing. That's something he hasn't done for years. It's like being back in high school or college…you know, talking on the phone all night with your boyfriend or girlfriend. We used to do that. Lord knows we racked up some hefty phone bills while in college. I don't know why, but it's been easier to discuss things this way."

David nodded his head and said, "I understand what you're saying. For some reason, talking on the phone or writing letters, even e-mailing, can be a great way to work through rocky times. Hey, all that matters is that you two are communicating. Don't dissect it too much."

Lizzy's eyes sparkled for a brief moment. "You're right. Know what else? Erik's even brought up the subject of visiting with Father Anthony, if I still want us to."

"You sound skeptical."

"I am. Erik's behaved a certain way for so long now, and all of a sudden he seems to be doing an about face. It's hard for me to believe it's for real."

"Be open, Lizzy. Give him the benefit of the doubt. People change; I see it almost every day."

She turned away and looked out the living room windows; her back rose up and down in rapid spurts, while her left forefinger rose to wipe away a tear. After a few moments, Lizzy's breathing slowed as she regained composure.

Her eyes were welled up when she turned back to David. "Erik's done this too many times before. He knows the right things to say. I'll believe he's really changing when I see it over the long haul. I'm tired of hearing about how he's going to change this or change that. It's time for him to put up or shut up. If this is just another round of bullshit to buy him some time, I won't stand for it. I'd hate to do it because of Christopher, but I won't have much—"

The phone rang.

"Excuse me."

Instead of answering the phone sitting on the coffee table, Lizzy headed to the kitchen.

Alone with his thoughts, David worried about the very real possibility of Lizzy calling it quits with Erik. *What can I do to help them?* He was troubled and felt helpless. More than anything, he wanted to tell Erik to hurry up and get his act together; that he was running on empty fumes. But would he be receptive to hearing this again? He sure as hell wasn't the first time.

When Lizzy walked back into the room, her mood had noticeably improved, at least outwardly. She was smiling. "All right, I asked you over for some food and fun. It's time for the kickoff – and more food." In her hands was a platter stacked with caramel fudge brownies.

"Oh, you angel," he said, eyeing his favorite sweet snack. Even though he was stuffed, he couldn't pass up these babies.

As they watched the teams' captains trot to the center of the field for the ceremonial coin toss, David said, "Hey, where's Christopher?" David had been so focused and preoccupied with drawing information out of Lizzy he had forgotten all about his godson. "Is he in his room? I'll go fetch him."

"No. That was Christopher on the phone. He called to ask if it was okay to watch the game at Larry's." David stopped in mid-bite, his eyes locked on to Lizzy's. "I spoke with Larry and he insisted, said he'd love the company. I hope you're not disappointed. Christopher sounded so excited that I just couldn't say 'No'." Then, a puzzled look flashed across her face.

David thought, Relax. Don't let her sense any alarm.

"What is it?"

"Oh, nothing," Lizzy said.

"Are you comfortable with Christopher watching the game there?"

"Yeah, I guess so. I really don't have much choice." There was little enthusiasm in her voice. "Today's just been one of those weird days."

"How so?" He said this way too fast, and Lizzy gave him a funny look.

"Well, around noon today, Larry called and said he'd like to set up a session with Christopher for one-thirty. I guess there was a bunch of cancellations because of the storm. What's odd is that Larry's never called me to schedule an appointment before. Anyway, I hesitated because of the roads and lousy driving conditions. But, Larry said that Christopher was very close to taking a big step in therapy and that it was extremely important to keep the positive momentum going from their previous sessions. That's all I needed to hear. When I got there, Larry said the session would probably last longer than usual and he'd call when they were finished.

"About three o'clock, he called to check in with me. Everything was moving along so well he wanted to keep going. I spoke with Christopher and he wanted to stay. David, he sounded really good. Also, Larry offered to give Christopher a ride home afterwards; around game time, Larry thought.

"You were right, David. Larry's great at working with kids, but he's also just a neat, down-to-earth guy. Outside of their sessions, he lets Christopher spend time over there. He absolutely loves being at Larry's house. Christopher's really bonded with Larry, which he says is the key to successful therapy. That's why he thinks it's the perfect time to increase the sessions to four times a week. Christopher's all for it. I think it's great because he seems to be getting back to his old self. And whatever the doctor says is best for my little boy is fine with me."

Lizzy paused for a moment and the puzzled expression reappeared.

"Is there something else, Lizzy?" David sat on the edge of the couch. His body was tense and rigid. Wildly, he thought, I can't believe this is happening! It's the same kind of grooming process Father Emery used with me. I've got to do something before Christopher and Lizzy are completely under Larry's spell.

"I guess there's also a problem with the snow; one of the hazards of living out in the country, Larry said. Apparently, the entrance to his private road is stacked up about six feet high with snow that the plows continue to move off the highway. Right now, the entrance is completely blocked. He said it happens all the time during big winter storms. His snow removal guy is supposed to come by a couple of times during the day to clear it again.

Now, Larry can't get hold of the guy. Larry's also been calling other services to come dig him out, but with all the snow and the football game, no one's around or willing to come over. The winds are blowing hard again and Larry said that causes the road to his house to become treacherous to drive on.

"It must have happened pretty quick, because when I dropped off Christopher everything was passable. If Larry can't get someone to clear things fairly soon, there'll be no other choice but to have Christopher stay overnight. I'm not real comfortable with that, but if it has to happen, I'm glad it's with Larry. Christopher's in good hands, and he'll probably have a great time."

David wanted to scream "No!" "No!" "No!" Instead, he watched as St. Cecilia's ran an option play to the wide side of the field. The Crusaders' quarterback, just before being tackled by a Taylorville player, flipped a perfect pitch to the trailing running back. Looking for an open lane to run through, the Crusaders running back took his eye off the ball for a split second. Fumble! Luckily, a St. Cecilia's offensive lineman batted the football out of bounds. The Crusaders retained possession, but lost twelve-yards on the play.

Lizzy yelled at the television. "Come on coach! Don't call an option on our first play! You gotta give our guys a chance to get comfortable in there. That fumble's gonna be stuck in the back of their minds all game now."

"You know, I could go get Christopher," David said.

While he spoke, the next play had already started: a roll out pass to the left side of the field. "Watch out!" Lizzy shouted, as a blitzing Taylorville linebacker blasted the Crusaders quarterback from behind. He held onto the ball, but the Crusaders were backed up to their own three-yard line. Lizzy and David were on the edges of their seats, but for different reasons.

Lizzy was so wrapped up in the game that she didn't hear his offer. He waited as St. Cecilia's ran a fullback trap up the middle for a few yards. Now, it was fourth down and twenty-two yards to go for a first down. The Crusaders punting unit ran out onto the field.

"What a way to start." Disgusted, Lizzy whacked a pillow off the couch. While picking it up off the floor, she looked at David; her face was flushed. "Sorry, I just get so caught up in these stupid games."

The Crusaders punter almost had his kicked blocked as the Taylorville special teams players attacked with a ferocious rush. The punt returner signaled for and made a fair catch at the Crusaders forty-one yard line. Immediately, the cable channel cut to the first blitzkrieg of TV commercials that would make the game last for hours.

This time, louder, David said, "Listen, why don't I run over to Larry's and pick up Christopher."

"Thanks, but let's wait and see what the conditions are like later. Christopher was pretty jazzed up about watching the game over there and I'd hate to burst his bubble. I'm sure Larry will be able to find someone to come out. Plus, I don't want you driving around in this mess and getting stuck in that car of yours."

With the commercial break over, Lizzy refocused on the game.

David reasoned, If I continue to push this, Lizzy's going to get suspicious and start asking questions. She's too sharp. Every fiber of his being told him to leave and get Christopher out of that house as fast as possible, before the manipulation that David knew was taking place with each passing second began to take root.

He rose from the couch. "Lizzy, I've got to make a call. Mind if I use the phone in the office?"

"Sure. Help yourself. Something wrong?" Lizzy had one eye on David and the other on St. Cecilia's defense.

"Probably not. I forgot to check the messages before I left." It was the first thing that popped to mind. He had to get away from all the noise and distraction of the game so that he could think clearly. Walking out, he thought, Lizzy will be distracted by the game, so I've got a little time to come up with something.

He closed the double doors to the office and began pacing around the room, desperately pondering what to do. Okay, he thought, stroking his goatee. Calm down and think. A plan began to sprout, and he stopped pacing. In a matter of minutes, it all fell into place. "I think it'll fly. I hate lying to Lizzy, but I've got no other option."

When he returned, Lizzy was standing and exhorting the Crusaders' defense to stop Taylorville from scoring. A graphic on the TV screen told David that the Tornadoes were on the Crusaders' eleven-yard line. Taylorville's quarterback dropped back to pass and was chased out of the pocket. He stopped and heaved a pass across the field for a touchdown.

"Four stinking plays," Lizzy groaned, as she fell back on the couch. "Our defense sucks." The camera panned the jubilant Taylorville sidelines. "Boy, we've got our work cut out for us. It's gonna be a battle tonight."

"Yeah, it is." He wasn't referring to the game.

As another commercial came on, David, who was standing behind Lizzy, said, "Hey Lizzy, umm, Larry called the rectory looking for me. He wants to enlist my help in finding someone to dig him out. Apparently, money's not talking because of the game, so he thought some holy persuasion might work. It really bothers Larry to be snowed in – you know, an emergency might pop up.

"I'm going to take off for a bit and round up Tom Meyer's help. I'm sure I can prod him into doing a good deed. Heck, all I might have to do is remind Tom that Larry will be very grateful, and generous." David paused and, like it was an afterthought, said, "Hey, since I'll be out that way,

I also can get Christopher. We could be back before the second half starts."

"Why don't you call Tom from here?"

"Well…I suppose I could," David said, not expecting such a logical response. He began to move toward the phone on the coffee table. Putting the receiver back in its cradle, he turned to Lizzy, and said, "No. I think it'd be better to go over there. Tom would be more likely to help that way. It's always harder to say 'No' to someone face to face."

"What if he's not home?" Lizzy had a perplexed look on her face, like a parent picking apart a child's lie.

David smiled. "Oh, I'm sure he's there watching the game." Before she could say another word, he rushed out of the room, retrieved his coat and gloves from the hall closet and stuck his head back into the living room. "I'll be back in a flash." He turned and ran out the front door.

Hopping into the car, he turned the key and, because of the bitter cold air, had to pump the gas pedal a few times before the engine sputtered to life. After backing out of the driveway, he looked toward the house and saw Lizzy standing at the storm door. He tooted the horn and waved, as if he was leaving to go get more chips at the convenience store down the street.

In a mad rush, David drove all the way across town to Tom Meyer's house, only to find no one home. Repeatedly, David rang the doorbell and banged on the front and back doors. Tom's old truck was sitting in the driveway with the slow plow blade attached. Frustrated, David thought, I'll bet he's at some bar watching the game.

"What a waste of time." David's fist slammed down hard on the Honda's hood. "Lizzy was right, I should've called." With the car idling, he climbed in and thought about what to do next.

On a hunch, he decided to make the drive to Larry's house. At best, David had forty-five minutes of travel time ahead of him. With the Honda's balding tires and the snow and ice that covered the roads, it would likely be much longer. *That's too much time,* David thought dejectedly. *I've got to—.* Then, an idea struck him.

"If I'm right, I won't need it, but just in case," David said. He turned off the car. "I don't think Tom will mind. After all, it is an emergency."

As he expected, there was no key in the ignition or under the floor mats or hidden on top of the visors. It really didn't matter, although David would have preferred it that way – it would have been neater, cleaner. Thanks to the skills he learned during his delinquent days, he twisted the two wires together and the truck rumbled to life.

The heavy vehicle handled the roads like it was a warm summer day and, less than thirty minutes later, he arrived at the entrance to Larry's property. David wasn't surprised at what he found. His hunch was correct: The entrance was plowed and open; completely cleared, as was the road that led to the house. He also noticed there was an abundance of sand and salt spread around the entrance and on the private road. This was what David had anticipated – and feared. He stopped at the entrance to the driveway, not moving forward.

Jaws clenched, he thought, *That bastard lied to Lizzy. He's lied to me and Father Anthony, and everyone in town. We've all been fooled and charmed by that snake. That's why it's so easy for him to chew people up and spit them out. The fear of being caught and uncovered for who he really is doesn't concern him one bit.* David's chest began rising up and down in quick, shallow breaths as he thought about the danger Christopher was being exposed to by an evil man that David once revered, just as his godson did now.

David was no stranger to this private road. He knew most every inch of it. During his sessions with Larry, David had learned to associate the trip up and down the pathway with goodness and healing. Still, he remained hesitant to drive up the lane. Not because of the danger posed by the packed snow and patches of ice that covered the narrow road – one wrong move might propel him into the surrounding woods. No, what frightened him was the uncertainty of what lay waiting at the end of this once friendly path.

The old engine sputtered as he prayed for strength; the kind of massive courage needed to sacrifice all that one believes sacred and whole. David didn't cower from these thoughts. It was as if time had stopped and he was frozen in place.

An eighteen-wheel truck came roaring by, much too fast considering the poor road conditions, and woke him from the warm cocoon of silent meditation. In the distance, he noticed the dark silhouette of an old pickup truck pulled over to the side of the road; he was sure it wasn't there when he first arrived. David was oblivious as to how much time had passed. It seemed a few seconds, but he sensed it was far more. Snapping out of his reverie, he felt peaceful, confident, unafraid.

Through gritted teeth, David thought with a renewed resolve, I'm willing. Lord my God, this is for Corey and all those that came before him, and for Christopher. That monster must be stopped. He slammed his boot down on the gas pedal. All four tires spun wildly on the hard-packed snow and ice, kicking up salt pellets and gravel until the truck gained traction and slung David through the entrance.

After nearly sliding into the forest while rounding the first of many sharp curves, David throttled back. Once traveling at a more reasonable speed, the mile-long climb went smoothly. The road wasn't in great shape. There were snowdrifts and patches of ice that would have impeded his passing had he been driving the Honda, but Tom's old truck blew through these hazards as if they didn't exist.

The road began to straighten a few hundred yards from the house, so David switched off the high beams. At about one hundred yards, where the forest opened up, he stopped and killed the headlights. David felt he needed an edge; he wanted Larry backpedaling. The surest way to pull this off was to catch Larry off-guard, so David concentrated on making his arrival a complete surprise. He put the truck in park and cut the engine.

David gave his eyes a few moments to adjust to the darkness before he slipped out of the truck. Walking over the driveway, he noted that it too was snow-packed, but plowed and clear. After a couple of deep breaths and a quick rehearsal of what he intended to say, David headed for the front door.

With his gloved hand shaking from both the bitter cold and apprehension of the unknown, David reached for the doorbell, hesitated, then pressed it hard and long. He waited. Nothing. Not a sound. He pushed again, this time pumping it over and over. Again nothing. He grew impatient thinking about Christopher. Opening the storm door, he pounded hard, while intermittently reaching up to clank the metal knocker.

Suddenly, there was Larry – hair wet, tightening the belt of a white silk robe. *I'm too late!* David thought. The sight of Larry sent David hurtling back to that day at Cather Lake. Even though David had cast aside the haunts that Father Emery had planted, the hate and rage still ran deep. Inflamed with fury, he knew he was capable of harming Larry.

"What the hell is...? David...what are you doing here?" The man composed himself with uncanny speed, but the dismay in his eyes could not be camouflaged.

David stayed strong and kept his emotions in check. The goal was to get Christopher out safely and if that meant placating this asshole, David would do it. "I'm sorry about the pounding, but—"

"The damn bell must be frozen again," Larry sniped. "It happens every once in a while in this kind of weather."

"I see," David said evenly. As he remained focused on Christopher's welfare, Father Emery's memory and the accompanying volatile feelings began to subside.

Larry broke out into a warm smile. "Now, what brings you all the way out here in these miserable conditions?" Behind him, David heard the sound of the sliding glass door open and thud shut. Larry whipped his head around and looked up the stairs toward the living room. David picked up on the quick gesture Larry made with his left hand, which was at his side, as if he was dismissing someone.

"I'm coming in," David said.

"Sure…sure. Let me go throw on some fresh clothes. I was just out in the hot tub. Go ahead and take a seat in the living room. I'll be right back."

David climbed the stairs leading to the living room. Fidgety and on edge, he couldn't stay seated. He got up to walk off the nervous energy. Cautiously, he inched toward the entrance to the kitchen, which was out of his view from the front door. Christopher was nowhere in sight. David peered out the sliding glass door at the hot tub where he first met Corey, then turned away at the memory. Looking around the kitchen, he noticed puddles of water leading toward the basement door. It was partly open. He was sure Christopher was down there, enchanted with Larry's lair. David walked over to the door and heard the TV speakers cranked up, a little voice was yelling, "Go! Go!" The game was clearly in full swing. He breathed a sigh of relief knowing that Christopher was safe for the moment.

"Now, what can I do for you?" Larry sauntered in, went to the basement door, and shut it.

"I've come to pick up Christopher."

"Excuse me?"

"I was at the Pattens when you talked to Lizzy. She said you were snowed in and needed help digging out, but no one was around." Larry's eyes opened a little wider. David read the fear and apprehension. He continued, "Well, here I am. Looks like a miracle's taken place though; everything's cleared – even salted and sanded."

With eyes darting back and forth, Larry slightly tilted his head to the right and left, as if stretching tension from his neck. Then, a bogus look of surprise spread over his face. "Hallelujah! It's about time. I thought I heard old Tom out there a while ago. He probably got my message and came over to plow during halftime. You can always depend on Tom Meyer to get the job done."

David thought, I've got the man's fucking truck you lying sack of shit. But he quickly quieted himself, reasoning, I'm here to get my godson. It won't do any good to call out Larry on this one. Just leave it alone.

"Lizzy's expecting Christopher back soon. I told her once we got you dug out I'd bring him home. So, if you would go get him—"

"What are you talking about?" Larry snapped. "Christopher's…listen, why don't you just go back to the rectory. I'll bring him home after the game like Lizzy and I planned."

David stayed put. "No. I'm taking him home – right now." One look into David's eyes told Larry all he needed to know about David's resolve. Larry's cheeks flushed red, and his breathing accelerated. David watched as Larry's eyes glassed over, turning wild, like an addict whose drug was being thieved. David was astonished as Larry, a man who always was in command and under control, transformed into a seething maniac.

"The fuck you are!" Larry exploded. "You think you can just walk into my house and do whatever you please? Get your ass out of here. I'll take the boy home like I planned with his mother."

"Larry, I know Christopher was in the hot tub with you, and I doubt he brought along a swimming suit to his therapy session."

"So what?" Larry shouted. "Christopher wanted to go out there in the snow. What's the big deal?"

Those familiar words hit David like a slap in the face, and he shot back, "You think Lizzy and Erik would approve of that! Was that part of Christopher's therapy, Larry?"

The man just laughed. "What? So you're going to tattle on me?" Another fit of evil laughter.

"If I have to, yes. There will be no more Corey's. I won't allow you to harm another little boy again."

Larry pushed David in the chest, knocking him back a couple of steps. He remained standing and continued to hold his ground. David was not about to back down.

"That was not my fault!" Larry screamed. "He was so fucked up, no one could have fixed him! You know that, you motherfucker!"

"So that gave you the right to use him like a whore, to satisfy your own sick desires? Larry, you sexually molested Corey – a goddamn little boy! You perverted fuck. You earned his trust, then broke his spirit. For crying out loud, you took pictures and shot videotape of a little boy. And now, because of what you did to him, he's dead."

Looking toward the closed door leading to the basement, Larry smirked, and said, "Yeah, I did those things, but you can't prove shit. Guess who's got the disks and videotape you stole?" His voice was cracking and becoming rough; flecks of spit splattered onto David's face and glasses. "After all I did to help you? You ungrateful little shit."

Larry began furiously pacing back and forth, like a rat lost in a maze. An awkward silence erupted. Cool it! David thought. I'm getting sidetracked. Just remain focused on getting Christopher the hell out of here. Stay calm.

Larry halted and smiled sinisterly. "There's not a goddamn thing you can do to stop me, superman. Face it; you fucked up. First, you broke into my house and that's a crime. You probably remember that from your younger days. Second, do you honestly think anyone's going to believe your bullshit? Come on, don't be such a naive asshole. If people had to choose between your word and mine, who do you think will win that one? Third, I told you about my…my sexual encounters with Corey during the sacrament of confession. Remember that vow you took? You say one word to anyone and, poof, you're no longer a priest. Are you willing to give that up?"

Uncertainty crept into David's mind and soul. He became lightheaded.

Larry chuckled. "I didn't think so. As I see it, the choice is really quite simple: Keep your mouth shut and you'll never have to make any decision."

Stop! David screamed in his mind. Do not be duped and intimidated by this man. "Larry, I made that choice long before stepping into this house tonight. If I have to sacrifice the priesthood to stop you, God knows I'm willing."

"I don't think it'll ever come to that. I believe I've heard enough." The strong, familiar voice came from the living room. Erik strode into the kitchen. "Where's my son you fucking puke?"

Fists clenched, eyes on fire, Erik approached Larry. He stepped backwards and stumbled, barely catching his balance. "I…we… It's all a lie! None of what you heard is true!"

Erik rushed Larry, throwing a vicious punch to his stomach. A bellow of air rushed from his mouth. Larry slammed into a barstool and fell to the floor. He lay in a heap, doubled-over and heaving, trying to catch his breath.

Erik was now in charge. David stood stone still, mouth and eyes agape, dumbstruck at his friend's presence. He managed to say, "I think Christopher's okay."

With Larry writhing on the ground, Erik walked over to David, put a hand on his shoulder and said with speed, "Lizzy said you might need help digging out – and I had to see you and my little boy. Thanks for the lecture. The truth hurts sometimes and, with my hard head, it takes a while to sink in."

Then, Erik turned to Larry and commanded in a slow, menacing voice, "What have you done with my son?"

Recovering from the blow, Larry scrambled to the basement door, opened it and slammed it shut. David could hear the man madly bound down the stairs.

"Oh, Lord!" David said. "Christopher's down there!"

For the first time since his arrival, fear radiated from Erik's eyes. "No!" he bellowed, running to the door. It slammed hard against the kitchen wall as Erik flew down the staircase.

Stunned, David paused a moment. Instincts kicking in, he ran and leaped down the steps three and four at a time, bouncing off the wall at the bottom.

There he saw Christopher in Erik's arms, both clenched in a tight hug. Where did Larry go? David wondered.

"Father David!" Christopher had a huge smile on his face. "You're here too? Look, my dad came home from work to watch the game with me!"

"Yes, he did," David said. "Your dad loves you very much."

Erik smiled in thanks, then motioned with his head to the room where the disks and tapes were stored. "In there."

"It's been a great game, Dad. There's only seven seconds left and if we make the field goal, we win!" Christopher clung to Erik, who with a bittersweet smile kissed his son on the forehead. My friend has returned, David thought.

Calmly, David said, "Why don't you two go finish watching the game in the living room. Larry and I need to talk in private."

Erik shook his head "No." David looked at Christopher and said, "Please, take him upstairs. Call Chief Gardner and tell him to get over here right away."

"You're right," Erik said. "Don't do anything foolish. Understand? I still need my best friend around to set me straight."

David smiled and nodded his head.

Erik jogged toward the stairway, holding his son close like the prized gift he was and said, "Hey, let's hustle, we don't want to miss the end of the game." Christopher jumped out of his father's arms and scampered up the steps.

David made his way over to the room. As he got closer, sounds of plastic cracking and glass breaking grew violently louder. Undaunted, David reached for and turned the doorknob. It was locked.

With a heavy heart, he rested his head on the door. "Larry, it's no use, the police will be here soon. You can't get rid of it. You know they'll be able to recover what they need."

The noises of destruction came to an abrupt halt. After a few moments, the rolling sound of a metal desk drawer opening and closing came from behind the door. Then, more silence. Now, all David could hear was the football announcer on the TV say, "The snap is clean, it's got plenty of leg—"

"Bam!" The sharp bang of the gun was startling and earsplitting. David fell to the ground. He lay motionless, hands covering his head. After a short time, he slowly and cautiously rose from the floor. On the other side of the door, the room was still.

David leaned against the wall and slid down until he sat in a heap by the door. He took off his glasses, letting them drop to the floor, and covered his eyes with the palms of his hands. The ache originated deep in the recesses of his soul. There was no way to suppress it; no way to stop the emotion from spreading, so David put up no resistance – something he had only recently been able to do. Rising to the surface of his skin, it burst forth in waves of tears and sobs – the kind that comes with both the great sorrow of a crushing defeat and the joy of a hard fought victory.

Twenty minutes passed before Chief Gardner and two deputies arrived on the scene. The men stayed in the background, letting the Chief make all the calls on this one.

Exasperated, Chief Gardner said to David, "You telling me that Larry Peck shot himself...because he's involved with child pornography?"

"Like I said, Chief, it's more than just pornography. I know it's hard to believe...hell, I still don't believe it. But I'm telling you the truth."

Chief Gardner stared hard into David's eyes, then said to his men, "Break the door down."

An officer kicked the door twice before the metal and wood holding the lock in place gave way. The other officer, revolver drawn, immediately leaped through the opening, swinging his gun to the left and right.

"No one, Chief," the officer said.

Chief Gardner stepped into the room. "What the fuck? Cooper?"

David looked around, stunned. He saw the closed back door. "He must have gone out that way. He was in this room, and I did hear a gun shot. Ask Erik, he'll tell you the same thing."

Chief Gardner looked at his two deputies. "Go check around out back." The two men shot out the studio door into the dark night.

The Chief took off his hat and ran a handkerchief over his forehead. "Look, I gotta see something...I need proof."

LITTLE VOICES

David nodded, then walked over and grabbed a videotape. "Follow me."

With Erik and Christopher still upstairs, David loaded the tape in the VCR and hit play. The first two scenes were like the ones he had viewed at the rectory. The third scene popped onto the television screen.

"That's...that's Corey Hansen," the Chief said. His arms dangled at his side as if lifeless; his shoulders slumped forward.

David noted that Corey looked older in this video. Again, the boy disrobed and laid naked on a couch. Then, like a snapshot, a man came into view in the corner of the screen to move the discarded clothes from the camera's eye.

"Rewind that!" Chief Gardner was back under control.

David rewound the tape and paused it just as the man appeared. There was no doubt: It was Larry.

The Chief looked at David, then at the paused figure on the screen. David felt the years of tension and bitterness dissolve between them as both realized that, for the first time, they needed each other's help.

"Where do you think he went?" Chief Gardner said.

David shook his head. "No idea."

The Chief looked back at David, "Listen...I—"

"Just catch the bastard," David said. The Chief nodded and followed after his men.

David scanned the damage in the room. The computer monitor sat smashed on the floor. Next to it lay the tower; a hole was blasted into its side.

Within a few minutes, Chief Gardner and his deputies reappeared. "Okay, we found some footprints and followed them for about a hundred yards. Looks like there was a struggle, then two sets of footprints led off into the woods. You recognize this?"

"That's Larry's gun; I've seen it before."

"Are you sure he was in this room alone?"

David ran a hand threw his hair. "He had to be."

Chief Gardner grabbed the toothpick sticking from his mouth and removed it. Kindly, he said, "Father, I want you to take Erik and Christopher back to their house. I don't think it's safe for you all to be here. Sit tight until you hear from me."

"Got it." David paused. "Be careful."

Chief Gardner smiled quickly and said, "Go on now."

Erik's car was barricaded in the driveway by two police cruisers, so David, Erik and Christopher hiked through the snow to where David had abandoned Tom Meyer's truck. As David was turning to enter the highway, he stopped and shined the headlights on marks he spotted in the snow. There were footprints leading across the road to the spot where David had earlier noticed a parked pickup truck; tire tracks circled around and headed back toward town.

"Oh my God," David said softly.

"What's wrong?" Erik said.

"Umm…nothing. Let's get you guys home."

When they arrived at the Pattens, David stayed put as Erik and Christopher climbed out of the truck. Erik walked around to the driver's side door, which David had opened. "Aren't you coming in?" Erik said.

"Gotta check on something, be right back." David slammed the door shut.

"Where are you going?" Erik shouted through the closed window.

"I'll explain later."

"I'm coming with you."

"Stay with your family." Before Erik could say another word, David ground the clutch into reverse and sped away.

Once at Neihardt Park, David turned on to the road that led to the playground. He quickly spied a fresh trail of tire tracks crushed into the snow. Arriving at the parking lot, David's headlights – high beams on – illuminated the driver's side of a parked pickup truck. Cautiously, David drove toward it. Ten yards away, he stopped when he recognized Reggie sitting behind the wheel. The giant of a man looked at David with surprise, quickly followed by contempt.

David slowly turned Tom's truck so the driver's side door was facing Reggie's. As he did this, David never took his eyes off the man. After putting the truck in park, David turned and looked out his front window.

"Jesus," he gasped. The high beams from Tom's truck lit up Larry's limp body hanging from a rope tied to the jungle gym – flesh exposed, pants down around his ankles.

Breathing in quick bits of air, David bowed his head. Slowly, he rose up and looked over to Reggie. He hadn't moved. David lifted his hand and motioned for Reggie to leave. Reggie didn't budge.

They locked eyes, each holding the others gaze. David mouthed, "Go."

Reggie nodded and moved on.

After a few moments, David peered out to the playground, taking in one final look. He made the sign of the cross and silently mouthed a short prayer. When finished, he slipped the clutch into gear and pulled away.

Author Biography

For more than a decade, Michael Sterba has worked at Girls and Boys Town, a renowned child-care organization founded in 1917 by Father Edward J. Flanagan. Reaching out nationwide, Girls and Boys Town helps troubled and delinquent children and adolescents grow emotionally, behaviorally, and spiritually. Sterba has had the opportunity to work on the front lines with at-risk youth as a direct-care worker and also as a consultant to the dedicated professionals that care for these challenging kids.

Mr. Sterba has written five non-fiction books in the child-care field: **Dangerous Kids**: **Foster Care Solutions: Practical Tools for Foster Parents**; **Treating Youth with DSM-IV Disorders**; **Issues in Quality Child Care: A Boys Town Perspective**; and **Boys Town's Psychoeducational Treatment Model**.

Little Voices is more than just a professional endeavor; it's a labor of love that reflects Sterba's beliefs and experiences developed over the many years of working with troubled children and their families – and as a devoted parent to his own children. While living in Omaha, Nebraska, the novel was written over a four-year period while Sterba balanced his roles as Senior Writer/Editor for Girls and Boys Town, husband to wife, Fae (a Realtor and owner of *Faemous Designs* jewelry), and father to son, Noah, and daughters, Hannah and Zoey.

Ordering Titles from Sensory Publishing. Inc.:

You can order this and other wonderful books directly from the publisher, just go online or call us!

www.SensoryPublishing.com

1-800-832-2823

Fiction:
Little Voices by Michael Sterba (ISBN 1058853-055-8)
The River Lethe by Perry A. Pirsch (1-58853-002-7)
The Justice Council by Oliver w. Holmes, Jr. (1-58853-048-5)
Incident on Jubal Mountain by Oliver w. Holmes, Jr. (1-58853-044-2)
A Common Place by Dale Gibble (1-58853-034-5)
Lost Bones of the Dead by Matthew Tuck (1-58853-006-x)

Non-Fiction:
MMURTL V1.0 by Richard A. Burgess (Technical/Computer)
The Euro-American Empire: Shadow Corporate Government in the Global Age by Larry Sullivan

Government Publication Series:
TMEP (Trademark Manual of Examining Procedure)

To be published when updates become available:

TBMP (Trial and Appeal Board Manual of Procedure)
MPEP (Manual of Patent Examining Procedure)
Title 37 of the Code of Federal Regulations
Patent, Trademark and Copyright Laws